MW00626915

# The Winnowing Winds

# The Winnowing Winds

_by_ ANN MARLOWE

_DODD, MEAD & COMPANY · NEW YORK_

1   2   3   4   5   6   7   8   9   10


Library of Congress Cataloging in Publication Data

Marlowe, Ann.
  The winnowing winds.

  I. Title.
PZ4.M34877Wi   [PS3563.A6739]     813'.5'4     77–3881
ISBN 0-396-07445-6

*For STEVE for everything*

By the winnowing winds that scatter the dust
And the clouds that are laden with rain
And the ships that skim swiftly over the seas
And the angels that apportion
    Yea! what has been threatened is true
    And the judgment will be upon you.

            ——*The Koran*

 *1*

AN ARCH of gray stone framed the landscape, the green slopes and blue sky and the haphazard patches of wild-flowers blazing suddenly like the jewel colors of a stained-glass window, as the little train emerged from the darkness of the tunnel into the valley of the Sarine. Or, as the river was called in my German-speaking part of the valley, the Saane.

My part of the valley. Well, it would be mine for the next ten months. Though I had not been back to Gstaad in as many years, already I felt a sense of homecoming, perhaps because Gstaad was the last place where Daddy and Conn and I had lived with Mother, that carefree thirteenth winter of my life. As the familiar scenes rushed past the windows, I poked tentatively among memories. To my surprise, the thought of Mother—the soft lilt of her voice and the unexpected flash of Irish humor in her gentle, dark eyes—was not painful. It was the other, more recent tragedy that would not bear thinking of.

In her own way, dear Kate had been right to propose my coming to Gstaad and taking up the teaching post that had so fortuitously fallen vacant the month before. Of course, being Kate, she doubtless felt the key to my rehabilitation lay in keeping busy. And with a full class-load of polyglot adolescents, I suspected that I would be busy indeed.

But my own reasons for accepting rested on another sort of therapy. Here in the comforting Swiss mountains, far from the hated sea, I would find what I most needed —an unbroken supply of peace and tranquility.

Or so I thought.

A burst of chatter and stale air from the smoking compartment propelled me to the platform. Smoothing the travel wrinkles from my sober beige suit and shaking my head at the lone expectant taxi driver, I picked up my suitcase. It could not be much more than a half mile to the school, and the walk would do me good. Three months of aimless idleness had taken their toll, physically as well as mentally.

Ahead along the Hauptstrasse the little electric train sped cheerfully over the trestle on its way to its destination twenty kilometers up the M.O.B. line. Pausing, I took a deep breath of the clean mountain air. Already in the first days of September it held a hint of autumn. The Swiss summer, it seemed, was a short season.

Almost without direction, as I rediscovered favorite shops and frowningly inspected the inevitable new construction, my feet took me along the main street and uphill past the Sporthotel and a dozen tidy wooden chalets to the cluster of imposing structures that was the Academy of the Oberland. A relatively new school, the Academy was already a considerable success, both financially and academically, and I noted with approval its settled, prosperous look. Flower beds ringed the massive old central building and the newer dormitories and dependencies. Red clusters of geraniums tumbled from window boxes and from great copper kettles suspended from the corners of the roofs.

It seemed only yesterday that Conn and I had watched these same dormitories being built and thrown snowballs at the piles of construction material, his shrill little-boy laughter carrying thinly in the winter air.

I choked back a sudden rush of tears. No amount of crying would bring back Conn and Daddy, that much I knew by now. I tightened my grip on the suitcase and walked slowly toward the main building.

A door marked "Office" pushed open easily and I stepped into the dimness of a long corridor. From somewhere off to the left a faint voice, British-accented, called:

"Ruedy? Is that you?"

As my eyes adjusted slowly, a chair scraped and footsteps followed the voice toward me. In a doorway a scant yard from where I stood a slender woman of medium height appeared.

"Oh," she said, startled. "May I help you?"

My first impression was that she resembled a mouse. Not that she was "mousy" or drab or at all unpleasant. She simply gave off an aura of soft brown timidity.

I smiled my most disarming smile. "I'm afraid I've arrived a day ahead of schedule," I said. "I'm Deirdre Sheridan."

"Oh yes, English and Drama," she murmured, neatly fitting me into a mental pigeonhole. "I expect you want to see Dr. Payne."

"If it's convenient." I tried the disarming smile again.

"Unfortunately he won't be here until late this evening. But we can surely work something out. I am Martha Payne." The headmaster's wife paused expectantly, and I dutifully acknowledged how pleased I was to meet her, how kind she was.

"I'll show you to your room, Miss Sheridan," she went on, indicating the door through which I had entered. I followed her outside and along a neat flagstone path to one of the newer buildings. "The girls' dormitory," she explained. "The Lower School girls are on the lower floor, the Upper School girls upstairs." She smiled faintly. "The younger ones are less likely to slip out the windows for midnight pranks. Not that we have discipline problems, but one can't be too careful. Here we are."

We had entered the ground floor, and now Martha Payne opened a door midway along the wide corridor that ran the length of the chalet-style structure.

"I expect you'll want to freshen up and inspect your new quarters. You share the adjoining bath with Miss Cline next door." She waited while I nodded approvingly, then said, "I'll send Ruedy to help you find your baggage. Then no doubt you'll want to rest until dinner. I expect you're tired from the long flight."

As she turned to leave, I said, "Not at all. I slept quite well on the plane." This was a direct lie, but I pressed on. "And thank you, but I won't trouble you for dinner. I'll be dining with my cousin Mme de Villiers in Saanen."

Her startled back receded as I considered what had made me dispute her on such a minor point, and whether I could indeed wangle a dinner invitation from Kate.

Normally I am able to hold my own against a strong personality, doubtless due to my theatrical training. But Martha Payne had by her own mildness maneuvered me into an even greater diffidence, at least until that last bland "I expect" provoked a rebuttal.

4

If this was the wife, what would I make of the great Dr. Payne himself?

I scarcely heard the first knock at the door.

Already I had unloaded my toilet kit into the near half of the medicine cabinet and mentally begun rearranging the sparse furniture. This by now was second nature, learned early from Mother and refined by years of practice as we followed Daddy's research grants from place to place, sometimes staying only a month or two before we were uprooted again. But the most unpromising faculty cottage or rented beach house invariably succumbed to Mother's instincts. Within a day she had fashioned a comfortable study for Daddy, filled vases with flowers, propped my battered rag doll on a pillow, and made a home. After she died, when school permitted and sometimes when it didn't, I carried on as best I could. Now I had only myself to do it for, but do it I would.

I had decided that the gay chintz bedspread would have to go. I'd look for a solid fabric, perhaps gold to pick up the richness of the fine Swiss wood paneling. And five meters more, I thought, for matching drapes in place of all that froth at the windows. A shag rug, brown maybe or dull green, throw pillows, some strong prints on the wall. Klee was Swiss, he would do perfectly.

The second knock came as I was tugging the massive oak desk from its place beneath the windows. I brushed a fallen strand of hair behind an ear and opened the door.

The tallish blond man who stood in the doorway was Swiss, there could be no doubt of that. The squareness of head and shoulders, the compact muscularity told of generations of mountain forebears. Even the cut of hair and clothes was slightly squared-off, testifying that the fashionable winter residents had not noticeably in-

5

fluenced the natives.

Then an open smile creased the bronzed face, the blue eyes lost their glacial coolness, and I decided that my visitor, squareness and all, was decidedly good-looking.

"Miss Sheridan? Ruedy Messerli. I understand you—" He broke off as his eyes fell on the heavy desk standing in the middle of the room. "Here, you can't manage that alone. Where shall I put it?"

I indicated a position along the side wall, and with two deft shoves he had it in place.

"Thank you," I said, and added, feeling some sort of explanation was due, "I really couldn't leave it by the window. I'd never get any work done with that glorious view in front of me."

Ruedy looked slightly puzzled, then smiled agreeably, and I understood suddenly that he saw nothing unusual in the mountains, that he had lived with this splendor all his life. I reflected how stolid and complacent the Swiss could be and wanted to shake him.

"The trunks haven't been delivered to the dormitories yet," he was saying. "Perhaps I can find yours more easily if you come with me to the box room?"

The British term sounded out of place in his American-accented speech. As I accompanied him across the central quadrangle, I wondered idly where Ruedy had learned his English, and what exactly was his position here. He might have been reading my thoughts, for he said:

"By the way, I'm officially the sports director, but that's only a full-time job in skiing season, so I do a few other things. Some gardening," he indicated the clipped lawns and neatly tended flower beds and shrubbery with a casual sweep of his square hand, "driving one of the school buses, building maintenance, repairs."

"It sounds," I said lightly, "as though you run the

school single-handed. What ever does Dr. Payne do?"

"Dr. Payne," said Ruedy soberly, considering, "is very good with ideas, I believe. But someone must look after *things.*"

At which point I resolved not to try joking with Ruedy again soon. Undoubtedly the Swiss had a sense of humor, but it was not constructed along American lines.

A crunch of tires on the deserted gravel driveway drew my attention to the little barred window overhead. Past the stacks of trunks and boxes within, I could see two pairs of gray-uniformed legs emerging from a sedate black Mercedes sedan.

The driver and his younger companion, who were unmistakably official, stood in earnest conversation for a moment, then disappeared in the direction of the office.

Behind me Ruedy was wrestling my trunk and foot-locker onto a baggage truck. I turned and resumed inspecting the cases surrounding me, some dusty from the summer's storage, some as newly arrived as my own. The labels bore addresses from California to Ceylon. There were the predictable number of Americans and British, and a surprising diversity of others.

Adam Ngomutu, Republic of Karanda. Surely this must be the son of the strong man of that emerging African nation?

Francisco Alvarez Quintana, Mexico, D. F. Lisa Kwan, Singapore. Jennifer Hearn, Saudi Arabia. Peter Duncan, Embassy of the Dominion of Canada, Ankara.

H.R.H. Haroun bin Sultan bin Muhammad, Qaiman. Another ruler's son. Qaiman, if I remembered correctly, was one of the tiny oil-rich states on the Persian Gulf, a hereditary sheikdom. And here were more trunks from the same address. These would be Haroun's sisters, Zora and Zafia. I wondered whether they would be as lovely and exotic as their names.

The click of high heels on the flagstone walk pulled my attention back to the window. A visibly agitated Martha Payne was approaching, accompanied by the two gray uniforms. The voice of the older one carried faintly into the cellar room.

". . . inspect the baggage to see that it has not been tampered with," he was saying, "and then have a look at the rooms that will be occupied by the boy Haroun and the little girls. Dr. Payne will be able to tell us what security arrangements . . ." The voice and the footsteps receded around the corner of the building.

I glanced questioningly at Ruedy. His jaw set a bit more squarely than usual, he wordlessly hauled the baggage truck up the ramp and into the sunlight. Beside the door stood the two gray-clad officials and Martha Payne.

"Nothing to worry about," the younger one told her. "Purely a matter of routine cooperation with a foreign government."

As they passed us and descended the ramp, I thought that Martha Payne did not look particularly reassured.

 *2*

"WONDERFUL, Kate. See you at six."

Replacing the receiver, I went back through the open door to the restaurant terrace, picked up my half-empty teacup and moved to the railing. Far below at the foot of the Wasserngrat the tiny chalets and neatly tended plots of ground had an unreal appearance, like an architect's model of an ideal Alpine village.

In the near distance lush green pre-Alps ringed the toy village. I traced the familiar names on the plaque attached to the railing—Wispile, Eggli, Videmanette. Beyond them, the higher Wildhorn and Oldenhorn thrust their rocky peaks, still bearing snow, above the timber line. Away to the south, the jagged teeth of the Dents du Midi shimmered in the afternoon haze.

Walking back to the upper lift station, I debated briefly whether to descend the Wasserngrat on foot, then decided the gentler lower section would be enough for the first day. Already my scrambles along the ridge had brought twinges to a number of long-forgotten leg muscles.

A middle-aged couple pushed through the door of the lift station, chattering volubly in German. Like a pair of Hümmel figures, they were perfectly matched, two round florid faces, two walking sticks, two tweed suits distinguished only by the man's knickerbockers and the woman's skirt. Identical stocky legs in knee socks ended in sturdy hiking boots that made my own sensible walking shoes look like ballet slippers. Without pausing, they set off down the mountain at an even pace.

The elderly lift attendant took my ticket and, deciding to address me in French, said:

"Those flowers, mademoiselle, where did you find them?"

I raised the bunch of purple and white blossoms happily for inspection. Not far from the path along the ridge, I explained, there was a shadowy crevice protected from the sun. There, in spongy ground beside a lingering patch of snow, I had found these late-blooming crocuses and gathered them for Kate.

"It's strange, isn't it?" I said. "In the valley, summer is already ending, but here where the snow melts late, these lovely flowers think it is spring."

"They are assuredly lovely, mademoiselle," the attendant agreed regretfully, "but—" He gestured at a poster tacked to the rough plank wall. In four languages it politely requested hikers to leave the wildflowers undisturbed.

Guiltily I promised not to repeat the crime, as the attendant fixed the safety bar in place and shoved the chair along the overhead track and onto the cable.

With the tops of the tall pines rising swiftly around me and the offending crocuses strewn loosely in my lap, I was glad that I had chosen the Wasserngrat today. The enclosed cabins of the other lifts in the valley would be welcome in the skiing season, but now the sun was warm on my back as the open chair dropped toward the sloping green pastures and the valley floor.

The chair bumped under a pylon and then settled into a more gradual descent, moving smoothly on the cable like an aircraft approaching a landing.

Suddenly I gripped the bar convulsively and felt my hysteria of the morning return, as strong and as senseless as before. The gentle slopes below me passed unseen. Through tightly closed eyes I watched again the broad expanse of Lake Geneva coming closer and closer, rising to meet the airplane, wide and wet and malevolent.

I had forgotten that the approach to Cointrin Airport would be over water, and it was the unexpectedness of it that finally snapped the last shreds of my self-control and sent me fleeing from Geneva, unable to spend an hour, let alone a day, beside so much horrible, hateful water. The night flight from Boston to Paris had been bad enough, but I had steeled myself and willed the plane hour by hour over the unseen depths below, not allowing myself to think of them. Then the sudden sight of the lake had assailed me.

It was worse than irrational, I knew, to feel such terror and loathing for what was, after all, only water. But I had felt it incessantly for three months, ever since the freak accident that had killed Daddy and Conn. I did not blame the boat's propeller blade that had sliced through the support lines, leaving my father and brother to die on the ocean floor. Even then, before their bodies had been recovered and brought back to the house near Woods Hole, I blamed the ocean itself. Daddy had devoted his life to the ocean's study. Conn, a promising marine biology major, would have joined Daddy in a brilliant career.

*11*

And the ocean had killed them both.

Dimly the sounds of the present returned, the scrape of the chair on its metal track, anxious voices. A pair of strong hands grasped my shoulders.

*"Fräulein, bist du krank?"* Miss, are you ill?

My eyes slowly focused on the interior of the lift station and the concerned young face of the attendant. Then they dropped to my lap. My hands lay tightly clenched, the knuckles white, and between them the crocuses, limp and twisted and crushed.

A last ray of late afternoon sun glinted on the picture window behind the wide, richly carved balcony. As I started up the long stone staircase leading to the chalet, Kate appeared on the balcony and called down:

"Deirdre, welcome back! You look marvelous."

Dear cousin Kate, with her unfailing buoyancy, would have said much the same thing if I had shown up with a broken leg. But I was indeed feeling better. The slow walk down the bottom half of the Wasserngrat had calmed me, and a cup of tea at Charly's Tearoom had had a restorative effect. If I could not match Kate's ebullience, I would at least not be gloomy company.

"I can't come down," she called. "I've something on the stove. Come round to the kitchen."

I mounted the steps past the ground floor bedrooms set into the hillside and met Kate, wooden spoon in hand, at the kitchen door.

"What do you think of my doorbell?" she asked, seizing a chain and whipping it from side to side. The chain was attached to the clapper of a massive Swiss cowbell, more than a foot across, which hung on its wide leather collar from a stout iron bar. "When the old one stopped working, the twins came home with this. Actually, I think

*12*

they're right. It does have more personality. Come on in."

She moved briskly about the kitchen, talking nonstop while she assembled a casserole. "There, that's done. Let's sit on the balcony until the light's gone. You've not seen a Swiss sunset in a long time. Vermouth cassis all right?"

As we settled into the comfortable chairs, drinks in hand, Kate kicked off her shoes and ran a toe meditatively along the carving of the balcony, tracing the cutout hearts and leaves.

"Deirdre?" she said tentatively. "Are you all right for money?"

"Oh, yes. The lawyers said I got a very fair price for the house on the Cape. You knew I'd sold it?"

I had sold it, in fact, with what I am sure was regarded as indecent haste, furniture and all. I had piled Daddy's papers into a trunk and delivered them to a colleague. A few mementos went into a small box. And then I had locked the house and walked away forever from that hated ocean-front property.

The price had indeed been a fair one. And the insurance money, the cursed double-indemnity insurance money I would have given anything not to receive, had all come to me too. Conservatively invested, it would yield an income which, while not lavish, still guaranteed modest independence. At a guess, I was probably better off than Kate.

"Well, if there's any delay, dear," she went on, "let me know. Since the twins are grown now, I'm really quite comfortably set."

The bland offer was typical of Kate. Heaven knew what sorts of economies she had practiced while the twins were growing up. Married in wartime London to Jean-

*13*

Paul de Villiers, a dashing fighter pilot with the Free French, she was widowed in the last days of the war, five months before the birth of the twins. The de Villiers, an old French family of diminished fortunes, could not help her much, and neither her widow's pension nor her own income was large. But on one point she was adamant. "Switzerland has not seen a war in five generations. My children will be raised here. They will not be victims of the next round of madness." It was the only reference she ever made to her own loss.

"How's Jeanne?" I asked.

Kate's reply was delayed by an "Oof!" as a large black and white cat leaped from the roof to the balcony railing and thence to her lap. "This creature is Cléopatre. She thinks she's irresistible. Oh, Jeanne's fine, and the baby is simply beautiful. Of course, since Théo's been posted to Brussels, I don't see as much of them as I'd like. Nor of Paul. I think you know he got the appointment to the Cantonal Hospital in Lausanne, which is close enough, but he's up to his eyes in work. That's why I'm so glad you could come, Deirdre dear," she said innocently, scratching Cléopatre's ears. "It'll be nice having family in the next village."

That was typical Kate too, making it seem that I was doing her a favor, when in reality I was doing exactly what she had decided would be best for me. For as long as I could remember, Kate had been rearranging other people's lives, subtly but resolutely, and seeing them submit with good grace.

Judging from the number of animals around the chalet, she also ran a one-woman SPCA. A yellow tomcat with a sadly battered ear inspected my ankles, then hopped to my lap, made a couple of circuits and settled down to purr.

From the village of Saanen below, the clear tones of a

bell striking the hour rose from the wooden steeple of the little white stucco church. Then the harmony was broken by the clangor of the cowbell at the kitchen door. The door banged, and a voice matching the cowbell in stridency called:

*"Madame de Villiers, êtes-vous là? J'ai le lait. Je le mettrai dans le bol."*

Kate rose, dumping Cléopatre unceremoniously onto the floor, and I followed. In the kitchen a woman, her feet in farm boots and her gray hair in a fiercely skewered knot, was pouring warm, creamy milk from a pail into a wide basin.

"Madame Bouchard," Kate said in fluent British-accented French, "I would like to present my cousin Mademoiselle Deirdre Sheridan."

*"Enchantée, madame,"* I said, taking the rough outstretched hand, as Kate placed the basin on the floor amid a chorus of meows.

"But how providential that your little cousin has come today!" exclaimed Madame Bouchard. "Of course she will want to see them. They are so adorable, and the eyes have just opened." She turned to me. "Kittens," she explained unnecessarily.

Kate gave me a curiously helpless look as we allowed ourselves to be propelled outside and along the level dirt path to the adjoining farm. Madame Bouchard wrenched open the door of a low shed attached to the barn, switched on a light, and motioned us to enter.

Blinking in the sudden brightness, the mother cat gently detached several tiny mouths, stepped from the worn cotton blanket and stretched voluptuously. Then she stalked around her brood, inviting admiration. She deserved it, for she was a magnificent calico, with yellow and black patches sharply defined against a pristine white ground, and a rakish buccaneer patch over one

*15*

eye. "This," announced Madame Bouchard, "is our Libérale."

"And a damned good name it is," Kate muttered. "That rotten cat—don't worry, Mrs. B. doesn't speak a word of English—that rotten cat is *very* liberal with her favors. It's a rare year she doesn't have three litters."

Madame Bouchard beamed and placed two of the wiggling kittens in my arms. I nuzzled them and made approving noises.

"Please, Deirdre," Kate said wearily, "don't encourage her. She already thinks I'm an automatic placement bureau. I'm at my wits' end to find homes for them. All my friends have at least one of Libérale's progeny, and I've got three. Of course, Libérale does produce marvelous kittens," she said, more warmly, "and I do think mixed breeds make the best pets. They're so affectionate, and intelligent too. And such wonderful company." By now her voice had assumed a suspicious enthusiasm. "Deirdre, don't you think—"

"Oh, no you don't Kate," I said decidedly. "I'm going to have my hands full enough with human young."

 *3*

DR. SIDNEY PAYNE shifted an orderly stack of folders to one corner of his desk, settled his tortoise-shell glasses more firmly on his thin nose, and with a neatly mani-cured hand leafed through the papers in front of him. From time to time he raised his pale eyes to me, as if checking that the description on the invoice tallied with the human merchandise delivered: hair black, eyes dark brown, height five-one, age twenty-three. He frowned, shuffled the papers together and said:

"Well, Miss Sheridan, we're very pleased to have you with us. I must say you seem, er, somewhat younger than I had expected."

I returned his gaze steadily and made no reply. There are some people who perversely confuse growing taller with growing up. I had ceased growing taller at the age of twelve, and Dr. Sidney Payne was not the first to imply that this showed a deplorable lack of character on my part.

"Still," he continued, "your credentials appear satisfactory. B.A. in literature cum laude from Wellesley, Yale Drama School, a year of varied experience in the New York theater." Once again his voice betrayed doubts about my character. "You will, of course, be responsible for student dramatic productions, and we look forward to a full season. So you'll only be expected to teach four literature courses and a drama workshop for credit."

As I digested this dubious bit of largesse, Dr. Payne said: "As you know, we prepare our students for both the American College Boards and the British G.C.E. examinations, so you'll be integrating the two sets of material in your courses." He went on talking about syllabi, standard texts, enrichment materials, team teaching projects, and the pile of books and papers on my lap grew steadily. "Naturally, being a late appointment, you've not had the summer to prepare your courses, and I don't expect you to have them blocked out immediately. But I would like to see lesson plans for the first month by, say, the day after tomorrow?"

I nodded assent, unable to speak. The numbness that had begun in the pit of my stomach had taken possession of my tongue and ears. I forced my attention back to Dr. Payne's words. He had launched into a small speech, no doubt meant to be inspiring, about the ideals fostered by the school. "We must instill in all our students a sense of discipline and decency, Miss Sheridan," he concluded. "Discipline and decency!"

He rose, indicating that the interview had ended, and I struggled to my feet, managing somehow not to drop anything from the cumbersome stack of books and papers. He moved to a board on the wall, detached a key and handed it to me. "Your key to the new auditorium.

Ruedy will be happy to show you over the lighting and backstage controls. Just let him know when you have a free hour." I wondered wildly when that might be, and suppressed an hysterical laugh.

"Yes, Dr. Payne," I said, as he held the door of the office, "thank you, sir." As the door closed firmly behind me, I realized they were the only words I had spoken in close to an hour.

Dropping the stack of books on the heavy oak desk, I sank onto the bed and pulled off my shoes. As the second one hit the floor, the bathroom door opened as if on cue and a cheerful American voice said:

"Hi, you must be Deirdre Sheridan. I'm Maggie Cline. We share this palatial suite."

Maggie looked the way she sounded, cheerful. She had a tip-tilted, freckled nose, wide blue eyes and a round face capped by reddish curls. She looked around the room with open curiosity, and her glance fell on the laden desk.

"I see you've met Old Payne-in-the-Neck. What do you think of him?"

"I think," I said dryly, "that he is a model of Discipline and Decency."

"Mmn, he thinks he's Arnold of Rugby. As a matter of fact, he's not a bad administrator. Unfortunately, he's also a fair historian. He keeps invading my American history classes to give a balanced viewpoint, which of course means British. Drives me crazy. But I don't think he'll give you any trouble."

"He already has," I said, and outlined our recent meeting.

"You poor dear," Maggie said sympathetically. "Have you ever done lesson plans? I suppose not. Wait a sec!" She dived through the door and reappeared a moment later waving a sheaf of printed forms. "Professor Cline's secret weapon. Neat little boxes, one sheet per course per week. I had them printed myself. Payne thinks they come from a school system in Cleveland." She smiled smugly. "Now aren't they a masterpiece of design? Just the right size, only room for the essentials, so you can get away with being awfully vague. That's just as well, because a class never goes quite the way you plan it. Oh, two hints. Abbreviate wherever possible. That makes the thing look like it's packed full of content. And whenever it looks a little thin, write 'Discussion'."

"Oh Maggie, thanks. You are a lifesaver."

"True," she said, not at all modestly. "I also do First Aid. There will be life-restoring coffee at four o'clock. Come next door for a gossip break. In the meantime, I leave you to your drudgery. Chin up!"

Heartened by Maggie's reassurances, I tackled the mound of books and papers, and gradually the task that had seemed overwhelming fell into perspective. As the days passed, Maggie was as good as her word, offering a steady stream of advice and encouragement, guidance and gossip. The few hours not taken up with faculty meetings and desk work were filled with her cheerful presence. Before I knew it, the week was gone, and the campus echoed with the shouts of a hundred excited young voices.

 *4*

THE DRY, precise voice of Dr. Sidney Payne cut across the babble of the Lower School girls filling the dormitory. "Ah, Miss Sheridan. May I present two of your charges?"

I rose swiftly from my desk and advanced to meet the slender girls who stood fidgeting uncomfortably under the avuncular hands the headmaster had placed on their shoulders. Even had they not been the last to arrive, I would have known immediately that these were the daughters of the Sheik of Qaiman. As we shook hands solemnly, I thought that they were indeed as lovely and exotic as their names. The elder, Zora, might be eleven years old, and her sister Zafia perhaps nine, but apart from the difference in age they were identical. With their delicate olive complexions and gleaming black hair and the dark, liquid eyes that really were almond-shaped, they looked like little princesses from the *Arabian Nights.*

The introductions were barely completed when Maggie appeared in the doorway and murmured, "Dr. Payne, could I see you for a moment?"

Left alone with the two girls, I smiled reassuringly and asked, "Is this your first time in Switzerland?"

Neither girl answered for a long moment, then Zora said in careful halting English, "It is the first time alone. We came in winters when our mother was alive." She swallowed hard and grasped her sister's hand, and I saw that Zafia's eyes too had filled with tears.

"Well then," I said brightly, "it won't be so strange to you. Shall we have a look at your room? It's just across the hall from mine. You're very lucky to have such a fine large room all for yourselves."

Not for the first time, I wondered about that. The Academy was a very democratic institution, but in this case royalty, even minor royalty, appeared to have its privileges.

As the girls inspected the room together and began to debate something animatedly in Arabic, presumably who should have which bed, I looked around me with a vague feeling of unease. The room had been changed since my first tour of the dormitory a week before. Of course, the bunks for four had been replaced with twin beds and only two desks remained, but the difference was not just in the furnishing. There was something else.

"Zora, Zafia, speak English!"

At the strange voice, I turned to see the graceful pair of girls, their spirits seemingly restored, converging with cries of welcome on a dark man of middle height. He gathered them to his side, then lifted his head and regarded me with eyes that were as dark and liquid as the girls' own.

For a full minute I bore his silent scrutiny, barely noticing the trim mustache over a firm mouth and resolute chin, the strongly modeled cheekbones under tanned skin. My attention was held by those deep eyes that probed and challenged.

"Zora, where are your manners?"

"I am sorry, Uncle Sadiq. This is Miss Sher-sher—"

"Sheridan," I supplied. "Deirdre Sheridan."

"Sadiq Yamali," he said, extending a hand that held mine as firmly as his eyes did. Then the scrutiny ended abruptly with a decisive nod, and his eyes crinkled in a smile that transformed his face from severity into urbane charm.

"I am delighted to know the girls will be in such good hands," he said.

A man of rapid judgments, I thought, as Sadiq Yamali turned his attention to the window behind me. I could still feel the pressure of his hand, and I was absurdly pleased that his opinion of me was favorable.

Dr. Payne's reappearance prevented further uncomfortable thoughts. "Ah, Mr. Yamali," he said, "do you find the arrangements satisfactory?"

Sadiq Yamali stared at the window for another long moment, gave that brief decisive nod I had seen before, and turned. His eyes rested on me for an instant and he smiled fleetingly, then said to Dr. Payne, "Perfectly satisfactory." I felt myself flush with pleasure at the implied approval as he continued, "Now if I might impose on your time for a few more minutes—"

"Of course, of course," Dr. Payne replied almost obsequiously. "Miss Sheridan, please help the girls to get settled, then come to my office in half an hour."

The door closed, and I set to work, placing stacks of winter clothing on the upper shelves of the built-in closet as little Zafia silently handed them to me. Zora, rummaging in a box of shoes, seemed more inclined to talk. But as I tried to draw her out, I found that I was paying only half attention to her carefully grammatical answers. The

*23*

other half of my mind was occupied by her disturbingly attractive Uncle Sadiq. I crossed to the window where he had stood, and wondered what Sadiq had been thinking about so intently.

Then I knew why the room seemed different to me. Last week, I was sure, the window had only screens and shutters. Now there had been added a finely wrought but obviously sturdy iron grille.

The murmur from the headmaster's office was punctuated by a scraping of chairs. The door opened and from the outer office I head Sadiq Yamali's voice clearly.

". . . not necessary to alarm the girls. Of course, Haroun appreciates the danger and I think he'll be quite sensible about it all. Oh, and while we're on the subject of Haroun." Yamali's voice took on a note of wry amusement. "He plans to work very hard for admission to Cambridge. It seems not to have occurred to him that his place is assured. I don't think, do you, that we need enlighten him?"

Dr. Payne chuckled appreciatively as they moved into the outer office, and Sadiq continued, "Thank you for your time. I'm sure you'll take all possible precautions. And, as I said, I'll be here from time to time to check on Haroun and the girls. I've taken a chalet on the Oberbort, and it's an easy matter to hop up for the weekend whenever I happen to be in Geneva."

"Splendid, splendid, Mr. Yamali. Good night and a pleasant journey."

"Thank you, Dr. Payne. Good evening, Miss Sheridan," he said, turning toward me. "I look forward to seeing you again soon. I hope you'll be able to give me good reports of Zora and Zafia."

"I'm sure I will. They are exceptional girls, as lovely and unusual as their names."

"Indeed they are. Your own name, if you will forgive me, is Deirdre, is it not?"

I nodded agreement.

"Also lovely and unusual." He took my hand and bent over it in a sketch of a Continental bow. *"Au revoir, mademoiselle."*

I sank gratefully onto the hard chair in Dr. Payne's office and struggled to collect myself. Really, it was too ridiculous. How much had I seen of the man, perhaps ten minutes? Hardly reason for a few words and the touch of his hand to make my knees unreliable. After all, a bachelor of his age—he was clearly in his thirties—would find such gallantry effortless.

Bachelor. There too it was ridiculous, the way I had—yes, admit it—quizzed an unsuspecting Zora about her fascinating relative. Artlessly I had remarked:

"How nice that your uncle was able to bring you here. He seems to be a great favorite of yours."

"Oh, Uncle Sadiq is not really our uncle," Zora replied. "Our mother was his cousin. He came to Qaiman after she married our father. He has worked in the government for many years, and he is more important even than Uncle Ahmed, who is our real uncle. Now Uncle Sadiq is very much Qaimani."

"Well," I persisted, "he certainly seems to be very fond of you. Has he no children of his own?"

Here I thought perhaps I had pressed too far, but Zora only seemed amused. "Uncle Sadiq? Oh no, he is quite a—*célibataire?*"

"Bachelor," I translated.

"Ba-che-lor," Zora repeated. "Yes, Uncle Sadiq is a bachelor. I think he has not time to be married. He is always traveling and very busy. Of course," she went on doubtfully, "our father is also very busy. But I suppose

*25*

that is different, because he is the sheik, and the sheik must have a—*héritier?*"

"Heir," I supplied. "And so he has Haroun and you and Zafia, and I am sure he is very glad to have you. But how is it that you speak such beautiful French?"

"We learned from our mother." Once again her eyes filled with tears, as they had at the first mention of her dead parent, but she pushed them valiantly back. "She was partly French. Uncle Sadiq also. They had grandparents from *le Liban*—Lebanon? So we learned to speak both French and Arabic from babies."

And that, I thought as I sat in Dr. Payne's office, went a fair way toward explaining Sadiq's continental chivalry. Probably he had been at least partly educated in France. The compliments that had pleased me so thoroughly were undoubtedly a simple Gallic reflex.

With an effort I forced my attention back to Dr. Payne. I had been listening to his words without really hearing them, as I mused about Sadiq Yamali, but now he began to speak of the very man who occupied my thoughts:

". . . expressed great concern about the safety of the boy Haroun and his sisters. It is about this that I wished to talk with you confidentially."

"Of course, Dr. Payne. But I don't understand. Does Mr. Yamali think that someone intends to—harm the children?"

"I'm not certain," he said hesitantly. "Nor, do I think, is he. But I confess I cannot dismiss his fears altogether. How can one, in these days of hijackings, kidnappings, political hostages? We must remember that the Middle East is a very troubled area. And that the Sheik of Qaiman is a very rich man."

"I see," I said slowly. "Then Sa—their uncle thinks there is danger of kidnapping?"

"It would be a possible explanation."

26

"Explanation, sir?" I asked, more sharply than I had intended. "Has there already been some sort of incident?"

"You are very quick, Miss Sheridan," said the headmaster with surprised approval. "There has indeed. The incident was ambiguous enough—the motive was not established, nor even whether it was intentional—but it was nonetheless disturbing."

"What happened?"

Dr. Payne considered for a moment. "You will not repeat what I tell you?"

"I will respect your wishes." I paused. "And Mr. Yamali's, I assume?"

"Exactly." Dr. Payne fitted his fingertips together and frowned at them, choosing his words. "Some weeks ago, as Haroun was driving not far from the city of Qaiman, his roadster was forced from the pavement by a larger automobile with four occupants. The boy showed great presence of mind, reversing the vehicle and placing some distance between himself and his presumed assailants. He was shortly joined by another car bearing a detail of bodyguards which, fortunately, the sheik had assigned to Haroun's protection only days before. The bodyguards emerged with guns drawn. The driver attempted to flee, and he was shot dead. The other three put up no resistance. When they were questioned, they maintained that the incident was an accident, caused by a steering aberration. Since then, they have been detained without charges in a Qaimani jail." His face showed profound British disapproval of such procedure. "But they have not altered their story. Of course," he continued uncertainly, "I believe the Qaimani authorities draw the line at physical torture."

I sat for a moment in silence, trying to grasp the details of Dr. Payne's dry recital. Then I asked, "But what about the attackers' car? Was it examined?"

"It was. And there was no evidence of steering malfunction. The car was new and powerful and very expensive. It had been purchased with cash shortly before by the man who drove it. There was no way to tell where he got the money. His companions, who insisted they had only gone along for a trial spin, said blandly that they assumed he had been blackmailing somebody. They were none of them of a very savory reputation."

Once again I sat for a few moments without speaking, while I searched for a point that had puzzled me. "You said the bodyguards had only just been assigned to Haroun. Then the attackers might not have known that the boy wouldn't be alone? That is, if the attack had been planned."

"Quite so."

"But why had the bodyguards been assigned to him?"

"Mr. Yamali did not say. Perhaps he did not know." Dr. Payne looked doubtful. "At any rate, they kept close watch over Haroun until his departure. And now it is our responsibility to see that no harm comes to him and his sisters."

Despite the gravity of the situation, I found myself suppressing a wry smile as I thought of Haroun bin Sultan bin Muhammad. I had met him only a scant half hour before, and yet I felt sure that this seventeen-year-old heir to the Sheikdom of Qaiman would find our conversation hilarious in the extreme. Oh, he would doubtless regard the headmaster's concern as reasonable and, indeed, no more than his due. But the idea that a mere girl such as I could entertain thoughts of "protecting" him, *that* Haroun would dismiss with contempt.

I could see him now lounging in the doorway of his sisters' room, a tolerant smile playing over his finely chiseled features as he watched us at our housewifely tasks. Shuttling between trunks and closet, I had studied Haroun covertly and wondered why I felt a mild antipathy toward him. It would be wise to quash such feelings, I knew, as he would inevitably be in one of my classes. And to be honest, it was not really antipathy I felt, rather an obscure resentment. But why resentment, I wondered. Reluctantly I owned the truth—it was because his sudden appearance had put a stop to Zora's innocent chatter on the absorbing subject of Uncle Sadiq.

I examined his face for traces of Sadiq and found the resemblance striking. Haroun might have been Sadiq's younger brother, or his son. There were differences, of course. Where the man had shown mature self-possession, the boy evinced only an adolescent cockiness. Still, I had to admit Haroun was a young man of considerable parts—confident, intelligent, alert. And there was no doubt that he had been born and bred to absolute rule. Something in his face proclaimed that he would not suffer fools gladly and that females were automatically included in that category until proven innocent.

His next words confirmed my suspicion. "Zora, Zafia, have you forgotten that Sadiq expects to take us to dinner in five minutes? I know that it is a Western custom for the women to keep the men waiting." His eyes flicked lazily in my direction. "But I had not thought you would adapt so quickly."

So, I thought, the gauntlet is thrown. Well, Mr. Haroun bin Sultan bin Et Cetera, you will have to meet the velvet-sheathed steel of American Womanhood.

Instantly I reprimanded myself. It was only natural for Haroun to be a bit bristly and arrogant. If he did not share the urbane charm and self-possession of Sadiq, there was an explanation. He was, after all, only seventeen.

In the headmaster's office, I asked Dr. Payne anxiously, "Does Haroun—appreciate the situation?"

Dr. Payne did not answer immediately, but when he did he spoke decisively. "I think he does. He seems to insist on regarding the attack as an isolated incident. That way he does not need to dwell on the possibility of a repetition. But he understands that any heir-apparent is vulnerable, and for the sake of his father's peace of mind, he has agreed to be particularly cautious. He knows that he must not go anywhere without company, preferably a staff member. Haroun's carelessness should not be cause for concern." He paused significantly. "But there are other causes. Zora and Zafia."

Oh no, I thought, impossible! Those two dark, almond-eyed little enchantresses. How could anyone want to harm them? Anyone who saw them must love them instantly. Even I, a total stranger, had been drawn powerfully toward them. To their father, those slender beauties must be—

Yes. Must be worth a great deal of money. Suddenly I saw the danger all too clearly.

"I noticed the iron grille on the window," I said tentatively.

"Ah, yes. I hope that will not cause too much comment." Again the headmaster looked doubtful. "If anyone should mention it to you, Miss Sheridan, it would help if you glossed it over with a rather vague explanation—a matter of Eastern custom, the cloistered upbringing of girls, that sort of thing." He regarded me speculatively. "I trust that your, er, theatrical experience will help you to carry it off."

As a matter of fact, I have never been particularly good at telling lies, chiefly from lack of practice. An angry retort rose to my lips, but I bit it back. In this case, I had no doubt I could and would allay suspicion for the sake of the young girls, and I unhesitatingly told Dr. Payne so.

"I gather Zora and Zafia—"

"—have been told nothing of this? It would serve no purpose to upset them. They are too young to understand. And in their case our watchfulness will not seem remarkable. The younger children are not permitted to leave the grounds unless accompanied by a staff member in any event. A little extra vigilance would be natural, especially as Zafia is our youngest student."

"Poor pet," I murmured sympathetically, thinking of Zafia's soft, frightened eyes. "She seems a bit—overwhelmed."

"Yes," Dr. Payne agreed. "I confess I had misgivings about admitting her. Oh, I think she'll do all right in the fifth form. Her tutoring has been excellent. But she is young for her age, and a long way from Qaiman. I hope, Miss Sheridan, that you will be able to win her confidence." He smiled across at me thinly, and I realized with surprise that, whatever my success might be with Zafia, I had won *his* confidence. I wondered what had caused him to revise his earlier uncertain opinion of me. Could the little he had seen of my work explain it? Or might it be, I asked myself with a sudden rush of pleasure, something Sadiq had said? He went on: "It is fortunate that you also are small and dark. Perhaps you will remind her of her home."

But as I recrossed the campus to my room and listened to the boisterous shouts of a hundred extroverted Western children, I thought that it would take a good deal more than my looks to make Zafia and her sister feel at home.

5

SILENCE had finally descended as the twenty Lower School girls settled themselves to sleep, and still my thoughts were occupied by the slender, almond-eyed Qaimani girls and, far too frequently, I told myself sternly, by their handsome uncle. I pulled the sash of my robe tighter and picked up my hairbrush for the ritual nightly strokes. Perhaps tomorrow I would find time to wash my hair. Tonight the firm bed in its snug wood-paneled alcove was irresistably inviting. But even that, I reminded myself, would have to wait. I had still not talked to Maggie, and it could not be put off.

I dropped my hairbrush on the dresser and turned to see, without surprise, that Maggie stood in the doorway. Already in the short week I had known her I had grown accustomed to her uncanny, almost psychic, ability to appear whenever she popped into my thoughts.

"Deirdre, come look!" she whispered.

I followed her into her cluttered bedroom, feeling my fatigue and apprehension lessen in the wake of her single-minded enthusiasm.

"Aren't they lovely?" she exclaimed, sweeping a hand toward a mass of long-stemmed roses with a vigor that threatened to overturn the vase. "A back-to-classes present, with the message 'Courage'. Now, isn't that just like Fred?"

I did not know whether it was just like Fred, but I forbore saying so. I did know that Fred was Maggie's fiancé in Cleveland, Fred had just received his medical degree, Fred was personable and brilliant and handsome, Fred was the center of the universe. In fact, I knew a great deal about Fred, since every third phrase from Maggie's lips was "Fred says."

"They're perfectly beautiful, Maggie," I said with what I hoped was equal enthusiasm.

"He's so marvelously thoughtful," she said contentedly. "He remembers the least little occasion. Thank heavens he's not going to be the sort of husband who forgets anniversaries."

"But, Maggie," I said, emboldened by her openness, "then why are you here? Why aren't you in Cleveland?" Why aren't you married now, I almost asked.

I did not need to voice the question. She answered frankly, "I couldn't stand being so close to Fred and not being able to get married, or even to see him without causing a family battle. My parents don't approve, you see, and—" She broke off with an unaccustomed frown, then resumed more brightly, "Actually, it's all for the best. Fred's doing his internship now, and I wouldn't get to see that much of him. And next June, when I'm twenty-five, I'll already have my grandfather's legacy, and then I can marry anyone I please. It won't matter whether my parents approve or not."

*33*

By now I had been so indoctrinated on the virtues of Fred that I exclaimed involuntarily, "But why on earth would they not approve?"

"Deirdre," Maggie said simply, "Fred's a Gentile."

I suppose my surprise must have been written all over my face. But Maggie simply laughed and said, "I imagine you thought you Irish had a monopoly on freckles and red hair. We're not all dark and olive-skinned, you know. Like you!" Her laughter now held double amusement.

In a moment I recovered and asked, knowing Maggie would not be offended, "What about Fred's family? They don't—"

"Mind that I'm Jewish? Lord, no! Of course, it was a bit uncomfortable until I explained that my family was Klein before the fear of Hitler changed the name. Fred's people are hide-bound Protestants. *They* were upset to think I was Irish, and therefore Catholic!" Suddenly Maggie's hand flew to her mouth, and her gaiety was replaced by contrition as she faltered, "Deirdre! I'm sorry, I didn't mean—"

This time it was my turn to laugh. "It's all right, Maggie. You haven't trodden on any toes. My family wasn't militantly Irish, and not Catholic at all. Daddy," I suppressed a pang, "was too devoted to the contemplation of God's creatures on earth to give any thought to formal forms of worshipping Him."

"He must have been a very nice man," Maggie said with rare solemnity. "Prejudice is so ugly, and so unreasonable. Look at us! Any anti-Semitic Irishman would accept me in a minute. But you, except for your name, you don't seem a bit Irish."

"Black Irish," I said lightly. "There are all sorts of theories. Some say we're the result of shipwrecked sailors who came from the Mediterranean a thousand years ago, or two or three."

*34*

"I can believe it," said Maggie judiciously. "You know, you do look Jewish. Or Arab. Even Qaimani, like those two darling little girls."

Instantly I remembered the chilling subject I had not yet broached. I had been wrestling with my conscience all evening, and it gave one last protest before I pushed it resolutely back. After all, my promise to Dr. Payne applied to only part of our conversation, and I was willing to breach even that if it meant an extra pair of vigilant eyes over Zora and Zafia.

"Maggie, listen!" I said urgently, and I related to her most of my conversation with Dr. Payne. She listened intently, and interposed a number of pertinent questions. And yet I had the feeling that she did not take the matter nearly as seriously as I had. Her questions all seemed directed toward proving that the fears Sadiq Yamali had expressed, the fears that were shared to some extent by Dr. Payne and wholeheartedly by myself, were quite groundless.

"You'll see, Deirdre," she said, once again her cheerful self. "Of course we'll all be careful, but I don't think there's any real danger."

As I went slowly back to my own room and crawled wearily into bed, I wondered whether anything in the world seemed real to Maggie. Except, of course, Fred.

I had almost drifted off when I heard a wail followed by low sobs. For a moment I thought it must be the Payne baby crying, the sound diminished by the distance from the headmaster's cottage. But as the sobbing continued, muffled as though by a pillow, I realized it was quite close at hand.

I listened for a moment longer, then slipped from the bed and pulled my robe on. In the dimly lighted hallway the sounds were clearer. They came unmistakably from

*35*

the room opposite mine.

Unwilling to startle the girls with a sudden light, I returned to my room and found a candle. Then I tapped lightly on the door and stepped inside, closing the door firmly behind me. In the candlelight that flickered as I placed the heavy wrought-iron holder on the nearest desk, I saw Zora perched uneasily on the edge of her sister's bed, holding the sobbing Zafia's hand.

Sensing instinctively that French would be more reassuring, I said softly in that language:

"Zora, Zafia, what's wrong?"

Zafia's tear-streaked face jerked from the pillow and she cried, *"Maman!"* Her soft dark eyes stared at me hungrily, and then she fell back to the pillow in a fresh fit of weeping.

"Hush, Zafia," her sister said. "It's only Mademoiselle Sheridan."

Crossing to the bed, I laid my hand on Zafia's thin heaving shoulders and spoke to her soothingly, still in French. Presently the storm of sobs diminished, and I looked a question at Zora.

"I think it was a *cauchemar*—a bad dream," the older girl murmured. "She woke up suddenly and started crying for our mother. Then you came in, and she must have thought you were—" Zora inclined her head toward the gold-framed photograph that stood on the bedside table.

I picked up the frame and studied the delicate, dark woman who looked out at me. Her features were more Oriental than mine, but the resemblance was undeniable. The same coloring, the same facial structure—we must even have been about the same size. Poor Zafia! Seeing me by candlelight, she must have thought she saw a ghost.

"Does she have these nightmares often?"

"Not so much now. There were more at first."

"How long is it since—"

"Less than a year." Quietly Zora told me of her mother's death in an automobile crash in Qaiman. She left me to infer that the body was somewhat mutilated, saying simply that Zafia had never seen her mother dead and could not accept that her absence was permanent. She kept looking for her to return, and tonight—

Tonight for one wild joyous moment she thought her mother had come back, and then she had been plunged into even worse grief. Because of me.

I looked at patient Zora, too young for the responsibility of mothering her sister, and at little Zafia, still crying quietly. When my own mother died, I had not been as young as they, and yet I had not recovered from the shock for many months. And my more recent loss was fresh enough that I could guess at the depths of their grief as I searched for words of comfort.

"Zafia dear," I said, lifting her thin shoulders and brushing the damp hair from her face, "of course you're homesick. This is a big change for you. But you aren't alone. You have Zora here and Haroun, and your Uncle Sadiq will be visiting soon. And you'll make lots of new friends. I hope that I shall be one of them."

By now her crying had subsided, and as she settled in my arms she lifted a wan smile to me.

"Sometimes," Zora said hesitantly, "when we were unhappy, our mother used to sing to us."

I smiled across at her, grateful for the suggestion. "Well, I don't know the songs your mother used to sing," I said gently, "but I do remember the songs *my* mother sang to me when I was your age." I began with "The Ash Grove." Then, one after another, the lilting Irish airs returned to me effortlessly. I think I must somehow, thinking of my mother, have infused the songs with her love and reassurance, for presently Zafia relaxed and

*37*

her head dropped sleepily to my shoulder.

I turned the pillow and eased her down onto it. "Are you ready to go to sleep now?" I whispered.

The little heads nodded.

"Good night then, Zafia. Good night, Zora." Impulsively I bent and kissed them both.

As I tiptoed from the room with the candle, I looked back once more at their delicate faces. The lines of grief were erased for a time. I was glad they did not know the danger that hung over them. They had enough to bear.

There must be no fresh tragedy in their lives, I thought fiercely. If I devoted every waking moment to watching over their safety and Haroun's, I would count the time well spent.

 *6*

A BUSTLE of activity on the stage echoed through the empty auditorium, Jenny's clear girlish voice rising in melodious counterpoint over Adam's firm baritone commands.

As I settled more comfortably into my tenth-row seat, propping the dog-eared script on my knees and flipping my notebook to a fresh page, I marveled for the dozenth time at the unflagging energy of these teenagers. In the past two months, it seemed that I had hardly had time to draw a breath, and now as I was just beginning to recover from our first production, already my troupe of young thespians was preparing, scripts in hand, to block the second.

With a final vigorous shove at a sawhorse, Adam called, "Places!" and the work began.

Thank heavens for Adam Ngomutu, I thought. Without encroaching on my authority, he had quietly assumed a good share of the responsibilities of production. Watching the sureness with which he manipulated both properties and players, I did not find it hard to believe that this boy's father, once having wrested control of his Central African nation, had enjoyed almost unopposed rule.

Even the transition had been accomplished with Adam's personal brand of self-deprecatory tact.

"Don't worry about a role for me this time, kids," he had said, as we met around a long table in the dining hall. "I already had the lead in the last one. And there aren't many plays like *Othello* floating around with a part tailor-made for someone as black as I am."

"Oh no, Adam," Jenny Hearn protested. "You have such a marvelous voice. You can't—" She broke off, considering the weight of his argument with sixteen-year-old judiciousness. "Well, maybe you're right. But at least say you'll do the prologue."

"I'll be glad to, unless someone else wants it. But what I'd really like to do," Adam said diffidently, "if Miss Sheridan and the rest of you don't object, is to act as stage manager. Miss Sheridan has so much to do that maybe I could be helpful. And that way I'd be part of the production, and I know I'd learn a lot."

And that, I thought, was pretty much the way it was working out. Except that I was learning a great deal more about Adam Ngomutu than he was learning about stage-craft. Of that he seemed to have an instant, instinctive grasp.

Of course, I reflected as I settled further into my seat, if thanks are due, the first are due to Jenny. Without Jen, I mightn't have had Adam in the group at all, or Haroun or Peter or a number of the others. Not that I had worried about a respectable turnout for our student theatricals. There are always girls who volunteer to do costumes while they hope to be offered parts, and the predictable number of show-off boys. But when Miss Jennifer Hearn opted for the stage, she brought with her the entire male contingent of the senior class.

Jenny's methods, when scrutinized, were not all that original. In the case of Peter, for instance, a toss of Jenny's honey blond hair and a languishing look from her softly fringed gray eyes would have led young Peter Duncan not only onto a stage but over burning coals. And once Adam and Haroun had been enlisted, it remained only for Jenny to suggest to the others that there was an "in" group and an "out" group, and theirs was the choice. But in snaring Haroun and Adam as the core of her company, she had indeed shown ingenuity.

"You see, Miss Sheridan," she confided somewhat after the fact, "it seemed to me that there's no sense putting on plays at all unless you have the best talent, and without Adam and Harry, we wouldn't have it. So I did the only thing I could. I appealed to their patriotism!"

I must have looked rather blank.

"I mean, they wouldn't have been interested in anything they thought was 'kid stuff'," she explained with an earnest attempt at maturity. "So I told them they had to consider their fathers' positions, and that some day they would be expected to assume an important role in world affairs. That's true enough. Harry *will* be sheik when his father dies, and Adam's father looks like he's set for life. All I did was point out the chance they had to perfect their public image—stage presence, voice control, holding an audience, that sort of thing. Things that will be important when they're political leaders. And you see," she concluded triumphantly, "it worked!"

Yes, it had worked, I thought as I jotted another note on the rapidly filling page, and *they* had worked. Both of

*41*

them. Adam, now consulting a sketch as he arranged straight-backed chairs to approximate the next set. And Haroun too. Haroun had devoted himself to this whole play-business with a seriousness that altogether surprised me. I had not expected him to accept direction so willingly from a mere female. Though, to be sure, there were still flashes of his male-supremacy outlook. I remembered the afternoon we had first discussed the project.

"The only problem I can see," Peter said, "is that there aren't enough girls' parts."

"That's the trouble with most older plays," Jenny said, "and this is no exception. At least it has a lot of characters. And anyway, we could always rewrite Crabtree as a female role."

"Or even two," Haroun contributed, with a sidewise glance in my direction. "It says clearly in the Koran that one man is worth two women."

"Sure, and a woman is worth three she-camels, I suppose," Jenny retorted.

"Oh, hardly that much," Haroun said lazily.

"Don't forget I live in Arabia too. I have a pretty clear idea of what the women are worth, and the camels *and* the men!"

"Harry, Jenny," I protested weakly.

"Sorry, Miss Sheridan," Jenny said. "But don't you think it's a wonderful idea? Please say we can do it!"

By that time, of course, I knew I had no choice. Jenny had already fired the rest of the group with her zest for the project, and her first innocent question had put the seal on it.

"Miss Sheridan, you're Irish. You wouldn't be descended from the playwright Richard Brinsley Sheridan?"

"I wish I could say I was," I laughed. "But there is a

relationship. An ancestor of mine was his cousin."

"Oh, but that makes it perfect, doesn't it, gang? Miss Sheridan directing one of her illustrious relative's plays, just two hundred years after it was first produced. And it's so appropriate—she's exactly the same age as he was then!" I felt myself flush, wondering just how Jenny had got hold of that particular piece of information. "By rights I suppose we should be doing *The Rivals*, but it's nowhere near as funny as *The School for Scandal*. And I don't think Dr. Payne could object just on the basis of the title," she went on guilelessly, "because it is a *very* moral play."

And so it had been settled, and the casting accomplished almost by acclamation. Jenny had found no rival claimants to the role of Lady Teazle, a circumstance which I suspected she had counted on. And Peter Duncan was easily persuaded to take the role of her husband Sir Peter. He claimed to be influenced by the fact that the name of the character was his own, so he would not be in danger of missing cues. But none of us present doubted his real motives: the chance of injecting an occasional husbandly caress into the role, and private rehearsals.

"And of course Haroun will have to do Sir Oliver," said Adam. "After all, he's supposed to have been out in India for years, so that perpetually tanned face of yours, Harry, is made to order."

Adam flashed a good-natured smile at Haroun, and Haroun returned it. How easily, I thought with a pang, this mixed bag of children accepted racial difference. If only the people of Bedford-Stuyvesant or Biloxi could do the same! Haroun's next remark reinforced my thought.

"Granted," he said. "And there's that tremendous line, '—how the plague shall I be able to pass for a Jew?'.

Coming from me, that should get a laugh."

The whole company dissolved in mirth.

And mirth still reigned now as I walked back up the darkened aisle and resumed my seat for the blocking of the third act. Well, I told myself, one problem I did not have to face with this group was constraint. A good half of my young cast had lost a parent through death or, more often, divorce, and all had been uprooted from their native soils, and yet they were remarkably self-possessed. Not a hint of stage fright.

Strange. The only stage fright I had noticed in these two months had been my own. That first day of classes had loomed like the jaws of Hell, and I, the same Deirdre Sheridan who had braved New York's critical off-Broadway audiences, had been hard put to keep my knees from shaking visibly as I faced a handful of teenagers. Happily, the ludicrousness of the situation struck me before it struck anyone else, and humor triumphed over horror. But my voice was still, I think, not as steady that day as it had been on opening night.

There was a slight movement in the darkness, and Ruedy Messerli dropped into the seat beside me.

"Hullo, Deirdre," he said quietly. "How is it going?"

"Hi, Ruedy. Very well, thank you, much faster than I had expected. These youngsters have remarkable talent."

"Mmn, maybe they have. They certainly seem to work very smoothly with you. I watched you during *Othello,* you know, and I was struck by the way you accomplished things. You'd let the kids show what they could do, and then you'd gradually bring out of them interpretations they must have thought they'd developed themselves. I think perhaps it is the director who is remarkable."

"Nonsense, Ruedy," I said mildly, wondering what had prompted this outpouring of flattery. I had never before heard him string so many words together at one time. "The credit belongs to the students. And to you," I went on warmly. "If you hadn't volunteered to take over the lighting, it wouldn't have been so successful. You did a wonderful job."

"You knew what effects you wanted, and you described them perfectly. I only pulled a few switches."

"You make it sound so simple. And that lighting panel is anything but simple. In fact, everything about this new auditorium is delightfully professional. That revolving stage—excuse me a moment."

I made my way to the pit, arbitrated a minor dispute, and turned back up the aisle to find Adriana Schiano bearing down on Ruedy from the opposite direction.

"Oh, there you are, Ruedy. I've been looking all over for you," she cooed, including us both in a glance of faint reproach. "You promised to help me with some stands for the sculpture class."

"Right away, Adriana," he said, then turned from the art teacher to me. "You wanted to discuss the sets, Deirdre. When do you think you'll be free?"

"I imagine we should finish in about half an hour. You'll be in Adriana's studio? Good. The three of us can get it all settled this afternoon."

Ruedy allowed himself to be borne off by an Adriana who looked, I thought cattily, a trifle triumphant, and I gave my attention to the stage. The blocking progressed swiftly, and it was not more than twenty minutes later that I called out, "Fine. We'll do the last two acts on Friday. And have your lines for Act One down by Monday."

Adriana's studio door stood open, and in the soft light cast by a single lamp she and Ruedy sat conversing animatedly in Italian about something which, I felt sure, had nothing to do with stands for any sculpture class. Adriana rearranged herself in her chair with a feline stretch that emphasized her rather full-blown Italian charms. Then she caught sight of me in the doorway and showed a brief involuntary frown of annoyance before saying in her richly accented English:

"Ah, Miss Sheridan. You took less time than you had predicted. How efficient you are!"

I felt my back stiffen, and considered the thinly veiled antagonism behind her barbed remark. There could be no other explanation than jealousy, pure and simple. But what cause had I given her? My relationship with Ruedy had progressed, it was true, to an easy friendship, but Adriana could hardly view the possibility of a deeper attachment between us any more seriously than I did. And anyway, I did not think that Adriana's interest in Ruedy was more than superficial. I shrugged mentally. There are some women who cannot bear to have any man pay the slightest attention to another female in their presence. Adriana Schiano, I concluded, was a prime example.

"I'm glad to find the two of you aren't busy," I said, then reprimanded myself inwardly for rising to Adriana's bait. "This shouldn't take long. Except for the picture gallery, the sets are quite simple, and they're all interiors." Briefly I sketched the requirements and concluded:

"The major problem is the sheer number of them. We can only set up three at one time. Even if we can work Charles' house as a split set, there will be five, and we'll have to change two at intermission. So it would be too cumbersome to have real bookshelves for the library. We'll have to use a painted backdrop. I hate to impose on you again, Adriana, but if you could assemble a crew of volunteers from your classes and supervise them—"

"I shall be delighted to be of some small help," she

replied silkily, but I could hear an undertone of resentment in her voice.

Now what ails her? I wondered with irritation. After all, she offered her services—in Ruedy's presence, as I recalled—quite freely. She couldn't think the one backdrop too great an undertaking. More likely, I thought, she would prefer to seem more important. On a sudden inspiration I said:

"You could be a great help! In fact, you could *make* the play. The picture gallery scene is crucial, and it'll fall flat if we have to depend on borrowed paintings. The portraits won't match the dialogue. So if—well, I know your painting class is doing portraiture now, so if you could talk them into adding wigs and period costumes, and producing a couple of pompous judges and a red-coated general and a girl in shepherdess dress—"

Adriana's expression changed instantly from an ill-disguised sullenness to wary interest. I had guessed well.

"We could even arrange a showing," I went on, "to coincide with the play."

Ruedy caught my eye, and caught my intention as well. "Of course, Adriana!" he said enthusiastically. "We could hang the paintings in the corridor outside the auditorium, and the intermission of the play would be the opening of the art show, the—what's the term?"

*"Vernissage,"* she said absently, her brow creased in concentration. "Yes, I think my students would enjoy doing it. But I hope, Deirdre, that you don't expect the quality to be too professional?"

"Not at all," I laughed. "The only one that needs to be any good is the portrait of Sir Oliver as a young man. That one really should look like Haroun. I suppose we could make do with tinting a photograph. But I'm sure he'd be glad to put on a wig and sit for the portrait if—"

"I'll do it myself," Adriana said decidedly.

"Wonderful! I hoped you'd say that." I slipped my coat on and picked up my ever-present stack of books. "According to the play, the painting is worth four hundred pounds. I think that's a bit steep, but if Haroun is as pleased with the results as I think he will be, you just may find you have a sale on your hands."

Adriana smiled complacently and waved a cheerful good-bye as Ruedy followed me out into the chill dusk.

"Admirable, the way you brought her around," he murmured. "I'll stick to what I said before. As a director, you are remarkable."

 *7*

THE FOLLOWING day was Wednesday, our free afternoon at the school. As I strolled back to the dormitory after lunch, I debated how to spend the glorious unplanned hours. First a long walk in the crisp autumn sunshine, and then perhaps an hour or two with the new novel Kate had loaned me.

But first I would look in on Zora and Zafia.

I paused in the doorway of their room and regarded the two slender figures sprawled together on Zafia's bed, their dark heads bent over a magazine. A wave of tenderness washed over me as I thought how precious these little Qaimani girls had become to me. The fifteen minutes I spent with them before bedtime was now ritual, and the high point of my day. And while I had from the beginning stayed close to them on the frequent school outings, what had begun as a safety consideration had evolved into an established and mutually delightful habit.

*"Massa' el-q'aire,"* I greeted them softly.

Two heads shot up and two treble voices chorused, *"Masaa' in-nuwr."*

"Thank you. I think everyone's afternoon will be bright. It's certainly a fine day. How do you say, 'The weather is beautiful'?"

Patiently they supplied the Arabic phrase and corrected my stumbling pronunciation.

This too had become ritual. At first I had suggested that Zora and Zafia teach me a little Arabic, in return for my help with the finer points of English, simply as a means of winning their confidence. But the project had been fruitful. Now Zora at least was able to chatter away happily with her schoolmates, confident that her grammatical lapses would be as easily forgiven as overcome. And I had mastered the formal Arabic greetings, a fair bit of counting, and the words for window and teacher, bed and doll.

"And what is this fascinating magazine that keeps you indoors on such a day?"

Zafia closed the cover and shyly handed to me a French periodical called *The World of Animals.* "We were looking at the pictures of the cats," she explained in her soft hesitant voice.

"They're adorable, aren't they?" I agreed. "Do you have many pets at home?"

Zafia frowned over the unfamiliar word.

"Pets? Is that family animals?" I nodded. "Oh yes, our father has many beautiful horses, and for the hunting the saluki dogs. But I like best the cats. I wish—" she trailed off wistfully.

As I looked down at the small, thin face, cloaked in reticence and shadowed by sorrow, I too wished. I

50

wished I could do something to restore the carefree innocence of childhood, to put gaiety back into those dear dark eyes.

"Wait here a minute for me?" I asked, and hurried along the corridor to the common sitting room where the telephone stood. I was in luck, and within the promised minute I was back.

"How would you two like to spend the afternoon in Saanen visiting my cousin? She's a very nice lady, and her chalet is absolutely full of cats."

I did not need to wait for an answer. The flash of excitement on their faces told me plainly. Zora and Zafia were bundled into warm sweaters and waiting for me almost before I had time to collect my purse.

At the main building I made an excuse to stop in the office, and the two girls stayed outside while I told Martha Payne our destination and Kate's telephone number. I returned to find them in animated conversation with Haroun.

"Sounds like great fun," he said. "Would you mind if I came too?"

"Oh, please do!" his sisters cried in unison, and soon the four of us were making our way down the twisting road to the village, the girls skipping hand in hand, while Haroun and I struggled to match their pace without serious loss of dignity.

"I wasn't trying to horn in, Miss Sheridan," he burst out suddenly. "But I have so few chances to spend any time with my sisters, and I don't want them to think I've deserted them. They've already had to face so much. And there's worse to come."

For a time I kept my eyes on the concrete sidewalk beneath our hurrying feet. Haroun's first astonishing words were still in my ears. This was a side of him I had not seen before, a sensitivity to the feelings of others—

first myself and then, unmistakably sincerely, his sisters. I stole a sidelong glance at him.

Haroun's face was now resolutely closed, as though he regretted his short speech. But why? Simply because he had shown consideration for the feelings of females? No, his love for his sisters was clearly genuine.

And then I really heard his later words—*there's worse to come.*

Could it be that Haroun, who blithely disdained all concern about kidnapping plots, was actually worried about the possibility? Perhaps he was. Perhaps he knew more than we had been told. And yet—somehow that did not seem to be the whole answer. There was something fatalistic in his statement, as though he *knew* some tragedy loomed.

Absorbed in this new question, I must not have been watching my footing. My low heel caught and I spun around, instinctively dropping my arms behind me to cushion the fall.

"Miss Sheridan, *êtes-vous blessée?*" cried Haroun, momentarily lapsing into French in his concern, as his two sisters raced back to us.

"No—no, I'm not hurt," I gasped, as I pulled myself into a sitting position and looked intently back up the hill. Then I mentally inventoried limbs and found that I was indeed all in one piece.

Three pairs of solicitous hands helped me to my feet and Haroun asked anxiously, "Are you sure you're all right? You look so pale."

Small wonder that I looked pale, I thought as I reassured them. I had just received a bit of a jolt. Not the fall, which was minor, but what I had seen as I fell.

Some fifty yards behind us a dark figure in workman's clothing was hurrying down the hill in our wake. As I fell, he abruptly checked his pace, his outline freezing in an attitude of profound startlement. A reaction that was, I conceded, natural enough.

But when I looked back up the hill scant seconds later, he had totally disappeared.

"The next bus is due in just over twenty minutes," Haroun announced as he emerged from the post office. "We may as well wait, even if the taxi gets back. He charges a bloody fortune."

Quietly pointing out to Haroun that he should practice his British slang on less tender ears, I suggested that we repair to Charly's Tearoom for a *coupe Danemark*. "After all, Cookie's meals are generally adequate, but desserts are his weak point. My treat!"

Twenty minutes later we stood outside the squat stuccoed post office opposite the railroad station and watched the bus pull in. The driver touched the horn briefly before climbing down to unload baggage and mail sacks. I studied the black symbol of a winding horn on the brightly painted yellow side of the postal bus, thinking what a long and orderly progress Switzerland had made since the first post coach had borne the symbol, even then invariably arriving on time.

Zafia and Zora found a pair of seats together, and Haroun and I settled across the aisle from them.

"I wish my English nickname had turned out to be something other than Harry," he remarked ruefully. "It seems to have unfortunate associations with the head devil."

"Old Harry, you mean?" I laughed. "I can see your point. You could always ask people to call you Aaron."

"The Hebrew form? Is that a common English name?"

"Well, perhaps not in Britain," I admitted. "But in New England, where I was born, there have always been a lot of Biblical names—Abraham, Elisha, Caleb. There was even a time when—oh!''

"What's wrong, Miss Sheridan? Are you really sure you're feeling all right?''

The bus driver already had his hand on the lever to pull the heavy front door shut when a last passenger swung aboard. He was a dark man of medium height, dressed in the electric blue that was virtually a uniform among European workmen. His back was almost completely to us as he spoke briefly with the driver, but something in the way he moved reminded me of the figure that had hurried down the hill behind us. When he turned, I caught a brief glimpse of his face. But the man on the hill had been too far away for me to be sure of a resemblance.

"Haroun,'' I whispered quickly. "That man who just got on the bus. Have you ever seen him before?''

He thought for an instant. "I think I may have seen him around the school. Why?''

"Oh, nothing. I thought he looked familiar,'' I said, as the blue-clad man moved quickly past us to the rear of the bus. With his dark coloring, I reflected, he looked as Arabic as my young companions.

I told myself sharply to stop imagining things. A man with dark coloring in blue workman's clothing was a common enough sight. Switzerland abounded in Spanish and even Yugoslav workers. And yet I knew I would be very relieved to get off the bus in Saanen and leave him aboard.

Zora and Zafia, chattering animatedly, were out of their seats before the bus came to a halt. Following them back along the narrow aisle, I noticed with surprise that the mysterious workman, as I had mentally termed him, was already descending the rear step. I had not been able to hear much of his conversation with the driver, but I thought I had caught the word "Rougemont," and assumed that was his destination.

As I watched, he stopped at the kiosk for a paper, turned slightly as he fumbled in his pocket for change, then disappeared around the corner. Well, that was that. He was gone, and I could stop my foolish worrying.

We set off up the narrow road beside the churchyard, the girls once again skipping ahead as Haroun and I labored behind.

"I'm glad to find I have an English name," Haroun said, picking up our conversation where it had been interrupted. "I wish I could think of an Arabic one for you. But there's nothing quite like Deirdre. It's Gaelic, isn't it?"

"Irish as Paddy's pig," I replied cheerfully. "Unfortunately, the girl of legend was a great source of troubles, but when I was born, my romantic mother was reading *Deirdre of the Sorrows,* so Deirdre I had to be."

"The same sort of thing happened to me," Haroun said. "I should have been Muhammad for my grandfather, but my mother wanted to name me for Haroun al-Rashid, and my father allowed himself to be persuaded. I'm afraid Father was a bit . . . uxorious."

"Haroun al-Rashid," I repeated. "The caliph of the *Arabian Nights.*"

"Arabian nights? Oh yes, the *Thousand Nights and a Night,* we call it. At any rate, my mother was more optimistic than yours in her choice of name. 'Al-Rashid' means 'the Upright'."

"Let's hope that inspires you during the skiing season," I said blandly, observing with a wicked touch of satisfaction that Haroun was at first reluctantly amused and then effectively silenced.

Calling to the girls to wait for us, and hearing their carefree answering shouts, I was glad they did not know how foolishly alarmed I had been only a few minutes before. And yet, as I remembered the man on the bus, my uneasiness returned. I had a vague feeling now that someone was mounting the road behind us. I must have heard some small sound, perhaps made by a farmer, or a dog. But as I placed my feet one before the other, I could not bring myself to turn to investigate.

Finally, with what I hoped was complete nonchalance, I reached into my purse and pulled out my compact. Holding it carefully in front of me, I brushed the grains of powder from the mirror inside the lid. Then I checked the angle of the sun from the shadows before me and calculated the slope of the road below. Deciding there would be no tell-tale glare, I raised the mirror and positioned it for a quick glimpse over my shoulder.

What lay back there was a man of dark coloring dressed in electric-blue workman's clothing plodding steadily up the hill.

"Haroun!" I said. "I—I think I have something in my eye. Would you look?"

Instantly he bent over me and pulled my eyelid gently back with a mixture of diffidence and solicitude that I would have found touching under any other circumstance. But at this point I was too busy maneuvering my compact into position for another look down the hill. With two perfectly sound eyes, I got a good view of the slope below and found it, as I had half-expected, totally empty.

"Thanks, Haroun. I think you've worked it loose. It feels better now."

I snapped the compact shut and dropped it into my purse. As we came up to the girls and turned the corner for the last bit of climb to Kate's chalet, I did not bother to turn for a last look downhill. I was quite sure our blue-clad shadow would not be visible.

8

GREETING the little girls with easy warmth, Kate turned
back to me expectantly for the introduction of her third
guest. When I pronounced Haroun's name, she hesitated a second and a flicker of speculation touched her
eyes. Then, inexplicably, she dropped into a profound
curtsey and said:

"Highness, this modest household is honored."

Good heavens, I thought, whatever has possessed my
cousin? Of course, the British are all notoriously royalty-
conscious. But dear democratic down-to-earth Kate?

"Madame," Haroun said firmly, raising her to her feet,
"no titles, please. It is my family which is honored. You
have shown great generosity in opening your home to
strangers, and I share my sisters' pleasure."

Kate's eyes held their familiar twinkle as she allowed
herself to be persuaded, and I had my answer. She had
achieved equality of rank as surely as if she had insisted

on it. But in permitting Haroun to confer it, she had not only fed his ego but captivated him as well.

Soon the three Qaimanis were chatting volubly with Kate, who pointed out the sights from her wide balcony, presented the members of her menagerie as they appeared, and provided cat cookies for Zora and Zafia to feed to Cléopatre, Samson, and the others.

In the kitchen a timer bell chimed and Kate, encumbered by a pair of cats, said, "Deirdre dear, could you pull the brownies out of the oven and set them to cool?"

Thinking that between my treat at Charly's and Kate's brownies it would be a miracle if the girls ate any dinner, I found a pair of potholders, lifted the pan from the oven, and set it on a rack.

"Thanks," Kate said as I returned. "Now that those are done, we can hunt up Libérale and her brood. I spoke to Madame Bouchard, and she said she'd be delighted for Zora and Zafia to meet them. They ought to be asleep in the tool shed at this hour." Briskly shooing the animals from her lap, she rose and began to fill the roomy patch pockets of her coat sweater with a variety of cat-related objects. Then, still talking nonstop, she shepherded us along the worn dirt path to the Bouchard farm buildings.

Stopping at the open door of the low shed attached to the barn, she peered into the shadowy interior and announced, "Success! They're all here. Now, remember to move gently, girls, so as not to frighten them." She snapped the electric light on and urged Zora and Zafia forward.

Hearing the soft cries of delight as the two slender dark girls fell to their knees on the worn cotton blanket spread on its bed of straw, and seeing the sparkle in the almond-shaped eyes Zafia raised gratefully to me, I did not regret the loss of my coveted free afternoon.

Nor, I thought, did Haroun. Regarding his small sisters, his face held a look of tender concern that sharpened the already strong resemblance to his Uncle Sadiq.

Sadiq! How long was it now since I had seen him? Except for a few hurried minutes the weekend before last, it must be a full month. And I had almost missed seeing him even then.

It had been a day of sunshine and crisp autumn air, like today. And, like today, I had sacrificed my free afternoon. Maggie's planned Sunday outing to Avenches with her ancient history class had swelled to two busloads. Ruedy was occupied on his family farm, a second driver was needed, and I gladly volunteered. I wanted to visit Avenches—called Aventicum when it was Roman capital of Helvetia—and as the drive was not much more than an hour, the unfamiliar Microbus should not be too much trouble.

I took the bus out for a trial run, testing the handling and the braking power while Maggie assembled the party, and pulled back into the driveway just as Haroun appeared and said breathlessly:

"I'm sorry, Miss Cline, but I won't be able to go after all. My uncle called from Geneva and he's taking Zora and Zafia and me out for the day."

A wisp of cloud covered the sun, and my spirits dimmed as quickly as the day. Sadiq was coming, and I would not see him! The more Zora and Zafia talked of their charming relative, the more fascinated I had become. Looking at the photograph on their night table, I often remembered his eyes holding mine when we first met, and felt them still.

Suddenly the excursion I had looked forward to became an odious chore. Haroun and his sisters would spend a whole happy day with Sadiq, while I had to convoy a load of unruly teenagers to explore some second-rate ruins.

As the day wore on, I managed to overcome most of my disappointment. After all, I had no reason to think Sadiq would even have noticed my presence. If he no longer seemed a stranger to me, that was all I was to him. And anyway, I reminded myself hopefully, there was always the chance he would still be there on our return.

After a picnic lunch the afternoon passed quickly. The students romped up and down the crumbling stone seats of the overgrown amphitheater, trooped through the small museum, ran along the top of the city wall, and drove imaginary chariots through the narrow gate. Their enthusiasm was infectious, and by the time I nosed the Microbus back onto the road to Gstaad, I found myself humming a snatch of a show tune. No need to examine the reasons for my ebullient mood, I told myself. I had simply enjoyed the afternoon. It had nothing to do with the possibility that I might soon exchange a few words with a dark, handsome man for whom I had conceived a foolish schoolgirl crush.

Still, when I had unloaded my high-spirited cargo and parked the Microbus behind the main building, I took a moment to run a brush through my hair, freshen my light eye makeup and check my navy pantsuit for wrinkles. I was glad that I had chosen to wear it today. Not only was it highly sensible for driving, but it was new and chic and it added inches to my height.

Inside the dormitory, I greeted the half-dozen girls clustered around a record player in the commons room and proceeded down the hall, deciding that it would be only natural to stop and ask Zora and Zafia how their day had gone. But when I reached their room and glanced inside, I found it neatly and impersonally empty.

Entering my own room, I closed the door with rather more force than I had intended and sat down at my desk to work on a stack of student themes. I read the opening paragraph of the first one perhaps five times, then shoved it impatiently aside.

"All right, Deirdre Sheridan," I said aloud. "Get hold of yourself. You can't concentrate for two minutes at a stretch. You look at a printed line and only see a pair of dark eyes above a trim mustache. Do you know what you need?"

A good shaking, I thought. Or better yet, occupational therapy. Busy hands, and all that.

So I pulled the workbox from under my bed and attacked the contents. Within twenty minutes I had hemmed the heavy gold drapes I had stitched the previous Wednesday, basted two pillows into their new covers, and was glaring balefully at the almost completed bedspread that billowed about me. Settling Indian-fashion on the new shag rug, I wrapped a firm tip of Scotch tape around the end of a length of cable cord, pierced it with a large safety pin, and began the laborious threading process.

I had almost reached the end of the final panel when there was a light tap on the door.

"Come in!" I called, working the thick cord through the last foot and pulling it free.

Zora and Zafia raced into the room, Zora perching in her habitual position on the end of the bed, while Zafia curled up in the easy chair.

"Oh, Miss Sheridan," Zora said, "we had such a wonderful afternoon! Uncle Sadiq took us to Lenk, and we walked up a mountain path along a lovely brook, and there was a bridge beside a big waterfall—"

"—and we had a picnic," Zafia contributed, "and we saw a marmot and a great many—*écureuils?*"

*61*

"Squirrels," said a masculine voice from the doorway.

As I whipped around to face Sadiq, the excitement that surged through me must, I felt sure, have been easily read on my face. But it was quickly replaced by dismay. After my careful primping of half an hour ago, Sadiq now saw me seated cross-legged on the floor in the midst of a welter of untidy sewing equipment. As I awkwardly extricated myself from the voluminous folds of the bed-spread and rose, I was unhappily aware that my hair was falling over my eyes and my trim navy pantsuit was dot-ted with gold thread and lint.

"My apologies for startling you, mademoiselle," he said easily. He smiled with the urbane charm I remem-bered, but his eyes held a glint of wry amusement that told me he had missed none of my discomfiture.

"I'm sorry not to have seen you this morning," he went on. "I'd hoped you would be able to give me the good reports of these two little minxes"—he grinned at Zora and Zafia in turn—"that you promised. Perhaps, if I'm not imposing too much, you might be free now for a while?"

I glanced at my watch and was debating how best to express my agreement without seeming too eager, when Zora came to my rescue.

"But, Uncle Sadiq," she cried, "we have dinner in ten minutes. You knew we had to be back before six-thirty."

"Ah yes, I had forgotten. But surely Miss Sheridan can make her excuses?" He darted a look at me, and I dipped my head in acquiescence. "So she will have dinner with me. Now, along with you. We shall go to your room and say good-bye while Miss Sheridan powders her hair and combs her nose."

I came very close to doing just that, as the pair of laughing girls disappeared across the hall with my self-appointed dinner date. Somehow I managed to brush my suit and twine my hair into an approximation of the loosely braided knot Mother had always worn to such charming effect low on the nape of her neck.

Minutes later I found myself, still breathless, trying to manipulate a strange seat belt as Sadiq piloted the rented car down the twisting road.

"You put your hair up," he said accusingly.

"Yes, I—"

"You shouldn't have. It doesn't suit you. You should be standing on the shores of the Irish Sea with the wind whipping through it. Or it should be streaming behind you as you race through the forest with Conchobar in pursuit."

"You know those old legends?" I asked with surprise.

"Not really. But I have read Synge and Yeats." He smiled deprecatingly. "In self-defense. The letters and telephone calls this past month have been so full of Miss Deirdre Sheridan that I felt I should at least arm myself with a bit of background."

I smiled in return. "I thought I was to report on the girls. But it appears to be working the other way."

"Haroun's contributed his share, too. You know, you aren't so very different from the girl in the legends. You seem to have bewitched my entire family." He slanted a grin down at me, and I felt the color rising on my neck.

Sadiq swung the car into the station parking lot and said, "Bernerhof all right? There's not much choice in the off-season."

"Perfect. The Bernerhof used to be our favorite. "We'd all have dinner in the cafe at least twice a week when. . . ."

"We?" Sadiq prompted.

"My parents and brother," I said shortly. "They're dead now."

He looked at me curiously for a moment, then took my

arm and said briskly, "Well, I *do* want you to tell me about the girls, so I'm afraid the cafe is out. Those beer-drinking, card-playing farmers make too much noise. We'll have to suffer with the white linen and silence of the dining room."

In the almost empty restaurant, the maître brought our cocktails and Sadiq lifted his glass to mine. "Cheers! I can really use this. A day with those children is more demanding than a round of negotiations at Whitehall or the Quai d'Orsay."

I tasted my martini, noting with pleasure that the bartender had for once put in more gin than vermouth. Looking at its twin in Sadiq's hand, I said, "You surprise me. I thought people from your part of the world didn't drink."

His eyebrows quirked upward. "My dear Miss Sheridan, how do you think I could survive in the Western diplomatic community if I didn't drink? The only saving grace about an embassy cocktail party is that it provides its own anesthesia." He sipped his drink meditatively. "It's true enough that Muslims aren't supposed to touch alcohol, any more than Christians are supposed to touch other men's wives. But they do. And anyway, I'm hardly a typical follower of the Prophet. My mother was a Lebanese Christian, and my father a Shi'ite."

"But then how—"

"Oh, that was no problem. The male Muslim is permitted to marry a Jew or a Christian, as my father did. Strangely enough, it wasn't my mother's religion which set me apart as I was growing up, but my father's." Sadiq looked across at me, and I made encouraging sounds to indicate that I was not bored. "Even our family name, ending in '-ali', indicated that we were Shi'ites, followers of the descendents of Ali, who was the husband of the Prophet's daughter Fatima. We've generally managed to maintain our claim to cultural superiority over the Sunni sect but, except in Persia, there are so many more of them than of us."

"Then you do consider yourself a Muslim?" I asked, hoping I did not sound too inquisitive.

He paused for a moment, then grinned broadly. "Shi-'ite yes, Muslim no. I am reminded of the French atheist who said, 'There is no God, and Mary is His mother'."

We were still laughing when the waiter appeared bearing an enormous tray. As he carved the roast saddle of venison and served the dozen vegetables, fruits, and sauces that accompanied it, our conversation shifted to Haroun and his sisters.

We must have touched on a dozen subjects in the hour and a half that followed—places we had both visited, books we had both enjoyed, world affairs and witchcraft —but I do not remember what we said. I only remember that the dark eyes across the table had an increasingly hypnotic effect on me and time passed far too quickly.

"I feel guilty," Sadiq said as he handed me out of the car, "for bringing you back so early. You've been a delightful dinner companion, and by rights I should be taking you dancing now."

"You'd need a genie in a magic lamp to arrange that," I laughed, feeling a wave of euphoria that the wonderful wine with dinner could not wholly account for. "In the autumn in Gstaad there isn't an open nightclub to be found."

"Then we'll have to wait for the civilizing effect of the skiing season. Anyway, I do have a meeting of the Refugee Commission in the morning, so I have to get back to Geneva tonight."

"And I have to tuck your nieces into bed now." I held out my hand. "Thank you, Sadiq. It's been a lovely evening."

He raised my hand and brushed it with his lips, softly said, "Good night, Deirdre," and was gone. I stood for a moment watching the taillights recede, then looked up at the stars winking whitely in the dark velvet night sky. The tingling of my hand where Sadiq's lips had touched it spread to my whole body, and I felt suddenly as though the mountain on which I stood had heaved itself into the heavens and placed me among them.

When I finally went in to say good night to Zora and Zafia, I found them nodding drowsily with the healthy tiredness that follows a day in the fresh air. I decided to follow their example and go to bed early. But it was only much later that I slept.

# 9

ABSENTLY, still thinking about Sadiq, I watched now as Zora and Zafia played with the three kittens that remained of Libérale's most recent litter.

Kate's ample pockets had produced an array of toys. Zafia was teaching two of the kittens, a tiger and a black-and-white, some sort of game involving a ball of yarn, while Zora dangled a catnip mouse before a little calico that was the image of its mother. Libérale, meanwhile, had removed herself to a corner of the tool shed and was washing herself, ostentatiously ignoring the fuss being made over her offspring.

Still absorbed in my own thoughts, I had not been paying attention to the conversation until Kate said forcefully:

"Then I don't see any reason why you shouldn't have one. Do you, Deirdre?"

I looked at her blankly and tried to recall what they had been saying.

"Of course not," Haroun said. "Dr. Payne could hardly object. Imagine, a school with a hundred students and not one animal. It's ridiculous."

"And a cat would be useful," Zafia said shyly, her eyes gleaming with excitement. "It would catch *les souris.*"

"Oh yes," Zora chimed in on cue. "I am certain that only yesterday I saw two mouses."

I signaled to Kate and shook my head urgently, but she returned my gaze steadily and said, "Well then, girls, the only question is which one it's to be. You choose while I talk to Miss Sheridan."

Following her outside the shed, I said heatedly, "Thanks a whole lot, cousin Kate. Now what am I supposed to do? You saw how they've set their hearts on having one of those kittens, and Dr. Payne will never agree."

"Then you'll just have to talk him into it, unless you want to disappoint them. Good heavens, Deirdre," she said with asperity, "if you thought there would be any problem, why didn't you say so when they first brought it up? You just sat there smiling and nodding."

Because I wasn't listening. Because I was thinking about Sadiq. But I didn't say that to Kate.

"Well, I'm sorry if I've put you on the spot," she went on more mildly. "But I assumed when you brought them here it was what you had in mind."

"Sure, Kate," I said with forced cheerfulness. "I'll do my best. Maybe it'll work out all right."

And perhaps it would. Perhaps, too, Kate was right to think I had intended this. I wanted to give the girls something to make them happy. Now it was up to me to see they kept it.

Inside the shed a mild argument was in progress.

"*Ce petit noiraud,*" Zafia said, "*est le plus beau. Voi ses bottes blanches et le plastron presque empesé!*"

"*Mais non,*" Zora insisted. "*Le tricolore! Il a des marquages frappants, et ce tache de noir sur l'oeil lui donne l'air d'un pirate.*"

"Please, my sisters, softly!" Haroun urged. "You are both right. The black one with the white bib is very elegant, like a gentleman dressed for a formal dinner. And the calico with the black eye-patch does indeed look like an engaging pirate. But somehow you must choose. Now, why don't you compromise on this little tigercat? Poor thing, nobody seems to want him."

"Not true," said Kate, scooping up the ball of striped fluff. "This little fellow is his mother's favorite. And Madame Bouchard did say she was willing to let Libérale keep one. Why don't we leave the tiger and take both the others? Zora and Zafia will each have her choice that way. And they'll be company for each other."

Soon Madame Bouchard had been informed of the adoption, and Zora and Zafia were triumphantly bearing their new pets back to Kate's chalet.

"How fortunate that the tiger just happened to be Libérale's favorite," I remarked.

"Yes," Kate agreed complacently. "I thought that was quite an imaginative touch."

"Oh well, I suppose it will be as easy to explain away two as one."

I occupied myself with the problem of winning Dr. Payne's approval while the children consumed brownies and milk, and Kate unearthed a covered picnic hamper and a soft cotton blanket and rummaged for her car keys.

As we ascended the steep path to Kate's garage, I thought with relief that the acquisition of the kittens had at least accomplished one thing. We would be driven back to Gstaad, and I would be spared the feeling of being followed constantly. Surely the man or men I had seen were harmless, and I had built a series of coincidences into a paranoid fantasy.

" . . . of course understand that the cats would be regarded as pets of the whole school," I said to Martha Payne, concluding a carefully rehearsed argument that had begun with my concern over the girls' reticence and homesickness and proceeded to their delight in the kittens and my conviction that they could be a great help to Zora's and particularly Zafia's adjustment.

"But if Zora and Zafia took responsibility for feeding them, then the cats would naturally consider them their special mistresses?"

"Exactly," I agreed warmly. "I thought that, as a mother yourself, you'd appreciate how important this can be for them, and you'd be the best person to broach the subject to Dr. Payne. You see," I confessed as we approached my room, "we've already brought the kittens back with us, more or less on approval."

Without waiting for Martha Payne to reply, I tapped lightly on the door and swung it open to reveal Zora and Zafia kneeling on the rug, supervising the kittens' first hesitant explorations of their new surroundings.

Zafia looked up apprehensively and pulled her black and white favorite protectively into her lap, but Zora gave me the grin of a born conspirator and, catching up the little calico, deposited it in the hands of a startled Martha Payne.

"Look, Mrs. Payne," she said with proprietary pride, "see how friendly he is. And how soft and beautiful."

We waited an anxious moment until the headmaster's wife settled the kitten in the crook of her arm and, stroking the tiny patchwork body, began to croon to it softly. As I had hoped, a British fondness for animals coupled with a new mother's weakness for all baby creatures won her over. Gently returning the calico to Zora's hands, she said:

"They're perfectly lovely, both of them. Have they got names yet?"

Zafia smiled her shy smile. "We were talking about that when you came. I thought for this little one, all dressed *comme il faut* in black and white like a so proper gentleman, perhaps we might call him Milord?"

"That's just exactly right for him. And the other?"

"Oh, that's easy," said Zora. "With the black patch over the eye like a pirate, he must be Captain Teach. Is not that a perfect name for a school cat?"

Adding my enthusiastic agreement to Martha Payne's, I refrained from pointing out that the name of Captain Teach was an unfair burden to place on a defenseless girl kitten.

Zora and Zafia, elated by the headmaster's wife's approval, eagerly showed her the purchases they had made on the way back to school. They soon had us both rearranging furniture in the commons room while they decided on the optimum placement of food bowls, litter box, and the big oval wicker basket. A group of students gathered to inspect the new arrivals, and Ruedy, dragooned from somewhere by an alert Zora, was being consulted about the practicability of installing a cat-hatch in the outside wall, when the straight and meticulously dressed figure of the headmaster appeared in the doorway.

"What in heaven's name is going on here?" he demanded.

Martha Payne detached herself from the group surrounding the kittens and hastily slipped her arm through her husband's. "Do come and see, my dear," she said. "We've just acquired two delightful additions to our

*71*

school family. This charming creature is called Milord, and the patchy little harlequin is Captain Teach. Now isn't that just the most marvelous name for a school pet?"

"Martha, you know that our policy—"

"—has just been changed," she said in a firm *sotto voce*. "For pity's sake, Sidney, try to look less grim! I'll explain it all to you later. Now steel yourself and pet the kittens."

Patting the two furry heads awkwardly, Dr. Sidney Payne said, "Very nice, I'm sure," and cast about for another topic of conversation. His eyes fell on me and, unaware for the moment at least that I was the principal architect of the outrage, he advanced toward me smiling warmly.

"Miss Sheridan. Just the person I wanted to see. You do play bridge, don't you?"

"Yes, sir. With more enthusiasm than skill, I'm afraid."

"Splendid, splendid. One of our parents will be visiting us the week after next, Jennifer Hearn's father, and I thought perhaps you might join us after dinner one evening for a few rubbers."

"Thank you, sir. I'd be pleased to," I replied, wondering whether his genial attitude toward me would be altered when he learned I had sponsored the kittens.

The dinner gong rang and, gratefully abandoning Dr. Payne to his wife's diplomacy, I turned to the task of persuading Zafia that she and Milord would both survive a half-hour separation. I could see that the wrench of parting would be even more drastic at bedtime.

It was, but it was then that I had my reward. When I went in to say good night to the girls, Zafia spontaneously slipped her arms around my neck in a joyful hug, and her great dark eyes at last held a gleam of pure happiness.

72

# 10

THE SLANTING rays of the late afternoon sun played on
the dull red of the roof tiles across the quadrangle as I
walked from the main building and headed for the auditorium. On the far side of the green expanse, a panel
truck was parked beside the new chalet-style building,
and two men were carrying a load of plywood sheets
inside. One of them was Ruedy, but though I wanted to
see him, he was not the reason I quickened my steps. The
other man, I thought from the way he moved, might have
been the one who had followed my little party of Qaimanis on our expedition to Kate's chalet in Saanen a
week ago.

Hurrying though I was, I was only halfway across
the quadrangle when the pair emerged and stood talking in the deepening shadows beside the auditorium.
Then Ruedy caught sight of me and started forward.
The other man touched Ruedy's arm, said something

quickly and, with a casual wave, moved off in the opposite direction.

"Hullo, Deirdre," Ruedy said, reaching my side. "We just came up from the lumber yard, and I think we have all the materials for the sets now. I hope you won't want them for ten days, though, because it's the end of the season, and my father will need me on the farm every moment I can spare."

"Well, you seem to have some help here," I said as casually as I could manage. "Who's your new assistant?"

"Assistant? Oh, you mean Abdullah. He's just been lending me a hand lately. He works somewhere up there." Ruedy waved a hand vaguely up the hill.

"Mmn?" I said encouragingly.

"For some foreigner who's taken a chalet for the skiing season. I think his employer sent him ahead to make sure everything was in order, but he won't be here for a while. The employer, I mean. So Abdullah finds time a bit heavy on his hands."

"But how did you meet him?"

"Oh, he just stopped to talk a couple of weeks ago, and we sort of hit it off. He's helped me with odd jobs since then. I guess the Arab disinclination to work was outweighed by a desire for company. Why the sudden interest? Are you partial to dark strangers?"

Ruedy was smiling easily, but as I met his eyes I saw in them a note of annoyance. Could it be jealousy? Or apprehension? Or simply a very Swiss dislike of being questioned?

Postponing conjecture for a more private moment, I said lightly, "No reason. I'm just struck by how many Middle Easterners we seem to have around here. Is your helper Abdullah another Arabian?"

"I don't think so. He's some sort of Arab, but he seems to speak French with a Moroccan accent. Anyway, there's no mystery about him. He's just a nice, shy fellow who's lonely for a little human contact."

Jenny's blond head was bent and her face creased in concentration as I dropped into step beside her. She looked up from the typewritten lines on the flimsy blue paper and said without preamble:

"Is this normal, Miss Sheridan? I mean, does everybody have the same problem, or do anybody's parents ever actually *approve?*"

I smiled faintly at her youthful despair and easily guessed her meaning. "Oh, I wouldn't worry too much, Jen," I said. "Remember, you're all your father has, and it's natural for him to be concerned. But I imagine he can be won over. He just wants to be sure you don't neglect the rest of your education and that you really know what you want." I thought of the wise and gentle counsel my own father had given me and my heart swelled, the pain mixed with pride.

"It isn't that," Jenny said, her tone no brighter. "I wouldn't mind if he had some real objections to my acting. I could meet those with arguments of my own. But he won't even take my ambition seriously."

"Come on now, Jenny," I reminded her, "he came a long way to see you in *Othello.*"

"Oh sure, I know he rearranged his business trip so he could be here, but that's the kind of thing Daddy has always done, ever since Mom died. This might as well have been my eighth-grade piano recital, as far as he was concerned. He refuses to admit I'm growing up. Well, I mean, you saw him. Isn't it obvious?"

I remembered Mr. Thomas Jefferson Hearn standing after the performance beside his daughter, no longer in costume but with traces of makeup still visible, as she accepted congratulations and compliments. Even in the

75

crowded faculty lounge he stood out, his short-cropped hair bleached lighter than Jenny's and his face bronzed by the sun. His gold-flecked hazel eyes looked down on her with affectionate indulgence.

My own attention was not on the tall, blond newcomer. I had seen Sadiq, exchanged a few words with him just after the performance, and my eyes strayed repeatedly to the door while I tried to hold up my end of the conversation. Fortunately, Jenny's father did most of the talking.

"Youngsters nowadays all have some kind of artistic leaning," he said in a soft drawl that suggested Texas or Oklahoma. "It seems to be a function of the age, don't you think, Miss Sheridan?"

I looked up at the tanned face. His smile was as soft as his voice, but behind the gold flecks his eyes held a hint of steel, and I guessed that T. J. Hearn did not enjoy being contradicted.

"You see," Jenny said now, lengthening her strides and waving her father's letter, "he thinks it's just a phase I'll outgrow. He doesn't stop to consider that I might have some talent. I do, don't I?" she said anxiously. "I'm not just kidding myself?"

"No, Jen. But talent and hard work are no guarantees. You still need luck."

"Sure, but I'll never know unless I try, will I? And the way Daddy is going, I won't even get a chance. Miss Sheridan, *would* you talk to him? Please?"

"Well, I don't suppose it could do any harm. He'll be here for a visit next week, is that right?"

"Oh no, it isn't just a visit. He'll be in Gstaad for the whole season. The oil company gives home leave, you know, four months every two years, and Daddy's going to spend them here with me. So," she concluded, "that'll give you plenty of time to work on him."

I suppressed a smile. Jenny clearly intended me to use

the same tactics she herself was learning to rely on. And why not? If my feminine charms had little effect on Sadiq Yamali, they might do better with T. J. Hearn.

Looking up at Jenny, I caught a sparkle of mischief in her soft gray eyes.

"Hi, I've brought your mail." Maggie dumped a pair of letters on my desk, then dropped into my easy chair as unceremoniously as she had dropped into my room. "After all, you don't check your box half the time, and I thought it might be important. Mind if I stay?"

"Of course not. What's new in the world of Fred?" I asked, eyeing the familiar long airmail envelope in her hand.

"Dunno. I haven't read it yet. You go on and look at yours while I open it."

Picking up the lighter of the two envelopes, I reached for my nailfile and slit the flap, wondering idly why Maggie, who normally treated the arrival of one of Fred's letters as an occasion for candlelight and strict solitude, was now suggesting a communal mail opening. I unfolded the note and found that it was from Martha Payne, confirming that I was expected at half past eight on Tuesday next in the apartments of the headmaster for bridge with the Paynes and Mr. T. J. Hearn.

As I pulled the desk calendar in front of me and noted the date, I saw Maggie regarding me expectantly over the top of Fred's closely written pages. I returned her gaze quizzically and picked up the other envelope.

My reaction must have been all she had wished for. I could feel the slow flush climbing up my neck to my face, and the hand that held the rich cream-colored stationery trembled as I noted the Paris postmark, the unfamiliar handwriting of the address, spiky and vertical in strong black ink, and the heavily embossed seal of the Legation

77

of the Sheikdom of Qaiman.

Maggie laughed merrily. "Well, well! I *thought* you sounded a bit too casual on the subject of the handsome Mr. Yamali. I see I was right."

"Don't be ridiculous, Maggie. This probably isn't personal at all, just something about Zora and Zafia. Oh, I admit I find him attractive, but I don't have any illusions about my importance to the girls' charming uncle."

"I hope not," she said. "I'm sure he's very practiced at making gallant compliments but, if you don't mind a word of advice from Wise Old Maggie, there are two reasons not to trust him. He's a diplomat and an Arab."

I smiled wryly. "You're biased. You think the only good Arab is a dead Arab."

"Not quite. But I wouldn't trust one just because he looked like Omar Sharif."

"He does not!" I said heatedly. "Sadiq doesn't have gap teeth."

By now Maggie was laughing uncontrollably. "Oh, Deirdre, if you could see yourself," she gasped, wiping tears from her eyes. "I suppose it was mean of me, but you *were* so baitable that I couldn't resist teasing you. Forgive me?"

"Sure, Maggie," I said weakly.

Suddenly she was on her feet, all contrition. "Look, I'm sorry, Deirdre. I didn't realize. If I'd thought it meant anything to you—" She flapped the letter in her hand helplessly. "I guess Wise Old Maggie's advice wasn't so funny after all."

"Maybe not, but it was still good advice. Don't worry, Maggie, I haven't any intention of letting a smooth Arab playboy break this sturdy American heart."

She and Fred's letter departed and I sat fingering the expensive embossed paper, postponing the moment of opening. I wondered how accurate my assurance to Maggie had been. If my head was soberly controlled, my emotions were less so. They were in fact in a thorough turmoil.

Gently I loosened the flap and drew out the heavy formal stationery. Sadiq's spiky masculine script wavered before my eyes, and it was some time before I could make out the words.

My dear Deirdre,

This note is unconscionably overdue. I'm afraid you thought me terribly abrupt the night of *Othello*, but I had barely time to kiss the girls and tell Haroun what an admirable Iago he made before flying back to Paris. I couldn't really afford even that much time, and I've been up to my eyes in work ever since. But that's no excuse for bad manners.

I gather you haven't been idle either, what with acquiring livestock for the school. The wires between Gstaad and Paris have been humming with the exploits of Milord and Captain Teach. In fact, though I hadn't planned to come down until December, Zora and Zafia have been most persuasive. The wenches have convinced me that a soirée at the Vicomtesse de Ribes' would be a dull affair compared with meeting their furred friends. So I shall be in Gstaad next Saturday.

Perhaps, if you are free, you might show your forgiveness by permitting me to take you to dinner then? I promise not to bring you back at nine this time.

Until next weekend—

S.

From the silent and shuttered ground station, the pylons of the Wasserngrat chair lift marched uphill bearing empty cables that swayed now in the stiff November wind. To the south a bank of threatening gray clouds fringed the dull white sky. I knotted my scarf more firmly and jammed my hands into the pockets of my windbreaker, hoping the rain would not resume at least for a couple of hours.

The ground beside the road was still spongy from a night-long downpour, and when I had crossed the narrow brook I decided to keep to the rutted farm track that wound along the hillside. It was no day for sightseeing or bird watching anyway, and this way I would keep my feet dry. It was the exercise that counted. With any luck the slopes would be skiable in a couple of weeks, and if I wanted to be ready, I had better find time for a good brisk walk every day.

It was shameful, I thought, the way I had let myself get out of condition. I had not even set foot outside the school grounds in almost four days, between classes and play rehearsals and being on duty for the last three nights running.

But then, it was in a good cause. Maggie had willingly exchanged duty nights, and now I was free all next weekend. I pulled Sadiq's letter from my shoulder bag and scanned the vertical masculine script. No matter how often I read it, I could find no encouragement for my eager anticipation. The note was written with easy informality, but it was hardly impassioned or even very personal. It was simply a means of passing a dull November evening in a dull Swiss village.

I folded the letter and dropped it back into my purse, and devoted my attention to the rudimentary road I was following. A few hundred yards ahead stood a massive farm complex, the front of the building a typical dark wood chalet, the back a barn. In the upper windows a stolid Swiss farm wife moved, dragging inside the pillows and feather beds she had set to air. As I approached, the last window banged shut, and except for a pair of raucous magpies, I saw no further signs of life for perhaps a mile.

The stony track crossed another brook and turned gently downhill. I was almost at the village of Turbach when a herd of cows appeared, driven toward a nearby barn by two men. Lifting a hand, I called out a cheerful, *"Gruetzi!"*

"Hullo, Deirdre," responded the younger of the two, and I saw with surprise that it was Ruedy. "What brings you to our part of the valley?"

"Out walking for my health."

"It seems to be working. You're the brightest looking thing I've seen on this dismal day. Come and meet my father."

Ruedy turned and spoke to the older man in the soft Swiss dialect that makes German almost pleasant to the ear. The elder Messerli extended a gnarled and cracked hand and said, *"Es freut mich."* He stood awkwardly a moment longer, then mumbled something about cows and hurried off after them.

"Swiss cows," I said, watching the sleek, fat brown and white animals depart, "are superior creatures."

"You've changed your tune," Ruedy said teasingly, leaning against a rail fence and lighting a cigarette. "I seem to recall a couple of weeks ago, when the Hauptstrasse of Gstaad was filled with these 'superior creatures' coming down from high pasture, you had some sharp words about what they did to conditions underfoot."

"Oh, that was just a moment of pique." I smiled sheepishly. "After I got my shoes cleaned, I got my sense of perspective back. Basically, Swiss cows are lovable."

"Are they? I hate them." For a moment Ruedy's face was animated by a fierce intensity, and then the emotionless Swiss mask was once more in place. "No, that's not true," he went on more slowly. "I don't hate farming. Sometimes, working in the fields in summer, I really enjoy it. But I don't want to spend my whole life at it, the way my father has. You see that slope?" He lifted a square hand to indicate the mountain behind us. "It all belongs to us, and it cries out to be developed. There should be a ski lift there, to open up the side with the northern exposure, and a restaurant, maybe even a small hotel. That's what I want."

"But Ruedy, I'm sure you could get backing. Why don't you do it?"

Ruedy threw his cigarette to the ground and crushed it with a muddy boot. No doubt he wished he had not said as much as he had, and I regretted my American inquisitiveness. But apparently he was used to it, for presently he answered.

"Because I don't want it to belong to some bank or syndicate. I want it to belong to me." He smiled ruefully. "I should have taken a leaf from my friends' book. Willy and Hans-Peter married American girls, and Willy's wife at least has quantities of money. That's what I need, a beautiful young heiress whose only wish is to marry a Swiss ski instructor." His voice took on a lighter note, as if to deny that he had meant any of what he had said. "Now, take yourself, Miss Sheridan. You wouldn't just happen to have a dowry of half a million francs?"

I laughed sharply, thinking of the irony. Here was Ruedy, who did not want his father's life, and who wanted a half million francs. And I, I had a half million francs I did not want, and I had them at the price of my father's life.

Ruedy mistook the cause of my harsh laugh and said, "No, I don't suppose you'd be teaching school if you did. Say, could I offer you a cup of tea? Father and I lead a bachelor's life out here, but I think we can manage that much."

"Thanks, Ruedy, but I'd better not. It doesn't look like the rain will hold off much longer, and I'll have to hurry to make the postal bus in Turbach. Could I take a rain check?"

"Sure, Deirdre. See you tomorrow." As I turned to leave, I thought I saw a shadow of disappointment cross his strong square face. Because I was leaving, or because I had heard his unguarded confessions? A hundred yards along the road I looked back and saw him, still leaning against the rail fence, staring fixedly at the ground.

 *11*

THE BRIGHT white sky over Bern still promised snow, but the late November air was crisp and clear as the students tumbled from the buses and made their way in happy chattering groups into the great square.

As it had been for a century past, Bern's annual Zibelemärit—Onion Market—was both a commercial occasion and a festive one. Crowds were milling about the Kornhausplatz. Here and there a traditional starched headdress framed a wrinkled face, and black-slippered feet peeped beneath a long black wool skirt. But in general the vendors presiding over the hastily erected wooden booths were distinguishable from the customers and curious tourists only by their cheerful green aprons.

And there were onions everywhere. Round onions and squat onions, small and large onions, onions with skins from the palest gold to the rich dark red of wine. Plaited into ropes, they hung from the awnings of the booths and lay in great heaps on the counters.

"Look at them," Zafia breathed, slipping her slender hand into mine. "Nothing but onions! How many, do you think?"

"Oh, thousands and thousands," Zora replied confidently. "Maybe even a million."

"And look at that vendor over there," said Haroun. "He's even wearing a string of onions for a necklace."

"You should talk!" Jenny retorted, tossing her long blond hair. "You've got more stuff draped around your neck than a Japanese tourist."

Haroun ignored her pointedly, squinting at the f-stop of his camera. Jenny winked at me, and I smiled back. Jen was right; Haroun was certainly heavily laden. In addition to the 35-mm. Leica he was now adjusting, he was burdened with a large leather case containing extra lenses and a light meter. The ensemble was completed by a man's purse, the increasingly popular shoulder bag sort.

"Ready, Haroun?" I asked.

"In a minute. I just want to get one more shot of this booth from below."

"All right, but there'll be plenty of time to come back here later. Right now we're supposed to be meeting by the clock tower."

"The Zytgloggeturm," Jenny said, raising her voice slightly against the clamor of vendors and buyers as we made our way among the booths of onions. "Isn't Schwyzerdutsch a *fun* language, Miss Sheridan? I mean, it's awfully quaint, but it's a lot prettier than German."

"Well," I said, "I have to agree that Zibelemärit sounds more graceful than Zwiebelnmarkt."

Ruedy's square hand waved at us as we fought clear of the last crowded aisle and joined the students milling about him. "Okay, is everybody here?" he said, counting heads. "Now where have Lisa and Cathy gone?"

The missing girls were soon located, and near us I saw the other busloads assembled, but still we waited. I looked at Ruedy and followed his patient gaze and then I smiled, understanding. The hands on the great astronomical clock stood at four minutes before the hour.

I lifted Zafia for a better view and Ruedy swung Zora effortlessly to his shoulders as the first bells pealed. Around us the students, even the blasé older ones, soon were laughing and clapping at the procession of cleverly carved figures jerking and jiggling their way across the medieval façade of the stone tower—Father Time with his hourglass, the crowing cock, the knight in armor, the jester with his tinkling bells—entertaining us as they had entertained fifteen generations of the good burghers of Bern. And of course there were the animated bears, ubiquitous symbol of the city, in this case a band of bear musicians. They had been my favorites ten years ago, and they were Zafia's now.

I had set her on her feet and was flexing my tired arms when a voice behind us said, "Hi, princess."

Zora and Zafia turned and looked up quizzically at the tall man with the expectant grin on his sun-bronzed face. But it was Jenny who whirled around and squealed, "Daddy!" She threw herself into his arms and hugged him for a long moment, then remembered her almost-seventeen-year-old dignity and detached herself.

"But what are you doing in Bern?"

"I decided to stop off at the embassy on the way to Gstaad, and figured I might catch up with you here. Looks like my timing was right."

"Super! We're going to the Bärengraben now. Want to come?"

"Sure, why not? They're nice bears, as bears go."

Jenny chattered incessantly, happy to be the center of

86

attention, pointing out the graceful sweep of the arcades we walked under, the uniformly handsome sandstone façades of the medieval buildings, the occasional pair of shutters in the slanting red and black stripes of Bern, the gaily playing fountains. And Thomas Jefferson Hearn, obediently admiring sights he had doubtless seen before Jenny was born, smiled down at her indulgently.

In five minutes we had crossed the Nydegg Bridge and reached the Bear Pits. Zora and Zafia, too small to fight the crowds around the vendors, enlisted my help and then, each armed with a bag of carrots, wormed their way to the railing.

The bears, sleek and brown and obviously well fed, begged and clowned, sitting up, standing, rolling over, sticking their heads between their legs. One agile fellow frolicked like a monkey high above the floor of the pit, swinging among the spars set at intervals through a bare tree trunk.

"Careful," I warned. "Don't lean over so far, Zora."

"Oh, the bears can't reach this high, Miss Sheridan. And besides, they're perfectly friendly."

"Maybe, but if somebody bumped you, you could go tumbling headfirst down onto that cement floor. Oh, look there!"

At the bottom of the tree trunk, a spar was missing, and through the hole a young bear, scarcely more than a cub, was playing peekaboo with the keeper. As the bear stretched himself to his full height and peeped through the hole, the keeper pretended not to be watching, and then suddenly directed a stream of water from a hose into the hole. The young bear chuckled, dropped to all fours, shook his head vigorously and began inching up the tree trunk again.

We watched the bears' antics for another twenty minutes, and then reluctantly gathered to continue our tour.

Once again it was Haroun who held us up, pleading that he wanted just a couple more shots of the Old Town from the end of the Nydegg Bridge. He adjusted and deliberated, now kneeling to catch the cathedral spire, now leaning over to get the sweep of the Aar and the old bridge below. He was still contemplating the possibilities when the rest of the party was well on its way across the bridge. Even Ruedy, bringing up the rear, was now a good thirty yards ahead of us.

I called to Ruedy to wait, and turned to urge Haroun to hurry. But my words abruptly changed into a small stifled scream, buried under Haroun's angry shouts.

*"Lâchez-le!"* he cried, struggling with a burly man in a black knit cap. More angry than frightened, he lashed out with a kick that caught his assailant on the shin, but the burly man retained his hold on Haroun's camera strap and managed to get an arm around his neck.

The uneven struggle soon grew into a melee of half a dozen shoving, shouting men. A passerby tugged at the arm of the burly man. A car pulled to the curb and its passenger, also wearing a black knit cap, leaped from the back seat and seized Haroun by the waist. Running back from the middle of the bridge, Ruedy shoved past me, with Jenny Hearn's father pounding behind him.

The scuffle would be over in a moment, I thought, and the thief subdued. But instead it continued and intensified. Everyone seemed to be shouting and shoving at cross-purposes, some trying to pull Haroun from the center of the tangle, some pushing forward toward his assailant. Soon the two black caps became indistinguishable from each other, adding to the confusion.

The knot of men swayed toward the curb, where the waiting car still stood, its back door gaping.

Suddenly Haroun ducked his head and broke free,

leaving the camera in the hands of his burly attacker. From the far end of the Nydegg Bridge a whistle shrilled, and an authoritative voice cried, "Halt!"

For an instant everyone's attention was directed toward the running policeman, and when I looked back, the two black-capped men were already inside the waiting car. It roared away from the curb while the burly man, the camera in his hand, was still groping for the door handle. Swiftly it rounded the corner by the Bear Pits and disappeared up the hill.

*"Was ereignet sich hier?"* the policeman demanded.

Everyone told him, all at once, and in an incomprehensible medley of languages.

"... *a saisi mon appareil photographique* . . ."

". . . must have been his accomplices . . ."

"... *und das Auto stand beim Bordstein* . . ."

". . . let them get away, dammit!"

*"I* let them get away? If you hadn't been shoving in the wrong direction . . ."

Finally the policeman obtained relative quiet, and asked whether anyone could describe the men or the car. There was another babble of voices, but eventually I was able to tell him that I had noted the license number.

He nodded approvingly and scribbled the number in his notebook. Then he frowned, flipped back through the pages of the notebook, and muttered in profound disgust, *"Gestohlen, gestern abend. Natürlich."*

Naturally. A gang of well-organized robbers, cool enough to operate in broad daylight, would surely provide themselves with stolen plates.

Attempts to describe the two men were no more successful. Everyone seemed to have conflicting impressions, and since the two men were dressed so similarly, and in winter clothing, it was doubtful that even a careful observer could have contributed much. The policeman methodically took down names and addresses, not looking hopeful.

Haroun, by now completely recovered from the incident, was surrounded by a cluster of his schoolmates and was receiving, without apparent modesty, their admiration for his bravery.

"Of course, it was foolish of them to think they could get away with it. I'd kept the strap around my neck. I'd never have lost the camera, if it hadn't been for all the well-meaning interference."

That wasn't quite fair, I thought. If it hadn't been for the "well-meaning interference," the black-capped men might have gotten away with more than just Haroun's camera.

They might, as Haroun said, have been foolish. To attempt such a clumsy snatch in broad daylight was either foolhardy or desperate. But the two men appeared to be neither.

If anyone had been foolish, it was Haroun. He had ignored a promise to his father, allowing himself to become separated from the group. If he had been more careful, the incident could not have occurred.

I resolved to have a brief word with Haroun, and a rather longer one with his Uncle Sadiq.

*12*

"GAME and rubber," said Thomas Jefferson Hearn, totalling the score with evident satisfaction. "Nicely played, partner."

"Yes indeed," agreed Martha Payne. "Might we have set it, Sidney?"

"Perhaps if I'd led a trump? No, no, it was there to be made—it wasn't obvious, but it was there."

"Well," said Hearn, pushing back from the bridge table, "I wouldn't mind playing all night, but you three have to get up in the morning. It's been a most enjoyable evening, Paynes. Thanks a lot."

Declining a final cup of coffee, Jenny's father helped me into my coat and we bid our hosts good night. As we stepped from the headmaster's cottage into the crisp night air, the frozen grass crunched beneath our feet. Across the quadrangle a streetlamp gave off a sphere of pale, cold light, and silhouetted against it we could see the first fine snowflakes sifting to the ground.

I took a deep breath and said, "Mmn, you can smell the snow."

"It's sure a welcome change from all that sand. I still have to get used to the cold again, though."

"How long have you been in Arabia, Mr. Hearn?"

"Jeff, please."

"Jeff, then," I amended.

"Oh, the better part of fifteen years. If you can call it the better part." Under his light tone I detected a more somber note, and then he was silent until we reached the door of the girls' dormitory.

"Well, partner," he said, "we'll have to do this again. We make a good team."

"Thank you, but I don't play in your league," I protested.

"Nonsense!" He grinned suddenly, the gold flecks in his eyes glinting in the light from the streetlamp. "We beat them, didn't we? Come on, say you will."

In fact, I had not done badly as Jeff's partner. He bid and played with imagination and relish, albeit with determination, and it had been fun. Besides, hadn't Jenny begged me to "work on him"?

"All right, Jeff, I'd like that."

"Great! Look, as soon as I line up a foursome, I'll give you a ring—no, the phone won't be in for a few days. I'll send Abdullah over with a message."

"Abdullah?" I asked, hearing my voice rise.

Jeff Hearn, noting my surprise but probably attributing it to the unusual name, said, "Yes. He's my man-of-all-work. You know, driver, houseboy . . ."

"Oh," I said, my voice normal again. "Did he work for you in Arabia?"

"No, he hasn't been with me long. But he seems like a dependable fellow."

Dependable, I thought a minute later, as I stood in the doorway and watched the tall, straight figure of Jeff Hearn stride through the thickening snow and turn up the hill. Dependable was a word I would have applied to Jeff himself. He seemed solidly and reassuringly American. If he thought Abdullah was all right, I was inclined to accept his judgment.

"Miss Sheridan, Miss Sheridan!" Zafia sounded full of eager excitement, and her tapping on my door was low but insistent.

Shaking my head to clear the remnants of sleep, I looked at the clock. It was almost seven. I reached over and turned off the alarm.

"Yes, dear, what is it?"

"Come and look. In the commons room. Hurry!" She did not wait for an answer but raced off down the corridor.

Jamming my feet into slippers and pulling on my robe, I snatched up my hairbrush and, trying to put my sleep-tangled hair into some semblance of order, followed.

Zora and Zafia were standing side by side at the window, their faces pressing against the panes, their breath fogging the glass. In the pale, blue-tinged dawn light, the world outside was covered in a soft silent cloak of snow.

Looking down fondly at the two little Qaimani girls who had seen snow so seldom, I murmured, "Beautiful, isn't it?"

"Oh no, Miss Sheridan," said Zora, with a trace of impatience. "Not the snow. Here, under the window!"

I pressed closer and saw, on the strip of bare ground protected by the deep overhang of the eaves, the two kittens. Huddled beside their cat hatch, an ingenious hinged construction installed by Ruedy with the reluctant consent of Dr. Payne, they stood regarding suspiciously the strange white phenomenon.

"Silly things, they're afraid of it," said Zora with eleven-year-old superiority. "Oh, look, there they go now."

It was Captain Teach—now nicknamed a more manageable Cappy—who led the way. She sniffed at the unfamiliar substance, tasted it, pushed it with a tentative paw. Then she stepped bravely in, and soon she was scooping out hollows and tossing the snow into the air until her black and yellow patches seemed sprinkled with sugar.

Milord, like his mistress Zafia, was more timid than his sister. He hung back, his nose a cautious inch from the cold white powder, and watched Cappy doubtfully. Finally he lifted a black and white paw and plunged it in. Within two seconds he had withdrawn it, turned and scampered through the cat hatch, and was standing trembling by Zafia's feet.

She picked him up and cuddled him to her chest, whispering quiet words of reassurance. Presently he stopped shaking and settled down to purr.

"Poor little Milord," Zafia said softly, "you've just gotten used to your world, and now it is all changed."

Her voice was full of sympathy, and I wondered whether she was thinking, as I was, that the same thing had happened not so long ago to her.

It was still ten minutes before rehearsal time, but dusk was already gathering as I entered the auditorium by the stage door and tossed my parka onto a folding chair. Onstage, all the overhead lights were blazing. Near the center Ruedy knelt with a tape measure in his hands. He called out in French, and on the far side I saw Abdullah pull the other end taut. Ruedy jotted a figure on a scrap of paper, reeled in the tape, and said:

"Hullo, Deirdre. We'll be through here in about five

minutes. We're trying to work out the lighting for that split set at Charles' house. It's a bit tricky, but we may be able to rig a chandelier—" He looked at the paper again, frowned, got up and wandered off.

I picked up my script and was glancing through the marginal notes I had made at the last rehearsal when the side door banged and the earnest voices of Haroun and Adam carried across the empty stage.

"Karanda's basically a one-product economy, too," Adam Ngomutu said, "and you've seen what's been happening to the copper market. It's not just my father who's worried. Even Kenyatta's in trouble. At least you've got OPEC to keep the prices up."

"Sure," Haroun replied, "but the oil won't last forever. We've got to diversify while the money's coming in, and it isn't easy. Building heavy industry means importing construction crews, which means housing them, which means—well, there are lots of problems. One of the biggest is fresh water, and most countries take that for granted. Karanda's lucky to have its agricultural capabilities."

"Yeah, but we have to import just about everything else. Hard goods, technology. We're spending everything we can afford having our people trained abroad. But it'll be at least another generation before we have our own teachers' colleges, medical school, technical schools. It all comes down to education."

"I know," Haroun agreed. "A century ago, not one Qaimani in a thousand was literate."

Adam snorted. "A century ago, nobody in Karanda had even *heard* of writing."

I felt a momentary twinge of guilt, listening to these two boys discussing the all but insoluble problems they would face when they returned to their respective countries. Our school play seemed frivolous by comparison.

*95*

True, both Adam and Haroun studied hard, and they needed some relaxation. And they were, as Jenny had suggested, gaining valuable poise in public appearances. But when I thought of the vast job of education that remained, I wondered whether they, and indeed I, might be spending the time better.

My musings were interrupted by the reappearance of Ruedy. "Hey, Haroun," he called, "what's the Arabic word for 'pulley'?"

"Need a translator, eh? Be right with you."

He crossed the stage and joined Ruedy and Abdullah, who gestured toward the ceiling and explained the problem in a mixture of French and rapid-fire Arabic. I caught some of Ruedy's end as they discussed the mounting of a chandelier over what would be the vestibule in the fourth act, but the technical terms were unfamiliar. At any rate the hall was rapidly filling with other members of the cast, and they soon claimed my attention.

It was more than an hour later, after a generally smooth rehearsal session, that Haroun bearded me.

"Miss Schiano wants to know how soon the costumes will be ready. She says she has to get started on the torso."

"How's the portrait coming?"

"We've had three sittings, and the head's about done. She won't let me see it yet, but she looks rather pleased with herself."

"Good. I think you can have the coat tomorrow, but I'm not sure about the lace cuffs and neckcloth. I'll check with Lisa." I paused, considering how to introduce the subject that interested me more. "By the way, thanks for helping out the lighting crew. The conversation sounded pretty intricate."

"Oh, I was glad to help. There were a few French

words for equipment Abdullah didn't understand, that's all."

"It must have been nice for him to be able to speak Arabic for a change," I said. "There aren't many Moroccans around here."

"Moroccans?"

"I gathered from what Ruedy said that he was some sort of North African."

"That's funny," Haroun said. "Judging from his Arabic, I'd have said he came straight from the Persian Gulf."

*13*

THE WAITER laid another log on the already blazing fire, refilled our wine glasses and discreetly withdrew. It was almost ten, and we now had the back dining room of the Alte Post to ourselves.

"I like this place," Sadiq said contentedly.

"It's charming. How did you ever find it in a little village like Weissenbach? We're only half an hour from Gstaad, but it's like another world."

"It's good for you to get away. Just a few hours with those two girls wears me out, but you have to keep up with a hundred of them all week long."

"Oh, I enjoy teaching, much more than I'd thought I would. But you're right, I can use a change. And this place is a delightful find. Some of those old hunting pieces in the *bierstube* are fascinating."

"I suppose. I don't particularly like guns," Sadiq said absently. "Fruit?"

I selected a pear from the wicker basket and, with a trace of longing for casual American manners, tackled it with knife and fork. Sadiq picked up an apple and regarded me quizzically.

"You look like a surgeon. I thought Americans didn't carve up their fruit."

"Oh well, when in Rome—"

"Europeans carry civilization too far," Sadiq said decidedly. His next words were melodic but incomprehensible, and as I waited for the translation, I saw that his eyes held a mischievous glint.

"I was quoting an old Arabic saying. 'Eating with a knife and fork is like making love through an interpreter.'"

He grinned suddenly, then bit into the apple with evident relish. My eyes dropped to the half-carved pear on my plate, and I found myself wishing the waiter hadn't put another log on the fire. It was much too warm already.

Sadiq, however, appeared quite comfortable, and our conversation continued on a succession of inconsequential topics over coffee and for much of the drive back to Gstaad. Finally we lapsed into a companionable silence. I settled back in the luxurious seat of the Citroën CX–2200, savoring the new-leather smell, and watching Sadiq's effortless handling of the powerful car. I knew that it was his own, for I had noticed the CD plaque that meant diplomatic corps.

Several kilometers passed while Sadiq concentrated on the driving and his own thoughts. Then he seemed to remember my presence.

"Comfortable? Getting enough heat?"

"Fine, thank you. It's a lovely car. Have you had it long?"

"Just drove it down from Paris. I'll leave it here for the

season. It's got front-wheel drive and hydropneumatic suspension. Should be a good mountain car."

"It sounds very—practical," I said.

Sadiq erupted in laughter. "But it's not a Ferrari? Confess, now, you're disappointed. But you're wrong, you know. We aren't all playboys." He paused, then added with mock seriousness, "At least, not full time."

We had passed through Schönried and begun the last sweeping descent to Saanen. Abruptly Sadiq pulled to the side of the road, switched off the headlights, and turned to face me.

I felt a momentary urge to giggle, remembering parked cars and earnest, awkward high-school boys. But my school days were past, and Sadiq was no boy.

"Deirdre," he began deliberately, "there's something we have to talk about. You've become very close to my family, particularly to Zora and Zafia. In fact, they've grown quite dependent on you. So I think you ought to know the truth."

While he chose his words carefully, my mind raced wildly over possibilities, each more fantastic than the last. I conjured up dreadful visions, filled with family taints and shameful secrets. But somehow I did not anticipate what he said next.

"Their father is dying."

"Oh, no!" I cried. But even as I protested, I knew it had to be true. I could hear Haroun's fatalistic words, and I knew now what he had meant when he said there was worse to come.

"My poor darlings. And of course they don't know?"

"No," Sadiq said. "Very few people know. It's not really apparent. There are long periods when the sheik seems in perfect health. But the bad spells are getting more frequent. It's some sort of rare blood disease, and even the doctors can't say how long he has to live. It might be a good few months yet, or it might be much less."

I was silent for a moment. Then I said, "No wonder Haroun was anxious to put his father's mind at rest. But I wish he'd take his promise more seriously."

"What do you mean?" Sadiq asked sharply.

I told him about the theft of the camera in Bern, and he questioned me minutely about the incident.

"You're right," he said finally. "Haroun was very foolish. I shall speak to him." Then he too fell silent.

"Sadiq?" I said tentatively. "If anything were to happen to—well, I mean, who is next in line of succession after Haroun?"

"The sheik's brother Ahmed."

"And if Haroun should inherit before he's of age, would Ahmed be the regent?"

"I don't know. I hope not."

"Would that be so—unfortunate?"

"Unfortunate! It would be a disaster. Ahmed isn't anything like his brother. Sheik Sultan is the best kind of enlightened ruler. But if Ahmed got his hands on the Qaimani treasury, he'd probably turn half of it into bombs for the Palestinian terrorists. Luckily, it would only be half," Sadiq continued bitterly. "Ahmed would want to keep the other half for his own pocket."

"Well, maybe the sheik won't name him regent."

"Maybe not, but blood ties are awfully strong there," Sadiq replied doubtfully. "And anyway, a lot can happen before Haroun reaches his majority. Ahmed's slick, and he's popular with the army. Of course, it isn't a very big army, but Qaiman isn't a very big state. All he'd have to do is win over a few key people, and you'd have a classic palace coup. He wouldn't even have to depose Haroun

*101*

openly. He could leave him as a figurehead, at least until Haroun showed signs of getting married and producing heirs."

"But aren't the Qaimani people loyal to Sheik Sultan and Haroun?"

"They seem to be, for what it's worth. But in practical terms, that isn't much. We don't have a history of—what's the word?—grass-roots political involvement. The tradition is more feudal, with power concentrated in a very few hands. And there are more means of bribery than just money. Ahmed knows them all."

"What about the sheik? How does he feel about his brother?"

"It's hard to judge," Sadiq said slowly. "I've done what I could, but I have to tread lightly. If I say too much against Ahmed, it'll only be put down as another piece of ambitious scheming."

I smiled. "You're rather cynical tonight, Mr. Yamali."

"I'm realistic," he said flatly. He stared out the window for a long minute, then turned back to me and spread his hands apologetically. "Sorry, I didn't mean to subject you to a lecture on the facts of Qaimani political life. Those are my problems. But I did want you to know how things stood, so if there's a phone call in the middle of the night—"

"Yes, I understand," I murmured.

Sadiq reached out and flicked on the lights. "Good heavens, it *is* almost the middle of the night. I'd better get you home, Cinderella."

"Of course. Mustn't let this nice new Citroën turn into a *citreuil.*"

Sadiq groaned at the pun. "Sometimes I question the wisdom of turning women into linguists. By the way, how's your Arabic coming?"

"Slowly, I'm afraid. We haven't had much time for it lately."

"I'll send you a book. That is, if—"

"Thank you. I'd appreciate it. I'll have more time once the play's over."

Sadiq put the car in gear and started down the long hill. "Next Friday, isn't it? Save me a good seat. Fortunately, I have quite a lot of business in Geneva in the next month, so I'll be able to get up here fairly often."

"Good. I know two little girls who will be extremely pleased," I said.

What I did not say was that there was a third girl who would be extremely pleased, and she was not as little as the others.

 *14*

THE NEXT day was sunny and unseasonably mild, and I decided to indulge myself in a good long walk. I had kept my resolution to get some exercise every day. Weekdays Cookie obligingly made up a sandwich for me, and I spent the lunch break working my legs back into shape for the approaching skiing season. I had already explored the nearby slopes of the Wispile and, across the valley, the more modest Eggli. But today I could afford a longer ramble.

It was not strictly true, I conceded privately, that I could afford the time. A stack of essays from the Modern American Lit class still lay ungraded on my desk. But there was no sense in kidding myself. While the three Qaimani children were with Sadiq in his chalet on the Oberbort, my mind would not stay on Faulkner or Fitzgerald.

I struck off down the valley, resolutely passing the

turning for the Oberbort, and began the long slow climb over Gruben to Schönried. The well-graded road was dry under my feet, and only a few patches of snow remained in the gullies and in the shaded patches beside the woods. Most of the area was open farmland. Soon the sun on my back, added to the briskness of my pace, became unpleasantly warm, and I removed my parka and tied the sleeves around my waist.

Below to the left, railroad tracks paralleled the road, and presently the little electric train rattled past. How much, I thought, had happened since I had climbed off it in Gstaad a dozen weeks ago! The cheerful little train had been a prophetic symbol, for I was finding, in the rewards of teaching and in the majestic but somehow peaceful beauty of the mountains, a measure of happiness once more.

And yet, I remembered, for the Qaimani children, the year would not be a happy one. The sun was still warm, but I shivered and pulled my parka on again.

The road was downhill now, and I passed quickly through Schönried and started down the main highway to Saanen. As I drew opposite the spot where Sadiq had parked the night before, I paused, reviewing the evening with mixed feelings. Then I shook my head impatiently. I had intended my walk to dispel such thoughts.

Kate was just pulling into the driveway when I reached her chalet, and her light-hearted greeting was as always infectious. She insisted I stay for tea, declaring over my protests that she would drive me back, and before long we were sitting by the fire exchanging news. On Kate's part, this consisted chiefly of the latest batch of snapshots of Jeanne's baby and a detailed and doting recital of his perfections. But eventually she asked about the kittens and their young mistresses, opening up the subject that had been monopolizing my thoughts all day, so it was completely dark by the time she dropped me at the school.

I was brushing my hair and reflecting that there wasn't really time to do anything constructive before supper when Maggie poked her head through the doorway.

"Aha, my stray lamb, you're back in the fold!" she said, waving an envelope at me. "Some Arab left a message for you."

I reached for the envelope, but Maggie snatched it back. "Uh-uh. Not until you tell me all about last night."

"Nothing to tell. We had dinner, that's all."

"Deirdre! If I take your duty night for you, the least I can expect is a blow-by-blow."

"All right, later. Now may I have the note, please?"

She handed me the envelope, then leaned against the door jamb and watched me expectantly.

I sighed. It was impossible to be annoyed with Maggie, but right now I wished she would take her gossipy good-natured self elsewhere.

"Maggie," I said patiently, "if you don't mind—"

"Okay, okay, I'm going. But remember you promised."

I closed the door gently behind her, slipped the single sheet of notepaper from the envelope, and felt a twinge of disappointment. Maggie's teasing had led me to expect Sadiq's spiky handwriting, but the slanting script that covered the page was unmistakably American. My eye ran down to the bottom and saw the signature "Jeff."

That explained it. The Arab Maggie had mentioned was Abdullah. I went back to the top of the page and read:

Dear Deirdre,
    We're in luck. I've met a retired English cou-
ple who seem reasonably with-it. He's ex-

106

Foreign Office, so they should play a good game, too.

How about a week from today? The theatricals will be over by then. (And thank God! This place is knee-deep in feathers and fans. I could have sworn, considering what I'm paying, that Jenny had a room at school.)

One benefit of our opponents' advancing age, from your standpoint, is that we can break at a reasonable hour. How about beginning at six? From what Jen says, Sunday supper at school is a chancy business anyway, so I'll have Abdullah put out a buffet, and we can play a couple of rubbers before and a couple after.

If the date isn't okay, let me know when would be better for you.

Yours,
Jeff

As I approached the kitchen, the door banged open, and, to the accompaniment of Cookie's bellowed "*'Raus!*", the two kittens scrambled past me. Inside, Cookie stood sharpening a wickedly curved knife on a butcher's steel with what seemed unwarranted energy. "*Ärgernisse,*" he muttered.

I picked up my sandwich and tucked it into my shoulder bag, thanked Cookie hastily, and retreated.

The kittens sat unperturbed a few yards from the door, grooming themselves in the bright noon sun. I stooped to scratch their ears. "Poor pussycats! Cookie thinks you are a nuisance."

Behind me I heard a short laugh, and I looked up to see Ruedy.

"I wouldn't waste my sympathy if I were you. Cookie's just keeping up appearances. Have you seen the bowls of 'leftovers' he prepares for them? This is the only place I know where fresh chicken livers are considered leftovers."

"Perhaps you're right," I conceded.

"Of course I'm right. Cookie's as bad as the rest of you. Those cats are thoroughly spoiled."

"Well, if that's spoiling, all pets and all children should be spoiled."

"Remind me not to ask you to be the mother of *my* children," Ruedy retorted. Then he looked uncomfortable. "Have a nice walk," he said abruptly, and hurried off.

I stood watching him speculatively for a few seconds, then went along the gravel driveway and turned uphill. As I passed Jeff Hearn's rented chalet, I remembered the brief note of acceptance in my purse and pushed through the gate. I was just slipping the note into the mailbox when the adjacent window swung wide.

"I swear they're making mailmen prettier all the time," Jeff Hearn drawled. "Come on in. The door's open."

"Thanks, but I can't stay. I'm off on my daily hike."

"Now that sounds like a good idea. Mind some company?"

"Not if you don't mind watching me eat my sandwich."

"Maybe we can do better than that. Wait a sec. *Abdullah!*"

Jeff pulled the window shut and reappeared in the doorway. "We're in luck. Cold roast chicken. Abdullah's wrapping it up now." He pulled a rucksack from the hall closet and began loading things into the pocket as Abdullah passed them through the kitchen door. Then he strapped a rolled blanket under the pocket and rummaged on the closet shelf.

"There it is!" He emerged with a sort of Tyrolean hat, adjusted it at a jaunty angle, and swung the rucksack onto his back. As we went out the door, he reached into the umbrella stand and extracted a quaintly carved and decidedly touristy alpenstock.

I laughed. "You look like a composite picture of the Alpinist. All you need is a pair of lederhosen."

"Oh no, not on this boy," he declared. "I've got ugly knees. Too many football injuries."

"Let me guess. Texas? TCU?"

"Right conference. It was the Aggies, though."

"Of course, Texas A&M. Geology. I should have known."

"What about you?"

As we walked steadily uphill I told him a bit about myself, then steered the conversation back to him. I wanted to know more in Jenny's interests, but I was also just plain curious. I asked, as tactfully as I could manage, how long ago Jenny's mother had died.

"Seven years," Jeff said. "Janet was an all-American girl. She didn't mind Venezuela so much, but she hated Arabia, everything about it. She was convinced she was going to die there, of snakebite or food poisoning or something."

"And she did die in Arabia?"

"No," Jeff said, his face impassive. "She died in Fort Worth. Of good old-fashioned American cirrhosis."

There was nothing I could say to that. I knew there were several causes of cirrhosis, but by far the most common was excessive drinking. She must have hated Arabia quite thoroughly. I wondered whether Jeff felt partly responsible.

We continued to climb for perhaps twenty minutes, and we were well above the middle station when Jeff slipped the rucksack from his shoulders.

"That's enough for me. I'm not in training the way you are." He tossed me an end of the blanket and we spread it on a level patch of meadow.

"I thought oilmen led outdoor lives," I said.

"I don't get out in the field as much as I'd like anymore. Too much desk work." He set an array of foil-wrapped packages in the center of the blanket and fished a couple of cups from the rucksack. "Wine?"

"Just half a cup, thanks. I'm a working girl, remember."

With appetites sharpened by the fresh air, we attacked the lavish picnic. The chicken was lightly spiced with cumin and other things I couldn't identify, and covered with a delicate fruit glaze. There were two kinds of sesame cakes. There was cheese, a tangy Appenzeller. And to round out the feast, plump dates still on the stem and a pair of the juicy clementines that make our American tangerines taste insipid.

As I packed the remains, Jeff stretched himself out on the blanket and folded his hands beneath his head. He looked lazily across the valley.

"There's an airplane over there, but I don't hear the engine. Glider, do you think?"

"Yes, they go up from the little airport in Saanen. It's late in the season, but with this weather, I suppose there are good updrafts over the Hornberg."

"God, wouldn't you love to be up there today?"

Remembering my last experience in an airplane, I clenched my hands involuntarily and shuddered. Then I said evenly: "The view must be magnificent."

"Ever done any skydiving?"

"No, have you?"

"Yeah, in Arabia. The first time I did it was on a bet. But then I got to like it."

"It must take awfully strong nerves."

Jeff shrugged. "It's something to do. That endless peninsula full of sand can get boring."

I suppressed a smile, thinking of the little Qaimani girls talking of their homeland. To them it was a place of infinite and exciting variety. But to Jeff Hearn it was simply dull. I remembered the day of my arrival here in Gstaad, and Ruedy's nonchalant acceptance of the Alpine grandeur that surrounded him. It was strange, I thought, how differently people saw the world.

As it turned out, that was the last of my daily mountain rambles. Tuesday dawned gray and nasty. Undoubtedly the Diablerets and the surrounding high peaks were laden with lovely fresh snow, if only they had been visible. But in the valley, at barely a thousand meters, we had nothing but steady bone-chilling rain.

My physical fitness program dwindled to a few diligent minutes of calisthenics, and my noon sandwich accompanied me to my desk. It was the only time I had to work uninterrupted. Every other minute, at rehearsals, between classes, at mealtimes, seemed to be filled with frenzied preparations for the play. I felt as though I were under siege.

"Miss Sheridan, we don't have enough lace for the cuffs," Lisa said.

"Miss Sheridan, can the chair be moved back a bit in Act Two, Scene One?" Jenny said.

"Miss Sheridan, how big should the parchment be?" Adam said.

"Deirdre, how do you want the screen hinged?" Ruedy said.

"Miss Sheridan, the hooks will have to be moved on the flats for the picture gallery. Someone forgot to allow for the frames," Adriana Schiano said.

"Miss Sheridan, the hairdresser says . . ."

Miss Sheridan, Miss Sheridan, Miss Sheridan . . .

But somehow, eventually, everything got resolved one way or another. And finally it was Friday evening.

*111*

 *15*

BACKSTAGE was barely controlled pandemonium as the stage-hands and cast worked to dismantle and replace two sets in less than twenty minutes. I heard some good-natured grousing, but most of my teenaged troupe were jubilant. They were playing to a virtually full house.

And it was an appreciative audience. There were faculty and students, parents and guests, but also a surprising percentage of the local English-speaking community. I had hoped the production would be well received, but I had somehow never considered the possibility of even a mild box-office success.

Now, at intermission, the success was being savored by Adriana Schiano. She deserved her moment of triumph. Her portrait of Haroun as Sir Oliver, occupying the place of honor between the great double doors of the auditorium, was a remarkable likeness, and she had succeeded in giving him the slightly forbidding expression the script called for. Even her pupils' paintings, lining the long wall opposite, merited the praise of the audience. What they lacked in technical competence they more than made up in élan.

I glanced at my watch as Adam appeared.

"All ready, Miss Sheridan," he reported breathlessly.

"Good. Ask Ruedy to dim the house lights."

The audience filed slowly back into the auditorium. Watching from an opening in the curtains, I picked out familiar faces. Jeff Hearn stood talking with Dr. and Mrs. Payne. My cousin Kate paused to chat with Zora and Zafia. But I saw nothing of Sadiq, and the aisle seat he had occupied during the first three acts was still empty when the lights finally went down and the curtain rose.

The paintings of Adriana's class, hastily transferred from the lobby, showed to good advantage against the wainscoting of the picture gallery set, and the auction scene unfolded to gales of laughter. Haroun especially was better than he had ever been in rehearsal. The role of Sir Oliver consisted largely of asides, and Haroun was clearly enjoying playing up to the audience.

The scene changed, and as the chandelier was lowered and illuminated, I reflected again how clever Ruedy had been. We had decided to substitute a simple hallway for the parlor, playing the scene before a scrim. The props were no more than a table, a cheval glass, and a fake doorway. But what might have been stark was transformed into opulence by the glittering chandelier. As the brief scene drew to a close, with Sir Oliver and Rowley at center stage, I moved forward beside Adam in the wings.

Then the lights went out.

In the sudden blackness, I heard a high-pitched, almost animal-sounding screech of protesting metal, followed by a resounding crash.

*113*

There was a moment of complete silence, then voices in the audience and onstage rose in confusion and alarm.

Adam reacted before I could, calling out in a firm tone of authority, "Everybody stay in your seats, please. We'll have the lights back on shortly." Then he said, lower but with equal firmness, "Gary, for God's sake, pull the curtain!"

Behind me, in the wavering glow of a cigarette lighter, I saw Ruedy fumbling with the cover of the master fuse-box. Groping in my purse for matches, I slipped past him to the trestle table that held the smaller props and seized a candelabrum. My hands shook as I lit the half-burned tapers. Shielding the flame as best I could, I hurried onto the stage.

A thousand shards of crystal reflected the candlelight. The glass seemed to be scattered over the whole stage. The frame of the chandelier, strangely, was hardly bent, and for an instant its glinting brass arms obscured what lay beyond. Then I saw the slumped form of Haroun, silent and unmoving.

I dropped to my knees, ignoring the broken glass, and set the candlestick beside Haroun's head. His wig was askew. From beneath it a trickle of blood ran along his ear and onto the floor.

Adam was beside me now. "Stand back," he told the gathering cast members, "don't touch him!"

"Adam, we've got to get a doctor," I said urgently, trying to make my mind work, trying to remember where the nearest telephone was.

And then the lights went on.

I was paralyzed. The sight of Haroun inert had been frightening enough by candlelight, but in the sudden glare I could see that beneath the makeup he was chillingly white. I told myself that I had to move, but it was an agonizingly long moment before I could do so.

*114*

As before, Adam was quicker to react. He parted the curtain, stepped onto the proscenium and said in a calm but carrying voice, "Is there a doctor in the house?"

A wave of hysteria swept over me. He must have read that in a play, I thought wildly. Life follows Art; he must know that one too.

Adam's voice went on, saying "minor accident" and "no cause for alarm," but I barely heard the words with their hollow reassurance. I stared into the wings, not breathing, not seeing. Until I saw Sadiq.

He pushed through the circle of children and knelt beside me. Suddenly I felt an overwhelming sense of relief. I do not know whether it was because of Sadiq's presence.

For at that moment Haroun slowly opened his eyes.

Fortunately, there *was* a doctor in the house. In fact, there were two of them. But by the time they arrived backstage, accompanied by the Paynes, Haroun was sitting up and insisting that he was perfectly all right.

The doctors applied themselves to dressing the cut on Haroun's head, peering into his eyes and checking his reflexes. Eventually they agreed that there were no signs of concussion and that Haroun should go to bed immediately.

"But that doesn't make sense," Haroun said. "You say I'm fine, and I feel fine. Of course I'll finish the play."

Jenny, covering her disappointment bravely, protested that the play was not important. But Haroun was firm.

"Look, it'll take a while to sweep up this mess. And I'm not even on again until Act Five. If it'll make you feel any better, I'll lie down until then. Okay?"

Promising to let the doctors check him again between acts, Haroun wandered off toward the drawing-room set to lie down on Sir Peter's sofa. I saw that Adam had the cleanup well in hand, so I too left, intending to look for Ruedy.

Sadiq was there before me. He held the end of a rope in his hand and was examining it minutely.

"I can't understand it," Ruedy said. "I suppose the wiring tore loose, and it must have caused a short circuit. But I don't see how the chandelier fell in the first place."

"Where was it attached?" Sadiq asked.

"This cleat here."

"Just wrapped around it in a figure eight?"

"No, we'd tied loops in the rope where it was to be raised and lowered. I wonder—" Ruedy called to Adam on the stage, then took the rope from Sadiq and pulled on it. With a tinkle of glass, the chandelier swayed upward and rose steadily as Ruedy drew in the rope hand over hand.

"The pulleys seem to be working normally," Sadiq said.

"Yes, and the loop looks okay too." Ruedy slipped it over the cleat and frowned. "Maybe if somebody accidentally stepped on the dangling end—" He shook his head in perplexity.

"Were there many people back here?"

"A few, I guess. I was working the lights. Maybe Abdullah knows. He was here a while ago. I'll ask him when I—"

Adam stuck his head around the corner. "We'll be ready in a minute or two, Miss Sheridan. Shall I go out and explain to the audience what happened?"

"That might not be a bad idea," I agreed.

"Is Haroun really okay?"

"I think so. I'm just going to check now."

Sadiq was close beside me as I hurried around to the idle set. I was resolved to keep a close watch on Haroun for the next twenty minutes or so. If he showed the slightest hint of discomfort or dizziness, he would not go on.

We found him standing before a mirror adjusting his wig.

"Haroun!" I said severely. "You're supposed to be lying down."

"I did lie down. I got bored. Here, look," he said, tugging at the side hair, "you can barely see the bandage."

"Oh, forget about the silly wig!" I exclaimed impatiently.

"Now, wait a minute. I'm very fond of this thing." Haroun removed the wig and smoothed it affectionately. "After all, it probably saved my life. Just think, if I were long-haired like Peter Duncan, I'd have been wearing my own hair. And then where would I have been without all this padding when the sky fell?"

"Yes, it could have been a much worse accident," Sadiq said evenly. "You were standing right under the chandelier, weren't you?"

"Pretty much. I must have heard something when the lights went out, because I jumped to the side. Anyway, it wasn't a direct hit."

"Did you see it, then?" I asked Sadiq involuntarily. "I didn't think you were watching."

He looked at me curiously, and I felt myself color. It must have sounded as though I was spying on his every move.

"Your seat was empty," I explained lamely, "but we couldn't hold the curtain."

That seemed to satisfy him. "I was waiting for a phone call, so I watched from the back of the auditorium."

"Did you see all the auction scene?" Haroun asked eagerly. "What did you think?"

"I think," Sadiq said, "that if you don't lie down right now, you won't get to see the footlights again tonight."

I rolled over, punched the pillow angrily, and looked at the glowing hands of the clock for the dozenth time. Three-thirty.

This was the first bout of insomnia I had suffered in the three months since my arrival. My days at the school were busy and active, and I normally sank into bed with a healthy tiredness and arose fresh and energetic. But tonight, when I was physically and emotionally exhausted, I could not sleep.

The little sleep I had was restless and troubled. I awoke repeatedly with vague memories of dreams filled with nameless terrors. It was better not to sleep. I resigned myself to wakefulness.

I started to get out of bed, meaning to check on Zora and Zafia. Then I remembered that they were not here. Sadiq, mindful of their concern for their brother, had taken them with Haroun to his chalet.

He had been right, I conceded, to whisk Haroun away as soon as the play was over. One thing Haroun did not need was more excitement, and it was a long time before the feverish cast and audience had finished discussing the events of the evening and dispersed.

I suspected, too, that he did not want Haroun to think too much about the accident until he had made up his own mind about it. Ruedy was clearly dissatisfied with his attempts to explain it, and Sadiq seemed even more so.

I tried again to remember exactly how it had happened. The lights had gone out before I heard the sound of the falling chandelier, I was sure. Of course, that might not mean anything. The wires could have torn loose as Ruedy suggested. But on the other hand, someone might have knocked the lights out and *then* unmoored the chandelier. In that case, he would have to be quite close to the rope.

Standing in the wings, I had had my back to the controls. Ruedy was at the lighting panel and had noticed no one either. He thought perhaps Abdullah might—

Abdullah! Why was I so ready to suspect poor Abdullah? Surely not because he was a foreigner and a servant. Probably it was just because I knew so little about him. Everyone who did know him seemed to like him. And he had not even been present in Bern.

Now why did I instinctively link the two incidents? Because of Haroun's involvement, yes, but they had nothing else in common. In Bern, it had been simply a clumsy theft. But even there, there was something strange. The clumsiness was inconsistent with the professionalism of the waiting getaway car. Unless the intention had not been theft at all. . . .

I remembered Dr. Payne's dry recital of how Haroun had been forced off the road in Qaiman. That link seemed more plausible. But the police in Qaiman could not shake their prisoners' story. And the police in Bern had had no luck in tracing Haroun's assailants, nor did they expect any. Even if Haroun had been a specific target, there was no way to tell who had hired the anonymous black-capped thugs.

Assuming they were hired. More likely they were just a gang of common thieves. After all, I reminded myself, America did not have a monopoly on lawlessness. The increase in crime in the past couple of decades had been appalling everywhere, even in Switzerland. And if they *were* hired, wouldn't their employer have been there to see the outcome? But who had been there? Just Ruedy and Jeff.

And Ruedy and Jeff were at the play, too, but—I wasn't making sense, even to myself. What happened at the play

*119*

must have been an accident. Ruedy had been right there, and that's what he thought. At least, that's what he said he thought.

My tired mind groped among the pieces of the puzzle, looking for a pattern, making random connections. Ruedy and Abdullah. Abdullah and Jeff. Haroun and Qaiman. Ruedy thought Abdullah was from North Africa, but he might have come from the Gulf. Jeff did, or near enough. But Jeff had nothing to do with it. He was in his seat watching the performance. Or was he? He might have left his seat. Sadiq had.

Sadiq! Was there no one my whirling brain exempted from suspicion? Sadiq had been waiting for a phone call. It must have been important. I wondered what could have been that important on a Friday night. It seemed a strange time. But no, I reminded myself. In Qaiman, Friday was the Sabbath. Probably the call had to wait until after sundown. That much at least I could explain.

I abandoned my attempts to make sense out of the rest of it. I was just too tired. Perhaps in the morning I would see things more clearly.

I dropped into a fitful slumber.

## 16

"Good morning. I hope I didn't get you out of bed?"

"Not even close," I replied truthfully. I had awakened from habit at seven and, knowing I wouldn't go back to sleep, had taken a brisk shower and dressed. I was just pouring a second cup of coffee when I was called to the telephone. "How's Haroun?"

"Fine, I think," Sadiq said. "He had a good night's sleep. Which is more than I can say for myself."

"I know what you mean," I agreed. "And the girls?"

"They're right here beside me and full of questions. First, they're sorry to have forgotten to mention it last night, but could you feed the cats?"

"Of course. I'll be glad to." I had forgotten about the kittens myself, but it was a measure of the girls' concern for their brother that they had not spared a thought for Cappy and Milord until this morning. "What's the next question?"

"The girls think it would be a nice idea if you could come up and have brunch with us. So do I. Can you get away for a while?"

"Why—yes, I think so."

"Good. What about getting a taxi at this hour? I don't think I—" Sadiq paused suggestively.

"Should leave the children? No, don't. I'll manage."

"Thanks. Oh, and one other thing. Would you pick up some bread?"

"Right. I'll be there in twenty minutes or so."

A full half-hour later I rounded the turn at the Palace Hotel, now shuttered and deserted, and climbed the last few hundred meters to Sadiq's chalet.

I had the bread, two golden braided loaves, under my arm, but I had been less successful in finding a taxi. Probably, I decided, all of Herr Kübli's drivers had gone hunting. It was a good day for it. The three-day rain had given way to a crisp clarity, and it looked like we would have to wait a while longer for snow. The ski-lift operators would be worrying, but I was pleased. The cold, clear air had quickened my blood, and by the time I pressed the doorbell I was feeling fresh and alert.

"Welcome to Chalet Bamby," Haroun greeted me. "Would you believe it? I told Uncle Sadiq he should buy the place just so he could change the name."

"On the contrary," Sadiq said. "It's a very appropriate name. It must be, because I know of at least three other Chalet Bambys in this village alone." He passed the bread to Haroun and helped me out of my coat. "Deirdre, I'm glad you're here. How on earth does one separate eggs?"

I followed him into the kitchen and found Zora and Zafia, dishtowels tied around their waists, frowning over a cookbook. They were glad to have me take command.

*122*

The three of us set to work assembling a soufflé while Sadiq escaped gratefully to the living room. It was not long before we joined him.

"It'll be done in twenty-five minutes," I announced.

"Good. That'll give you a chance to sit down and relax. It was a nasty trick, inviting you for a meal and then making you cook it." He handed me a tall frosty glass of tomato juice and picked up another for himself. "Girls, why don't you set the table now? And Haroun, you'd better help them. They can't reach the top shelves."

Haroun gave us a knowing look as he left with his sisters.

Sadiq lifted his glass toward mine in a silent toast. I tasted the tomato juice, which proved to be a Bloody Mary.

Sadiq smiled briefly. "Haroun has a suspicious mind. But he's right. I did want us to be left alone. I want to ask you about last night."

I told him, trying to be as accurate as possible, what I remembered of the incident.

Sadiq nodded thoughtfully. "What about this Messerli?"

"Ruedy? Surely you don't think he had anything to do with it? He's so reliable."

"But what do you really know about him?" Sadiq persisted.

I toyed with my glass and reflected. "Not very much," I admitted. "I mean, you know the Swiss."

"Yes," Sadiq agreed. "I don't put much stock in national stereotypes, but I've never known a Swiss who wasn't reticent about himself."

"But why would Ruedy want to—"

Sadiq shrugged. "There's always money."

I thought of Ruedy asking me jokingly if I had a dowry of half a million francs. Still, I was unconvinced.

"What's your impression of Jeff Hearn?" Sadiq asked abruptly.

"Jeff?" I thought a moment. "He's pretty much what you'd expect a Texan to be. Hearty and self-confident and, well, open. He does things with dash." I looked at Sadiq and couldn't resist saying, "He plays a lovely game of bridge."

Sadiq frowned, and I went on hurriedly, "Jenny's crazy about him. On the other hand, I gather his wife drank herself to death. I don't know much about it. I get the feeling there's a reckless streak in Jeff, but it may just be a pose. Or maybe if you work in the oilfields long enough you get used to danger. He claims he's glad to see the end of Arabia for a while. Still, he has an Arab servant with him."

"Yes." Sadiq got up and paced across the room. "I've heard a bit about Hearn from other sources, and what you say fits. He's a hard one to figure out. I could bear to know more about Mr. Thomas Jefferson Hearn."

When I reached the gate of Jeff Hearn's chalet the following evening, I paused, remembering Sadiq's words.

Jeff and Abdullah stood in the kitchen in earnest conversation. Framed by the wintry darkness, the brightly lit view of the interior through the uncurtained window was as vivid as a stage set. I took some time fumbling with the latch before I passed through the gate and started slowly up the walk. Telling myself that I had no intention of spying, I nonetheless kept my eyes on the window. The scene before me was intriguing.

Jeff's face was plainly visible as he gestured and expostulated. Abdullah's back was to me, but from the set of his shoulders he seemed to be maintaining a stubborn position.

I wondered what they were arguing about. Probably some household matter. Whatever it was, Abdullah stood his ground. Either Arab servants were a breed apart, or this was not a typical employer-employee relationship.

Jenny burst out the door and pelted down the steps, nearly knocking me over.

"Oh, Miss Sheridan! Sorry, I didn't see you. Are you okay?"

"Fine. What's the big rush?"

"Got a paper due tomorrow, and it isn't even started. Hey, Miss Sheridan." She dropped her voice. "Have you talked to Daddy?"

"Not yet, Jen. I think I'd better work up to the subject gradually."

"Yeah, I guess maybe." She looked doubtful, then brightened in adolescent optimism. "I'll keep my fingers crossed. Gotta run now. 'Bye!" And she was off down the road, her coat flapping behind her.

Jeff's open American grin was back in evidence when he greeted me at the door. I followed him into a bedroom where I put my coat. Then he left me to repair my windblown hair while he admitted the other guests.

The Penfields were a pleasant couple with an interesting background, and we sat in the living room chatting for a few minutes before moving to the bridge table. I had been looking forward to the game, but as it progressed I became aware of a hint of tension diminishing my enjoyment. The Penfields did not seem to notice anything. They played steadily and well. And Jeff too was playing with his usual combination of dash and determination. But every so often, when he glanced at Abdullah, the lines of his jaw tightened.

Abdullah hovered in the doorway, ready to serve us. He was politely attentive to all of us and deferential to

Jeff. And yet I was relieved when, after we had finished the buffet and been served coffee, Jeff dismissed Abdullah for the night.

We played for another hour or so, and then Mrs. Penfield confessed that she was tired and the game broke up. Saying that if I would wait a bit he would walk me home, Jeff went to the door with the older couple.

When I returned from rinsing the coffee cups and stacking them in the kitchen sink, Jeff was pouring himself a hefty drink. "You've got time to stay for a nightcap, don't you?" he asked.

I checked myself on the point of refusing. I didn't really want a drink, but it was barely ten o'clock, and I had promised Jenny that I would "work on" her father. If I intended to influence him in favor of her acting ambitions, I had better lay the groundwork. So I settled into an overstuffed chair and accepted a mild Scotch and soda.

"The Penfields seem like agreeable people," I remarked.

"They're nice enough," Jeff said. "But I'd rather have a little more action. I hear there are some strong games in town. You interested?"

"You mean for money?"

"You wouldn't have to worry about that part. I'd take care of your stake."

"Oh, I couldn't let you do that!" I protested.

"Sure you could. It's all ill-gotten gains, anyway. I'm on a hot streak. I went down to Evian last night, and it was like I had that roulette wheel on a leash."

Not wanting to commit myself just yet, I shifted the subject slightly. "Did you take Jenny down with you?"

"Jenny! I wouldn't take her to a place like that!"

He was quite vehement. It was clear that where Jenny was concerned, no pedestal was too lofty. And yet, I reflected with a flash of pique, he didn't see anything wrong with involving *me* in his high-stake gambling.

"And besides," Jeff went on, "you have to be twenty-one to get into the casino. Not that Jen's that far off. She'll be seventeen next Saturday. God, it makes me feel old!"

He ran a hand through his short, sun-bleached hair and groaned in mock despair. He must be pushing forty, I thought with surprise. He certainly didn't look it. When he grinned, his deeply tanned face was entirely boyish.

"By the way, that reminds me. I need your help, Deirdre. I want to arrange a surprise party for her birthday. I thought you could tell me who to invite."

We turned to discussing plans for the party, and Jeff was working his way through a second stiff drink when I noticed that it was almost eleven. Reminding him that I had classes to teach in the morning, I went to the bedroom to get my coat while he began turning out lights.

I was standing in front of the dressing table mirror knotting my scarf when I saw him lounging in the doorway.

"Now there's a fetching sight," he drawled. "Just what every well-appointed gentleman's bedroom needs."

I flushed, and to cover my awkwardness I said lightly: "I thought in Arabia you all had harems."

"That's okay for quantity. I was thinking about quality."

"You forget, Mr. Hearn, that I am a proper schoolmarm."

"I wonder. I'll bet there are depths of passion in your Celtic soul." He looked at me steadily, a glint of amused challenge in his gold-flecked eyes.

"At the moment," I said, "there are depths of fatigue in my Celtic bones." I picked up my coat and put it on.

Jeff grinned. "Okay, Cinderella. We'll take you home."

As we walked down the hill toward the Academy, I thought of Sadiq, who had called me Cinderella too. In most ways, the two men could not have been more different. And yet, with his streak of recklessness and his provocative speech, there was no denying that Jeff Hearn was a very attractive man.

The next day was the first of December, and in Gstaad it was the first real day of winter as well. The snowflakes that settled steadily on the ground were plump and heavy. At lunchtime the students were already building snow forts and busily stockpiling ammunition.

I found Ruedy, as I had expected, in the ski room. He reached into a rack for a pair of skis, unclipped them, and wiped them carefully. Then he clamped them bottoms-up on the workbench and began to file the edges. He was engrossed in his work, and I stood for a couple of minutes looking at the array of equipment. Lining the two side walls were pegs supporting skis and poles, dozens and dozens of pairs of them. The far wall was given over to neatly labeled pigeonholes for boots. The center of the room held benches, and when I walked in and sat on one of them, Ruedy glanced over and said happily:

"Hullo, Deirdre. Catching ski-fever?"

"Everybody is. Do you think this is really going to last?"

"Absolutely. Even the weather forecast says so. If it keeps up like this, we'll have a solid meter of base by the weekend. We were afraid we'd have to move the preseason instructors' school somewhere else, but now it looks like we'll have perfect conditions."

"Are you going to be teaching in it?"

"Not this year. Just a classroom session on safety equipment. I'll be too busy here."

128

"It looks like the contents of this room alone would keep you busy for more than a week."

"Oh, they'll all get done. Which ones are yours? I didn't see them."

"I have to buy a new pair. I decided it wasn't worth shipping the old ones. I brought my boots, though."

"Yes? What kind are they?"

"Venerable old Raichles. They date back before all this plastic and foam. To give you an idea how old they are, they only came in one color—black. But I wouldn't trade them. They're as comfortable as old slippers."

"That's not the point. They won't give you the proper support. You ought to get a pair of . . . well . . . of course, if you need new skis . . ." he floundered.

I tried not to smile. Ruedy, with what amounted to a Swiss reflex, had thought immediately of money. For all he knew, I couldn't afford new boots as well as skis. Poor Ruedy was painfully embarrassed.

"I do, Ruedy," I said briskly, "and I'd appreciate your advice. Would you have time to come down to Hermenjat's with me and help me choose them? I don't know anything about these new bindings."

"Sure. Whenever you say," he agreed eagerly.

"I think I'll keep the old boots for a while, though. I don't need all the latest equipment, the way I ski. I'm happy to leave the racing to the kids."

Ruedy picked up a rubber ski clip and began stretching it mechanically. "Did you know we're going to have a racing team this year? I'm supposed to coach them."

"That should be interesting. Are you getting a lot of response?"

"Oh yes, quite a bit. Even Haroun's going to try it. Just for fun, of course." Ruedy chuckled. "He says he's too old to think of serious competition. But he wants me to start training his sisters. He says if they start now, they can ski for Qaiman in the '84 Olympics!"

"Well, and why not? Royalty have brought home medals in riding and sailing."

"Not in skiing."

"I don't see the difference."

"More competition. Skis cost less than sailboats or show jumpers."

I had no answer to that. Somehow, with Ruedy, things generally came back to money. I remembered Sadiq's remark, and it reminded me why I had come.

"Ruedy," I said casually, "did you ever find out any more about how that chandelier came loose?"

"No," he said abruptly. He seemed to take the question as a personal accusation.

"I thought Abdullah might have noticed something."

Ruedy stopped bristling. "No, I asked him. He wasn't even there when it happened. He'd just gone outside for a cigarette. Of course, there was no reason why he shouldn't. He didn't have anything special to do."

"No," I said mildly, "there was no reason for him to be there."

Ruedy considered my remark for a moment, debating whether to take umbrage again. Finally he said: "Anyway, Abdullah doesn't speak English, so he wouldn't understand what was going on." He threw the ski clip on the workbench and picked up the big aluminum file. Drawing it deliberately across the bottom of the ski, he said, "I doubt we'll ever know what happened."

 *17*

THE STREETLIGHTS were already on as we made our way among late-afternoon shoppers, their umbrellas raised against the snow, and entered the warmth of the sport-shop.

"From what you tell me," Ruedy said, "I think you'd be better off with compacts."

"You mean short skis?"

"Not really. Compacts are your own height, so they're not that much shorter. But they're a tiny bit wider and they have rounded tips, and they make skiing a lot easier."

"But I've been skiing on and off since I was ten on regular skis."

"That's what I mean. If you learned so long ago, you're probably used to keeping your weight too far forward, and your skis too close together too. With compacts you'll naturally develop a better equilibrium. So even if you go back to slightly longer skis after a season or two, for more speed, you'll find you have much better technique."

I digested this while Ruedy turned to greet the proprietor. He explained my needs in melodic Schwytzerdutsch, introduced me rather as an afterthought, and moved to the bank of skis.

"Had the lady considered how much—" the proprietor inquired delicately.

"Not really. How much will good bindings cost?" I asked Ruedy.

"Maybe two hundred, two-fifty."

My God! I thought. That's almost a hundred dollars. I hadn't realized it was that long since I'd bought skis. Then I reminded myself that I could afford a dozen pairs if I wanted. I was still not used to having money.

"Then I suppose up to five hundred for the skis," I said.

Ruedy's eyebrows rose slightly, but he said nothing. He pulled a couple of skis from the display rack, and the two men compared their merits while I listened. Eventually they turned to consult me.

"Not those," I said decisively. "I don't like the color."

Ruedy's reaction was once again confined to his eyebrows, and I did not bother to justify myself. He could wear bright orange skis if he chose; I was not going to have my equipment clash with every item in my wardrobe. I had never been a snow bunny, but there were limits.

"What about Kneissls?" I said. "I always liked those."

"An excellent line," the proprietor agreed immediately. "You'd be interested in the Freestars. Here, you see the bottoms have the same transparent Racing Base as the competition models."

I was more concerned about the color of the tops.

Luckily they were an unobjectionable black, and I agreed to the choice without further discussion. Then, to mollify Ruedy, I left the selection of bindings and poles to him. Before long I had approved the order, specified the initials to be engraved on the skis, and been assured that everything would be ready by Thursday.

"Well, that seems to be it," Ruedy said. "I have to pick up a couple of things at Pernet's, but it won't take me long. Why don't you wait here where it's warm, and I'll bring the car around?"

"Thanks, Ruedy, but I have some more shopping I'd like to do, too. And I've already taken too much of your time. I don't mind walking back, really. I'll enjoy it in the snow."

And no doubt I would have enjoyed it. But by the time I finished shopping I was too late, and too laden, to do anything but take a taxi. I had to dump my packages and rush to make dinner.

An hour later I spread my purchases on the bed and surveyed them happily. I had wandered into the back of the sportshop after Ruedy left, intending to buy a pair of ski gloves and perhaps some extra thermal underwear. But then my eye had fallen on a magnificent sweater that would be perfect for après-ski. The salesgirl caught my growing enthusiasm, and soon I was trying on half the stock of the shop. I wound up with the sweater, not one but two pairs of gloves, a couple of turtleneck pullovers, and a pair of impractical but stunning white pants.

I was standing in front of my mirror in the *pièce de résistance,* a quilted navy outfit put together with an array of white industrial zippers and topped by an outrageously rich-looking white fur hat, when Maggie popped through the communicating door.

"Deirdre, that's fabulous!" she exclaimed. "Good Lord, it looks like you bought out the entire town."

*133*

"No, just Hermenjat's," I said contentedly.

It was true, I thought as I turned once more before the mirror to admire the trim lines of the ski suit, that in scarcely an hour I had parted with almost two months' earnings. But I had worked hard for it, and except for what I had spent decorating my room, my expenses had been minimal.

Perhaps I had been extravagant. But I had not felt so deliciously feminine for ages.

I was still unrepentant Saturday morning as I shouldered my new skis and started up the road from the school. The navy and white outfit made me feel not only chic but also warm and comfortable, and I was eager to try out my new equipment. The weather had finally cleared the preceding afternoon. Now a timid sun picked out jewel glints in the fresh snow, though at ten o'clock the air was still early-morning cold.

As I came abreast of Jeff Hearn's chalet, the door opened and Jeff hailed me. "Hi, Deirdre! I tried to call you, but you'd just left. Come in a minute?"

I propped my skis against the fence, clumped up the freshly shoveled path and, knocking the snow from my boots, followed him inside.

Jeff sat on a carved bench and began pulling on a pair of heavy socks. "Everything all set?"

"I think so. Lisa has rounded up a good stereo and a bunch of records. That's all these kids need for a party, that and a mountain of food. Jenny doesn't suspect?"

"Not a thing. I told her I'd pick her up at quarter after six to take her out to dinner. I figure I'll drive about five miles, then discover I forgot my wallet and have to come back."

"Perfect. By then everybody will be here ready to shout 'surprise'."

"Right. Where are you bound for now? I thought I might catch up with you on the way to the lifts, but you were going uphill."

I explained. Walking in ski boots, even my comfortable old ones, was not easy. If I remembered correctly, this way I could cut across to the top of the trainer lift. Then, by using the intermediate t-bar, I would make my way in progressive warm-up runs to the bottom of the Wispile cablecars. "And if you don't mind deep powder," I concluded, "you can leave the *piste* in the middle of the last descent and wind up on this road again."

"Very neat," Jeff said, "but I don't recommend it today. The Wispile will be too crowded with instructors. Jen said the whole school is going there this afternoon to act as guinea pigs for them. That's why I'm not worried about her coming here and seeing the party preparations."

I knew that Ruedy had arranged for the students to serve as demonstration classes, and I planned to join them later in the afternoon, but for now I was free. One advantage of my heavy schedule was that I was exempted from monitoring Saturday-morning study hall. Today it was a particularly welcome respite.

"What do you say we try the Eggli? The blue trail is nice and easy for the first run," Jeff said. "Strap your skis on top of the car while I get my boots."

I obeyed, hoisting my skis up beside Jeff's with a sigh for dead chivalry. Despite his years abroad, Jeff was a thoroughly liberated American male. He might hold a door when it occurred to him, but it didn't occur with any dependability.

He came into the garage and muttered, "Damn that Abdullah! He's disappeared again."

"He's over at the school," I said. "I saw him in the ski room looking for Ruedy."

Jeff frowned and said something under his breath. I wondered whether that was what he and Abdullah had been arguing about the previous weekend.

"Hop in," Jeff said, tossing his boots on the back seat. They were a shiny new model, blue molded plastic with knurled buttons in place of the lower clips. "Can't drive in the things. The spoiler's so stiff you can't press the accelerator. Can't walk in them either."

I smiled faintly, knowing that Jeff was only sounding fashionable. He had gone out and bought himself the most professional pair of racing boots he could find, so he could have the pleasure of grumbling about how uncomfortable they were.

He backed the car between the high banks of snow, then braked and rolled down the window as Abdullah approached up the middle of the road. Jeff spoke to him in Arabic, but I caught the words "today" and "telephone."

Apart from something about two o'clock, I missed the exchange that followed. Then Abdullah grinned and asked a question in which I distinguished the word for female teacher.

Jeff's reply was brief but emphatic, and translated as something between "so what" and "forget it." He rolled up the window, clashed the gears and drove down the hill swearing under his breath, still in Arabic. I decided it was perhaps as well I didn't understand that part.

I wondered idly why Jeff put up with Abdullah. Their relations did not seem particularly harmonious lately. Perhaps Arab servants were often difficult, and Jeff was simply used to it. He was undoubtedly used to paying his help virtually nothing. That may have been the chief point in explaining Abdullah's presence. It would not have weighed strongly enough with me.

We had always, I reflected, had household help when

we lived in the Caribbean and the Mediterranean. After Mother's death, I had continued to deal with them as she had, treating them as respected co-workers, with unfailingly good results. But perhaps Arab society was different, and such treatment would not work. Nevertheless, it would be interesting to try running a household in, say, Qaiman along such lines. Not that it was likely I would ever be called on to do so.

Jeff's thoughts were in the same part of the world, for he asked about Haroun and his sisters, their adjustment to the school and their activities. He sounded genuinely interested, but I felt a sudden possessiveness about the Qaimani children, and I answered him in general terms. Then, thinking I had been abrupt, I added that they took great pleasure in the frequent visits of their Uncle Sadiq.

"Oh, him!" Jeff said shortly.

"You know Mr. Yamali?"

"I've met him. And I've heard a lot about him around the Gulf. I wonder what his angle is. You never know what these Arabs are thinking."

I did not know what Jeff Hearn was thinking, but where Sadiq was concerned, it was clearly uncomplimentary. "I would have said," I suggested diffidently, "that Mr. Yamali was rather Western."

"Maybe. He sure seems to have a high opinion of himself. And he's so smooth he must polish himself every morning."

I did not answer. This was the first independent opinion of Sadiq I had heard, and it presented a picture quite different from the one I had formed. But strangely, in Jeff's comments, I could find nothing to contradict.

"Race you to the bottom," Jeff said, and took off straight downhill. I shrugged and followed, not attempting to match his pace. I was used to my new skis now, but

I still did not think the third run of the season was a particularly prudent time to go flat out. Jeff shouted *"Piste!"*, boomed over a crest and was out of sight.

He was leaning on his poles and laughing when I skidded to a stop beside him. "Not bad for a girl," he said. "Ready to go up again?"

We passed the ticket-taker and flashed the celluloid-encased passes that we wore on strings around our necks. The photograph on mine was depressingly unflattering, and I quickly unzipped my jacket and tucked it back inside. Jeff continued to toy with his, and as we stepped into the tracks and were borne uphill, he remarked:

"These things are quite a bargain. How many lifts do they cover? About forty?"

"They're not the bargain they used to be. I remember the first year I was here, a season pass was about seventy dollars."

"Don't talk about inflation," Jeff groaned. "That reminds me. I picked up a new novel the other day, and the author had a character in Switzerland paying for a drink with a five-franc note."

"That is funny," I agreed. "There have only been five-franc coins ever since I can remember."

"That wasn't the funny part," Jeff said. "The funny part was, he got some change."

When the lift deposited us at the top of the Eggli, Jeff jabbed the tip of a pole to release his bindings and stepped out of his skis. "Let's slog on over to the restaurant and claim a table before the lunch crowd gets too heavy."

"I thought they weren't due to open for a couple of weeks."

"Have you ever seen a Swiss pass up the chance to

*138*

make money? Of course they're open. Come on."

Jeff was right, and an hour later I was finishing my second cup of coffee and wondering how I would ever summon the energy to stand up, let alone ski again. "I should never eat *rösti,*" I sighed. "It's pure calories, but I can't resist it."

"You don't have to worry about your figure," Jeff said automatically. It was an inaccurate and typically male remark, but nonetheless welcome. "Anyway, you'll burn it up in one run."

He reached under the table and refastened the clips of his boots, then stood and led the way outside. As we reclaimed our skis and walked toward the cablecar station, he said, "This will have to be the last one for me. I have a couple of errands to run. But if you want to keep on skiing, I can come back for you any time after three."

"Thanks, Jeff, but I don't—"

I was interrupted by a piercing wolf whistle. My head turned involuntarily. It is the natural reaction of any girl; if the whistle is not meant for her, she wants to assess the competition. But this time I wished I had tamed my instincts, for I was looking straight into the eyes of Sadiq Yamali.

It was a moment before I realized he was more embarrassed than I was. And then I saw Haroun standing beside him, an impish look on his face.

Jeff and Sadiq greeted each other and shook hands perfunctorily. By tacit consent the three of us ignored Haroun.

"Jeff," I said, "I'm not sure how long I'll want to stay, so don't worry about coming back."

"If it's a question of Miss Sheridan getting home, I'll be glad to drive her," Sadiq offered.

"Thanks, Yamali, I'd appreciate that," Jeff said in a

tone of voice that conveyed just the opposite. To regain the initiative, he added, "Then I'll see you tonight, Deirdre?"

"Right. And thank you for the lunch."

Jeff laid his skis on the ground, stepped into the bindings and, with a wave, plunged down the beginning of the expert trail. To his natural recklessness there was now another element added, and by the time he disappeared in a spray of snow, he was skiing at the fine edge of control.

Sadiq looked after him for a moment, appreciating the display for what it was. Then he turned to Haroun.

"Well, young man," he said. "I think you owe Miss Sheridan an apology."

"But it was meant as a compliment," Haroun protested innocently. "Besides, dear uncle, it was you who pointed out to me how ravishing she looked."

Sadiq pressed his lips together and looked at the sky.

"What are you doing here anyway?" I asked Haroun as a diversion. "I thought everyone was going to ski together on the Wispile today."

"Oh, I begged off so I could ski with Uncle Sadiq."

"And I am beginning to regret it," Sadiq said. "Well, we came to ski, so let's ski. Perhaps it will keep you out of mischief." He picked up his skis and began to walk away.

"Hey, where are you going?" Haroun called.

"Over to the Schopfen run. If you think that without any warm-up you can go down the black trail like that daredevil Hearn, you are mistaken."

He stalked off, and I followed, with Haroun bringing up the rear. Sadiq's face was rigidly set. I had never seen him angry before, and it was a disquieting sight.

We had our skis on before Haroun caught up with us and, without waiting, Sadiq nodded to me and started down the hill. The physical activity seemed to dissipate his anger, for soon he slid to a stop to wait for Haroun. As I pulled up beside him, he shook his head ruefully and muttered, "Spoiled brat."

"Oh, he's not such a bad kid," I said.

"I know he's not. I guess sometimes I'm unreasonable. But I have such high expectations for him."

Sadiq's face was almost paternal as he watched Haroun slip the loops of his poles over his wrists and push off. He picked up speed, heading toward us, and I thought how splendid he looked, slim and athletic and full of the eagerness of youth. He was directly above us when he lifted over a hummock and pivoted gracefully and then, without warning, pitched sideways.

He fell toward us with incredible speed, rolling over and over in a spectacular eggbeater, arms and legs flying, one ski swinging in great arcs at the end of its strap, the other still attached to his boot and gouging the snow each time he flipped over.

I did not have time to move. I only had time to hear Sadiq cry out, and then the bright white snow went black.

# 18

WHEN the world came back, it was at a crazy angle. The first thing I saw was my skis, crossed tips-up against the sky. But they did not seem to be attached to me. My legs lay flat on the ground. Then I saw that the skis had been planted above me in the snow.

That made sense. They always planted the skis in a cross when there had been an accident.

I turned my head sharply to the other side. For a long minute I saw nothing more. Then the exploding pinwheels steadied into winking points of light that receded slowly to reveal Sadiq's face. Other people hovered behind him, but I did not recognize any of them. Somehow that did not seem quite right.

Sadiq's lips were moving, but I could not hear what he was saying. I reached up to push the fur hat back from my ears. My arm hurt. I moved it experimentally, testing the wrist and elbow. It was sore, but it seemed to work.

142

I tried the other arm. That was better. I closed my eyes and concentrated on trying to hear.

When the sounds began to come back, I opened my eyes and said, "Haroun? Is he—" My voice sounded very far away.

"He's all right," Sadiq answered faintly. "Don't try to talk. The luge will be here right away."

"Luge? I don't need. . . ." I raised my head and tried to sit up.

"Hush. Lie still." Sadiq pushed me gently back. He slipped off his jacket, rolled it and eased it under my head.

"I'll be . . . okay . . . in a minute," I said, the words coming with difficulty. "I just . . . had the breath . . . knocked out of me."

"You had more than the breath knocked out of you. You were unconscious for a couple of minutes. Now take it easy." He brushed a loose strand of hair from my face. "Can you move your arms?"

"Yes, they're fine."

"Legs?"

I shifted my hips cautiously, then the knees. Something about the left leg felt a little strange, so I postponed it until last, hoping it would get better. Right knee okay, right ankle, toes, left knee. Left ankle. Pain shot up the leg.

I bit my lip and flexed the ankle again tentatively. It was worse when I moved it laterally.

"What is it?" Sadiq asked.

"I think I've hurt my left ankle."

"Keep it still. The luge is coming now."

Haroun arrived before the luge did, crunching up the hill, his skis over his shoulder. He must have rolled quite a way below us. He did not seem to be injured, except in his self-esteem, but he was distinctly annoyed. He

*143*

planted his skis in the snow and looked questioningly at Sadiq.

"Oh, no," he said when Sadiq told him. He dropped on one knee beside me. "God, I'm sorry, Miss Sheridan. I don't know what to say."

"It's all right. It wasn't your fault."

"Sure it was. If I'd only—" He stood up abruptly. "No, damn it, it wasn't! Sadiq, look at this." He turned toward his skis. "I thought maybe I hadn't closed the binding properly. But these settings are a full eight points apart. No wonder I lost a ski on the first turn. If I ever get my hands on the joker who—" He broke off, punching an angry fist into his other glove.

Sadiq peered at the settings of the bindings. "When's the last time you checked them?"

"I just adjusted them yesterday. And they can't move by themselves."

"No." Sadiq was silent for a moment. He started to say something, then changed his mind and said, "Well, better put them right. We have to ski to the bottom before we can go to the hospital with Miss Sheridan."

Strong hands were now lifting me onto the toboggan-like sledge. I was probably the first casualty of the season, but the rescue team worked with the impersonal efficiency of long practice. Soon I was wrapped in a cocoon of quilts and canvas and strapped to the luge, my injured leg cradled in a protective cage. The attendants grasped the poles at the ends and directed the luge steadily downhill, their skis snowplowing to brake the descent.

I protested when I saw the ambulance, but Sadiq was adamant. Even if his car had not been halfway around the mountain at the cablecar station, he said, he would have insisted I stay on my back until a doctor looked at me.

So I allowed myself to be borne past the lumber yard,

through the village of Saanen, and up the curving drive to the Bezirkspital.

I was still on my back an hour later, resting in an anteroom and waiting for Sadiq. My ski boots were on the floor beside me and, propped against the wall, a pair of shiny aluminum crutches.

It had been a bad moment when they got the boot off, but it was accomplished quickly, and before long the X rays were taken and developed. When the doctor came back, he was beaming. In tones he might normally have used to announce the birth of twins, he confided that I was suffering from nothing more than a mild concussion, a few bruises, and a rather nasty sprain.

Now the ankle was firmly bandaged, and I was feeling sufficiently recovered to wish they had not had to slit the inner seam of my pant leg.

Then I reproved myself for worrying about my new clothes when I might at this moment have been wearing several pounds of plaster. I was lucky and I knew it, though my relief, and Sadiq's, had been mild compared with Haroun's.

When Sadiq returned, he was alone. "I've cleared everything with the desk," he said, "and the doctor says you can leave."

"Where's Haroun?" I asked, pushing myself up gingerly.

"My place, with orders to stay there. I don't want to worry about him anymore today," Sadiq said grimly.

I started to say something, then thought better of it.

Sadiq placed a large box on the couch beside me. "You can't go out in this weather with nothing on your feet. Try these on while I put the others in the car." He picked up my ski boots and crutches and left abruptly.

I tipped back the lid and parted the folds of tissue

paper, but I did not try them on right away. I just looked at them. They were the most beautiful pair of boots I had ever seen. I stroked the long, silky white fur, then lifted them carefully from the box. They were fur inside too, a soft, warm brown, and they laced all the way up, so despite my swollen ankle, they would be easy to get into. I turned them over. Even the size was right. I remembered Sadiq toying with my discarded ski boot before he left to fetch his car; he had thought of every detail.

I was holding the boots on my lap and smiling gently when behind my shoulder Sadiq said, "Are they all right?"

I looked up into his anxious face. "Sadiq, they're absolutely lovely, but I can't accept them."

"Please. I wish you would. You've been rather thoroughly battered by a member of my family. The least I can do is gift-wrap the damage."

He sounded so earnest that I did not protest very hard when he slipped the boots on, laced them and helped me up onto my good leg. I turned to reach for my crutches, forgetting they were no longer there. But Sadiq slid an arm around my back, swung me off the floor and, before I could say anything, carried me out through the lobby to the waiting car.


I shifted the telephone receiver to my other hand, glanced through the commons room window at the sunset, and positioned my foot more comfortably on its pillow. "I know, Jeff," I said, "it's a shame. I was looking forward to it. If it were just a quiet evening, I'd disobey the doctor. But the last thing my head needs is four hours of rock music at full blast. So there it is."

"Well, take care of yourself."

"I will. Ask Jenny to save me a piece of the cake."

There, I thought as I hung up, that's all arranged. I

146

had wondered what I would do about finding a substitute chaperon for Jenny's party. I knew Maggie was away for the weekend in Leysin. Then I had looked at the duty roster and seen Adriana's name down for tonight. That solved everything. As long as I let her pretend she was doing me a favor, she would be glad to have me sit quietly by the office switchboard with a book while she joined the handsome Mr. Hearn in supervising his daughter's party. Also, I had an idea that the presence of the voluptuous Adriana Schiano would go a long way toward reconciling Jeff to my absense.

So that was settled. What wasn't settled was the mystery of Haroun's safety bindings. I thought back on what Sadiq had said.

It had been a half hour from the time he delivered me to the dormitory until he reappeared. I had installed myself in the commons room, a stack of pillows behind me and under my ankle and a pile of examination papers on my lap. Sadiq stamped the snow from his boots, dropped his anorak on a chair, and sat down opposite me.

"I've collected your things and put them in the ski room," he said. "Mrs. Payne showed me the way. I took the opportunity to ask her a few questions."

I waited for him to continue.

"That place is open all the time, isn't it? Anybody could go in there."

"I suppose so. Nothing around here is locked except at night."

He slumped further down in his chair, his shoulders hunched forward. "I don't understand it. There doesn't seem to be any kind of pattern. I thought after the first couple of incidents—you know what happened just before Haroun left Qaiman this summer?"

I nodded.

"And then that business in Bern. It looked like they might both have been kidnapping attempts. That's bad enough, but at least you know what you're dealing with. I talked to Haroun, and he has been more careful."

"But now there have been two accidents in scarcely a week," I said.

"And that's at least one accident too many. But they don't seem to have anything in common with the previous things. That's what baffles me. I can't find a connection, and there *has* to be a connection. It simply can't be coincidence. And yet, it's as if there are two forces at work, two completely different mentalities."

"I think I see what you mean," I said slowly. "The kidnapping attempts, if that's what they were, were well planned and cleanly set in motion and—professional. But these last attacks, they're—"

"Malicious. And capricious. That falling chandelier could have killed Haroun. But the ski bindings were more like—a shot in the dark. He didn't even get hurt." Sadiq looked up suddenly, apologetically.

I smiled in wry agreement. "That's true." I thought for a moment, then said, "You know, Sadiq, there is one common element—Haroun."

"Well, obviously. That's what we've been talking about."

"I know, but—what I mean is, if it were a question of kidnapping, wouldn't the girls have been equally likely targets? Of course," I acknowledged, "we have kept a pretty close watch on them."

"*You* have, I know," he said warmly. "You barely let them out of your sight."

"That's not exactly a hardship. I love having them with me."

And now, two hours later, they came through the commons room door. They had high color in their cheeks, and they were laughing as they recalled the spills they had taken. Zora started to relate one particularly funny mishap. Then she noticed my propped-up foot, and broke off to ask what had happened. I explained that I too had had a spill and, having further to fall than they did, had foolishly managed to twist my ankle.

They stood for a moment with concern on their faces, then Zafia wordlessly left the room. She returned with Milord in her arms. In what I knew was the ultimate gesture of consolation she could offer, she placed him on my lap. Milord crawled up under my chin, nuzzled me, then went back to my lap, where he proceeded to make a nest in the examination papers and curl himself into a comfortable ball.

Zora and Zafia pulled chairs close to me and asked in hushed tones if they could do anything.

"Hey, you two," I laughed, "there's no need to whisper. I'm not dying, I just sprained my ankle. Tell you what. You get the kittens' supper, and then I'll hear all about what you did today."

When Zora brought the supper bowl, Milord immediately lifted his head and began to unwind himself. But before he hit the floor, Cappy, ever ahead of her brother, had streaked into the commons room and was tucking into the food. I chuckled and turned to see them better, shoving the pillows back and swinging my feet to the floor. Before long the kittens had licked the bowl clean and were doing the same to themselves.

Presently Cappy paused in her ablutions. She cocked her head in my direction. After a moment's consideration, she walked over to circle my feet. I swung my left leg back onto the safety of the sofa and watched, fascinated, as Cappy and now Milord examined my remaining boot. Milord, uncharacteristically, made up his mind first and began to lick the long, white fur.

"Look," Zora crowed, "he thinks he's found a new friend!"

"Of course he does," I said. "After all, it's furry. And it moves." I wiggled my toes, and Cappy pounced on the boot, engaging it in a playful tussle.

We watched the antics of the kittens and the fur boot until Martha Payne came in with a dinner tray for me. That signaled the departure of the girls for their own meal.

Left alone, I contemplated my solitary tray and my solitary thoughts. My spirits dropped precipitously.

If only, I wished desperately, I could take an eraser as I did in the classroom and wipe out that last exchange with Sadiq! I had tried to shove the memory of it aside. But now, more than two hours later, every word and inflection echoed in my ears.

He had risen from the chair opposite me and begun to pace restlessly back and forth to the window. "I keep looking for a common factor," he said. His right hand was clenching and unclenching. "You'd think it would be easy to narrow the field. But it could be any of a number of men." He glanced at me and smiled crookedly. "It could even be a woman."

"Now just a minute," I said in feigned indignation. "If you mean me, I hadn't even heard of your troublesome cousin Haroun when that business in Qaiman happened. And if we're looking for alibis, your own wouldn't bear too close an examination!"

Sadiq stopped pacing abruptly. His hand no longer clenched. He stood absolutely still, facing halfway toward me, staring straight ahead. His jaw was set in the rigid line I had seen earlier, and he scarcely breathed.

When I finally found my voice, it sounded strangled. "Sadiq, I'm sorry I said that."

"So am I," he replied quietly.

150

"I—I didn't mean it the way it sounded," I faltered. "I should have known better than to joke about something like that. It was unforgivable."

He stood still a moment longer, then picked up his anorak and walked to the door. He did not turn. "No," he said, his voice carefully controlled, "not unforgivable. But not easy to forget." He closed the door gently behind him.

I stared at the hard smooth blankness of the door for a long time. Then I dropped my face into my hands. I had not cried in months, but I came very close to it then.

By eleven o'clock that night my spirits were little improved, and I was dead tired. I should, I knew, have gone to bed. Martha Payne would have taken over the office. And if I insisted on sitting up, I should at least have spent the time reading the latest novel I had borrowed from Kate. But I had forced myself to work on papers and lesson plans, in some obscure effort to punish myself. By the time I finally picked up the novel, I could not concentrate on it, and I abandoned myself to bitter reflections and self-recrimination.

When the older students began to filter in, I roused myself and tried to assume an expression of interest. As they signed the late-permission book, they chattered about Jenny's party, which, they all agreed, had been "fabulous."

The last to come in were Haroun and Jenny herself. Their voices heralded their approach to the office.

"I mean, did you *see* her?" Jenny said indignantly. "Batting those big black Latin eyes of hers at both of them, Daddy and your Uncle Sadiq, at the same time? And smiling so demurely. She hasn't got a demure bone in her body. Oooh!"

So, I thought, Adriana Schiano had enjoyed the party

as well. I felt a sharp twist of jealousy. Sadiq had undoubtedly gone along to keep an eye on Haroun, but he had stayed for other reasons. I had sent Adriana to Jeff's with good grace and a touch of curiosity, but I had not intended her to sink her clutches into Jeff and Sadiq too.

"I think it was shameful," Jenny concluded.

Haroun laughed unrestrainedly. "Listen to who's talking! The biggest flirt in the school."

"Well, I like that!" Jenny snorted. I could picture her tossing her long blond hair. "Just remember, I'm the same age as you are now. You ought to treat me with more respect."

They came into the office, Jenny flouncing and Haroun grinning behind her. His grin faded when he saw me.

"What are you doing up?" he demanded. "You should be in bed."

I smiled in weary agreement. "As soon as you sign the book, I will be."

"You've got a lot of nerve, bossing Miss Sheridan around," Jenny told Haroun. "From what I hear, she'd be in one piece if it weren't for you."

"I am in one piece," I murmured. "And it wasn't Haroun's fault."

"No," he agreed, ushering Jenny out, "it was just some silly practical joke."

I sighed as I snapped out the desk light and struggled up onto my crutches. Practical joke? Haroun sounded as though he had convinced himself it was nothing more.

 *19*

I CLOSED the bluebook, scrawled B— on the cover, and dropped it onto the pile at my elbow. Thank heavens that batch was done, I thought. I was heartily sick of reading about the Whiteness of the Whale. In fact, I was sick of everything from Chaucer to Cheever. And there was still another set of examination books to come. The students complained about term finals, but as far as I could see, they were every bit as hard on the teachers.

I shoved back my chair and hobbled to the window. The noon sun looked warm and inviting. I wished I could be skiing, or even taking a good brisk walk. But my ankle was improving with frustrating slowness. I had played bridge once more with Jeff, and one evening he had taken me to a movie, but apart from that, I had not been out of the school. The last twelve days had positively dragged.

Jeff pulled into the school driveway as I watched, and

Adriana came around the corner, her skis over her shoulder. She looked annoyingly healthy and carefree. Being the art teacher, she had no finals to worry about. There was no reason why she should not go skiing with Jeff. Still, I felt a disturbing resentment. Adriana had been uncommonly sweet to me lately. Knowing Adriana, that meant she thought she could afford to be patronizing.

Maggie came in as my eyes fell on the beribboned azalea plant that had been Jeff's get-well offering. It looked a little dry. I reached over to my desk for the carafe and spilled some water into it.

"I hope you're not planning to eat that thing," Maggie said. "Fred says azaleas are poisonous."

"My only plans, as you well know, are to look at it," I said. "It's pretty, and it lasts longer than cut flowers."

I had had to throw those out days ago. They had arrived on the Monday after my accident, a vast armful of tea roses. The accompanying card bore a single word in spiky script, "Forgiven." By then Sadiq had gone back to Geneva, and I had not seen him since.

The single word haunted me. It was stark and uncompromising, and it had a cold ring to it. It meant what it said, but it was not what I wanted to hear. I did not delude myself. Sadiq was not allowing me back into his good graces. He was merely being scrupulously fair.

"Come on, gimpy," Maggie said. "If we're going to be on time for lunch, you need a head start."

She handed me my coat, and then my crutches, and held the door for me. I followed her down the corridor and out of the dormitory, trying to put more weight on my left foot.

Maggie's incessant chatter floated back to me. She was flying to Cleveland in two days for the Christmas holidays, and her conversation alternated between the delightful prospect of seeing Fred and the inevitability of battles with her family. I stifled a sigh, thinking how lucky she was to have a family at all. My first Christmas without Daddy and Conn loomed unbearably bleak.

As we crossed the quadrangle, Ruedy fell into step with us. He observed my progress for a few moments, then said:

"Hey, you're really getting adept at handling those things, Deirdre."

"I can think of things I'd rather become an expert at," I answered dryly. "You know, Ruedy, I'm beginning to think you were right. If I ever get off these crutches, I'd better get myself a new pair of ski boots, something good and firm."

"Yes," he agreed. "With a weak ankle, you'll need more support."

"I wish I'd listened to you and bought them two weeks ago."

"On the contrary. Though I don't like to encourage female stubbornness," Ruedy said, grinning with heavy Swiss humor, "you were probably lucky to be wearing your old boots. That is, if you insisted on being knocked over from a standstill. With racing boots, you might very well have snapped the leg above the boot top."

"Gee, thanks, Ruedy," I said with a grimace. "You do know how to make a girl feel better."

We entered the dining hall and were immediately accosted by Mr. Carstairs, the music director, with questions about the next evening's Christmas pageant. Luckily, a choral program was planned, so the responsibility was mostly Mr. Carstairs', but there was to be an accompanying *tableau vivant*, which meant that Ruedy and I had been rung in for lighting and costuming. Between settling last-minute costume problems, administering and grading one more exam, and making out final reports, I

*155*

was kept busy all that afternoon and well into the next.

It was after five o'clock on Friday when I went in to help Zora and Zafia pack the last of their clothes for the Christmas holidays.

The task was complicated by the presence of the kittens. I was all for shooing them out. But Zora and Zafia, facing a two-week separation from their pets, would not hear of it. So Cappy and Milord stayed. They tangled themselves up in scarves and belts. They made pawprints on stacks of freshly folded blouses. And they discovered that half-filled suitcases made quite wonderful lounging cushions. It must have been a full hour before we managed to close the last lid.

"What time is your Uncle Sadiq coming for you in the morning?" I asked, ranging the suitcases against the wall.

"Oh, we are going to his chalet tonight," Zafia said. "Because we leave for Qaiman as soon as there is light tomorrow."

"It will be nice for you to have his company on the trip home."

"Company!" Zora laughed. "He won't be much good for company. He'll be too busy flying the plane."

"Then you're not going by commercial airline?" I asked, surprised.

"No, we're going in Uncle Sadiq's plane. Oh!" she exclaimed, her hand darting to her mouth. "I wasn't supposed to tell anyone. But I'm sure Uncle Sadiq didn't mean *you.*"

I was not as sure as Zora was. Even where the girls were concerned, I was no longer in Sadiq's confidence. It was not fair, I thought angrily. A few harmless words —but they had proven not to be so harmless. Perhaps it really was my fault. Even with Ruedy, I reminded myself, I had often found that jokes did not translate. And Sadiq

*156*

came from a vastly more alien part of the world.

There was a knock on the door, and one of the girls' schoolmates entered. "Your brother's in the commons room," she said. "He wants to show you something."

Both girls brightened in anticipation. Zafia raced out the door, and Zora, pausing only to say, "Come on, Miss Sheridan!", followed, with Cappy and Milord at her heels.

I hobbled after them, putting as much weight on my left ankle as it would bear, using a single crutch as a cane. I was determined to give the ankle exercise and get rid of the remaining crutch by Christmas.

When I reached the commons room, Haroun and his sisters were clustered around a wicker basket. It was wrapped in cellophane and done up with a gay satin ribbon. Nestled in excelsior was an array of Eastern delicacies.

"It was addressed to me, but it must be for all of us," Haroun said.

"But who sent it?" Zora asked, untying the ribbon and removing the wrapping. She crumpled the cellophane into a crackling ball and tossed it to Cappy, then dangled the ribbon before Milord's outstretched paws.

"I don't know. It came by messenger. I looked for the card, but it must have fallen off."

"Oh look, Haroun!" Zafia exclaimed, her dark eyes shining. "Pastries and nuts and sweetmeats, and that looks like mint tea. Let's have one of these first."

"Zafia, not now," I said firmly. "You'll spoil your appetite. You know how hard Cookie's been working on the Christmas banquet."

"Just one, Miss Sheridan?" Zora pleaded.

"Later. It's time to feed the cats and go to dinner. Now put the basket on the table, and let's not have any arguments."

The girls looked at me reproachfully, but they obeyed without further protest.

The students emptied the auditorium with record speed that evening, heading back to the dining hall. Backstage the members of the chorus hung their robes haphazardly on the long rack and hurried after. The Christmas pageant was over. It was nine o'clock, party time.

Adam, in the Moorish costume he had originally worn for *Othello,* tossed his headdress into a box of props and ducked out the stage door. Jenny followed him, calling over her shoulder, "Come on, Haroun, stop looking at yourself in the mirror. If we don't watch out, the little kids will eat everything before we get there."

Haroun made a final adjustment to his outsized turban as his sisters romped up to him, each holding a hand of their Uncle Sadiq. "Haroun," Zora said approvingly, "you looked magnificent!"

And he did. When he had heard Adam remark the week before that Balthazar was traditionally played in blackface and he already had a costume, Haroun had immediately volunteered to take the part of another of the Three Kings. No doubt he considered himself a cut more royal than Adam, and he had spared no effort on his costume. He had even found a mammoth paste ruby somewhere to serve as a clip for his turban. He looked every inch the Oriental potentate. Now he was basking in his sisters' admiration.

"And wasn't the Payne baby a sweet Christ Child?" Zafia said.

"If you like babies." Haroun scowled. "It's a good thing they talked Mrs. Payne into playing the Madonna. For a while I thought even she wasn't going to be able to keep the little brat quiet."

"Oh Haroun, you always have to sound so—unsentimental!" Zora said with unexpected wisdom. "Hurry up, we're missing the party." She tugged at his silk sleeve, and the three of them went off to join their fellows.

Sadiq lingered while I straightened a few things and shut the stage lights. He looked a bit uncomfortable, I thought, though he could not possibly have felt as awkward as I did. Finally he said:

"How's the ankle coming?"

"Better, thank you. It's more a question of inconvenience now than discomfort." My voice sounded stiff even to me.

We set out across the moonlit quadrangle and the silence lengthened as I searched for a new topic. Then we both started to speak at once and broke off in confusion. Sadiq inclined his head politely toward me.

"I haven't thanked you for the lovely roses," I said.

"They were hardly an adequate apology. I'm afraid I was guilty of overreacting that afternoon. I'm sorry."

"Not at all, it was my fault. I should not have spoken as I did."

My words sounded so priggish and insincere to me that it was no wonder Sadiq did not reply. As we walked slowly toward the dining hall, I found myself leaning more heavily than usual on my crutch, and I checked myself. I would not indulge in such an obvious bid for sympathy.

"Will you be going to America for the holidays?" Sadiq asked presently.

"No, I have no family left in the States." There, another bid for sympathy—stop it, Deirdre! "I'll be spending Christmas with my cousin, Kate de Villiers, in Saanen."

"Ah, then perhaps I shall see you when I get back from Qaiman."

*159*

"I understand you're flying the children down yourself. That is, Zora didn't mean to tell me, but—" I stammered.

"Deirdre! Of course it was all right for her to tell you. When I said she shouldn't mention it, I didn't—" He paused, sounding genuinely concerned. "I hope you don't think we've been keeping secrets from you."

I stopped, pretending to adjust my grip on the crutch while I considered. No, I didn't think the children kept anything at all from me. But I was no longer sure just how far Sadiq's candor extended. When I did answer, it was obliquely:

"I can understand that you're worried about security."

"You bet I am. The airlines are better than they used to be, but too much can still happen. This way, nobody knows when and where we're going. I won't file my flight plans until the last minute. And when I hand those children over to the sheik's bodyguard, I will be very relieved."

"How *is* their father?"

"About the same, I gather. But telephone calls aren't very satisfactory. I'm anxious to see for myself how things are going."

"Will you be staying in Qaiman until the children come back?"

"No, not that long. But I hope to manage ten days or so. Fortunately, not much will be going on here around the Christmas season, but in Qaiman it will be business as usual. And there are a few things I've promised myself to look into."

Sadiq's voice was grim, and as I stole a glance at him in the moonlight, so was his face. But then it relaxed and he said:

"By the way, there's another promise I haven't forgotten—to take you dancing. How soon do you think that ankle will be ready?"

"Oh, I expect I'll be able to trust it in a week or two."

"Then how about—" he began, consulting a mental calendar. He frowned. "I suppose you're busy for St. Sylvestre?"

"New Year's Eve? No, I—I haven't made any plans."

"Good! Some friends over in France," he gestured vaguely toward the southeast, "have invited me to a rather posh party that sounds amusing. Will you come?"

"Thank you, I'll be happy to," I said, carefully keeping my voice from putting into the words all the emphasis I felt.

Sadiq said something about arranging the details later, and then our conversation was ended by our arrival at the dining hall.

The long tables had been pushed back, and in the center of the room, where the swags that decorated the ceiling converged, a large, bulbous object was suspended. It was draped in a bedsheet, with a cord hanging down, like a sculpture ready for unveiling.

Dr. Sidney Payne climbed onto a chair and called for attention. He checked his footing nervously, cleared his throat and said, "Parents, honored guests, faculty, and students, good evening. As you know, we at the Academy of the Oberland are fortunate in numbering among our school family students from many corners of the globe. One of the most distant and exotic is Mexico, represented by Francisco Alvarez Quintana, who has kindly offered to share with us tonight a Christmas custom from his sunny land. Pancho?"

Dr. Payne descended awkwardly from his chair, and Panchito scrambled up in his place. Seeing that all eyes were on the shrouded object, and the younger children were already squirming toward the front of the circle, he made his explanation brief but showmanlike. "And

*161*

that," he concluded, seizing the dangling cord with a flourish, "is what we call a piñata."

Panchito yanked the cord, and the folds of sheet slithered to the floor. Although he had substituted for the basic earthenware jar a thick shell of papier-mâché, in all other respects Panchito had achieved a highly creditable version of the traditional piñata. He had chosen to decorate it as a ceremonial mask, and the paint and bright bits of paper were augmented by a crown of gaily colored feathers.

"Stand back and leave room underneath," Panchito directed. "We all take turns hitting it. The smallest person in the room goes first."

Zafia moved shyly forward, urged on by her sister, and took the stout section of broom handle that Panchito held out to her. Blindfolded and turned about, she stood on tiptoe and gave the piñata a gentle rap. Then she handed the blindfold and stick to Zora and slipped through the crowd to stand between Sadiq and me. She was pink with embarrassment. It was bad enough to be singled out, her face said, but to be singled out because you were the littlest and least significant of all!

Zora felt no such reticence. She was allowed one whack, and she made it a good one. The others followed suit, and soon cracks began to appear in the decorated shell. By the time the stick passed to the Upper School, the piñata was well battered and dented. It was Jenny who delivered the *coup de grace*. With unerring sense of direction, she laid the stick across two deep cracks and sheared the bottom off.

The contents of the piñata cascaded onto the floor, and the students dropped to hands and knees, scrambling after the candies and trinkets. Even Zafia summoned the courage to join in.

The confusion ended with the entrance of Cookie,

dressed in a Santa Claus suit, wheeling a cart that bore two immense punchbowls. Trays of cakes and cookies had appeared on the long tables lining the walls. In the corner, Martha Payne placed a stack of Christmas carols on the record player.

Zora and Zafia made their way back to the corner where I sat quietly observing Adriana Schiano flaunt her charms before Jeff Hearn. Sadiq was watching the same scene, and I thought I saw his mustache twitch in amusement.

Then his attention was claimed by Zafia, who nudged him shyly and said, "Now, Uncle Sadiq?"

He nodded absently, took a small package from his pocket and handed it to her as Haroun joined us. Zafia turned toward me, but it was Zora who said in obviously well-rehearsed words:

"Miss Sheridan, in your country Christmas is a time when you receive gifts from people who love you. Zafia and I will be far away, but on Christmas Day we want you to have something from us."

I smiled and took the package from Zafia's gentle hands, then caught the two girls in a quick impulsive hug. "I'll put it under my cousin Kate's tree tomorrow," I promised, "and I'll open it the very first thing Christmas morning."

My eyes were threatening to get misty, but Haroun forestalled that. Whipping from his gaudy silk sash a thin tubular object wrapped in gold foil, he bowed and presented it to me.

"Not to be outdone," he said with a grin. "I trust you'll accept this in the spirit in which it is intended."

I looked up and saw the familiar mischievous glint in his eyes. I had a pretty good idea in what spirit his offering was intended, and I reflected that in Haroun's case, a separation of a few thousand miles when the gifts were opened might be barely sufficient.

Sadiq had been looking on indulgently, but there was an edge of impatience in his voice now when he said, "All right, girls, let's say goodbye to the Paynes and collect your suitcases. You won't be getting enough sleep tonight as it is."

I followed them out of the main building and along the path to the dormitory, intending to put the packages in my room and kiss the girls goodbye before returning to the party. Slowed by my crutch, I was several yards behind them when Zora reached the door, pushed it open, and began to scream.

 *20*

ON THE floor the basket of Eastern delicacies rested on its side, the contents tumbling out, excelsior scattered everywhere. The bag of mint tea was ripped open. A trail of leaves extended from it, mute testimony to what had happened.

Cappy lay senseless in Zora's arms. Her paws were splayed, her tiny head lolling, her chest quivering in shallow yet alarmingly rapid breaths. Her eyes were scarcely open, but through the slits the whites showed blue. Zora's desperate pleadings could not rouse her, and a flood of tears fell unheeded on the soft furred body.

But stricken though we all were by the sight of Cappy unconscious, it was Milord who really terrified us.

Milord acted possessed.

His little black and white body arched and twisted in a frenzy, as though invaded by a host of demons. He turned this way and that, he leaped in great wrenching somersaults, he threw himself convulsively to the side, eluding all our efforts to grasp him.

Then he began to run backwards, faster and faster. But no matter how hard he tried to back away from it, he could not leave behind the torment that gripped him.

"Sadiq!" I screamed, raising my voice above the cries of the girls. "Get a blanket or something! We have to get them to the vet right away. You catch Milord while I telephone." I dragged the instrument toward me and snatched up the receiver. "Hurry!"

Sadiq's head jerked up in surprise at my commanding tone. Then he caught sight of my face, and my urgency communicated itself to him. He turned and plunged down the corridor. Within seconds he was back, a bedspread in his hands.

He slung the bedspread over the tortuous writhings of Milord, directing Haroun and Zafia to hold the corners. Then he carefully worked the struggling cat into immobility, with the head loosely shrouded and the limbs tightly and repeatedly bound. Milord's struggles were weaker now, although his head still jerked spasmodically, and shudders rippled through his makeshift straitjacket.

Sadiq looked up and started to ask a question.

"Later," I said, my voice firm. I shook my head at him sharply, flicking my eyes toward the girls. "The first thing is to get the kittens to the doctor. Can you bring the car right around to the door?"

"But what—"

"I'll take care of it," I said levelly. I tucked the telephone receiver under my chin and began to shove the candies and pastries back into their basket.

Sadiq watched me for a moment, then his eyes widened and he nodded and left abruptly.

Thank God, I thought, he understands. He understands at least enough not to ask questions in front of the girls. And they must not know!

I finished gathering the contents of the basket and turned to scooping the scattered tea leaves back into their torn bag. "The doctor will want to know what made them sick," I said, forcing myself to keep talking, to fill the time until Sadiq returned, to keep the girls from asking questions I could not answer. "It must have been the mint smell that attracted them. They probably thought the tea was catnip. Haroun, will you help me with this? We don't want to leave any lying on the floor."

"Right," he said, bending to help me. His voice was quiet and controlled, but the eyes he raised to mine were filled with anguish.

I no longer had to wonder whether Haroun understood. It was all too clear that he did. He had probably understood before Sadiq did. Someone had sent him a basketful of poison.

I had almost given up on the switchboard when Martha Payne's voice came over the line with a breathless, "Yes?"

"Martha, get me Dr. Werren, quickly please. The cats have gotten into something and they're sick."

"Oh, dear! I do hope it's not—just a minute. Wagner, Wehrle, here it is." I heard her dialing. "It's ringing now. Is there anything I can do?"

"Thanks, no. I'll call you back when I can. Oh, and don't mention it to the others, all right? No sense upsetting people."

Haroun gave me another anguished look as Dr. Werren came on the line.

"Dr. Werren, this is Deirdre Sheridan at the Academy of the Oberland. The kittens have eaten something that has made them quite ill. May we bring them around to you now?"

"Of course, of course," the vet said briskly. "What are the symptoms?"

"One of them is comatose. The other seems to be going the same way, though he was uncontrollably frenzied a couple of minutes ago."

"My God! Any idea what it was?"

"*Ich glaub' es war—*" I paused, summoning up my rusty German. What I wanted to say I could not say before the children in French or English. "*—absichtliches Gift,*" I concluded.

There, I had said it. Deliberate poison.

"*Gift?*" Dr. Werren repeated incredulously. But I knew I had not mistaken the word. When I had first learned it, I had been intrigued that the same word could have such a happy meaning in English and such a deadly one in German. Now it was not just intriguing but horrifying. For the tempting basket with its cellophane and ribbon had concealed the deadly sense in the guise of the happy one.

"*Sicher?*" Dr. Werren persisted.

"Yes, I'm sure."

"Well, get them down here fast. I'll turn on the outside lights."

Just as I hung up, the headlights of Sadiq's car swept the windows of the commons room. Zora and Zafia, each with her pet in her arms, ran to the door and out. Haroun hesitated, holding the bag of tea in his hand. Then, finding no pocket in his outlandish costume, he tucked the bag into his wide silk sash and hurried after them.

"Haroun!" I cried. "Don't go without me. I'll be right back."

I snatched up the basket with its lethal cargo and raced down the corridor. I forgot my crutch, I forgot the screaming pain in my ankle, I forgot everything but the need to hide the basket safely away.

Once in my room, I dropped the basket on my desk, shot the bolt on the door that connected with Maggie's room, and seized the never-used key to the hall door. Locking it behind me, I flew back to the commons room and out to Sadiq's car.

Please don't let it be too late, I prayed as I ran. Please don't let the kittens die. The girls have lost their mother, and they're about to lose their father. It's so little to ask. Please.

On the drive to Dr. Werren's, I concentrated on framing my first crucial remarks to the vet, trying to choose German words as different as possible from their French or English counterparts.

Except for my street directions, no one spoke. Sadiq devoted himself to driving with all speed. In the back, the girls wept forlornly. And Haroun struggled to hold Milord, now in the throes of a fresh wave of violent convulsions. Finally we swung up the last hill and into the yard of the Werren chalet.

The vet stood framed in the open doorway, his wife hovering behind him. The children were out of the car almost before it had stopped, Zora rushing toward Dr. Werren with the limp form of Cappy in her arms, Zafia anxiously clinging to the side of Haroun with his thrashing burden. I pushed open the passenger door and hurried to overtake them.

Everyone was talking at once, and it was a moment before I was able to force myself on Dr. Werren's attention. Then I blurted out the words I had been practicing:

"Doctor, the children don't know about the poison, and we don't want them to know, so please discuss it only in German."

Dr. Werren's eyebrows shot up, and he looked behind me questioningly.

*"Richtig,"* Sadiq confirmed.

I turned and gave him a grateful half-smile, but he did not return it. He added, still in German, "I just wish I knew what was going on."

By now Dr. Werren had taken the writhing bundle of cloth from Haroun and was delivering a barrage of instructions to his wife, interspersed with questions to the rest of us.

"You don't know how long ago they ate it? Any idea what it was?"

"Whatever it was," Haroun said in careful schoolboy German, "it was in this." He drew the bag of tea leaves from his sash and held it out.

Dr. Werren told Haroun with seeming indifference to drop it into the pocket of his smock. Grasping Milord more firmly, he said, "Sit down. This may take some time." He turned toward the inner office. "Monika, set up an I.V. and start the . . ." The door banged behind him.

There was no clock on the wall of the waiting room, and the minutes stretched into what seemed like hours. I wished I could manage a look at my wrist watch. But Zora and Zafia, seated on either side of me on a long bench, each held one of my hands tightly in a despairing search for reassurance.

On the far side of the room Sadiq and Haroun sat in quiet conversation. Haroun seemed to be recounting the incident of the basket, but much of the time he spoke in Arabic, and even when he shifted to French, his words were pitched so low that they carried only indistinctly to where I sat with the girls.

Presently Haroun joined us. "Uncle Sadiq wants to talk to you," he told me. I nodded, squeezed the girls' hands, and relinquished my place on the bench to him.

He settled himself wearily between his sisters and placed his arms around them protectively.

I stood before Sadiq, waiting for him to speak. The muscles of his jaw were tight, and there were deep lines of strain around his eyes, but his voice was even as he said:

"Where is the rest of the stuff now?"

"Locked in my room."

Sadiq nodded approvingly. "Good. That was quick thinking."

"Sure, when it was too late. But I should have suspected—"

"No, Deirdre, don't blame yourself," he said with a gentle smile. "You reacted very well. You were quite right to protect the girls from knowing." He gave a small sigh. "If only I'd been here when—well, there's no sense worrying about that now. As soon as we can leave here, we'll have to get on to the police. For all the good they'll do," he concluded philosophically.

"Oh, Sadiq, do we really have to? Won't that mean the girls will find out what happened? Anyway, they can't be left alone, especially not tonight."

"No. Is there any chance you could—"

We were interrupted by the return of Dr. Werren. He shook his head almost imperceptibly and asked us which cat belonged to which girl. Sadiq told him, and we moved across the room to join the children. Sadiq slid onto the bench beside Zora, while I took my place by Zafia. We faced the vet in a solid row, as though the five of us, by force of numbers, could reverse what he was going to tell us.

Dr. Werren bent down in front of Zora, took her hands and spoke gently in French. "You know that the cats ate something which was bad for them, and it made them very, very ill. Cappy was already in a deep sleep when you

*171*

brought her here. Well, Zora, she just stayed asleep and —and quietly died. I'm sorry."

Zora sat quite still for a moment. Then she pulled her hands from Dr. Werren's and turned to bury herself against Sadiq's chest. Her thin body trembled all over and her shoulders heaved in an erratic rhythm, but she did not make a sound. And the rest of us did not dare to break her silence. Sadiq held her tightly, rocking her in his arms. Haroun sat biting his lip, his eyes even more anguished than before. And Zafia wept quietly, the tears forcing themselves through her fingers and down over her slender wrists.

Finally Zafia raised her face to Dr. Werren. Her grief for her sister was mixed with both fear and hope as she asked haltingly, "Wh-what about Milord? Will he—"

"I don't know, Zafia." The vet placed a tentative hand on her shoulder. "You see, while he was so active, we couldn't give him a sedative, because it might have made it worse later. So we had to wait. Now he's gone to sleep, the way Cappy did. And we'll just have to wait some more. We'll keep him warm and watch him and hope for the best. That's about all we can do."

"How long—" Zafia gulped.

"I don't know that either, little one. Probably not until sometime tomorrow. Why don't you go home to bed and try to sleep? We'll watch him, and if there's any change, we'll call you."

Zafia nodded, her tear-streaked face numb. I felt numb, too. But as I sat holding her small, cold hand, I felt my numbness fade, to be replaced by a helpless anger. It simply wasn't fair. All I had wanted to do was to give the girls something to make them happy. And I had only succeeded in causing them more sorrow. It would have been better if I had never taken them to Kate's that day—

Kate. Of course. Kate would step into the breach. I rose and whispered to Sadiq.

Kate carried the last of the girls' suitcases from the dormitory and slung them onto the back seat beside my overnight bag and her own.

"So," she said, sliding behind the wheel and guiding her car out of the school driveway, "you want the girls to think it was something that was just bad for cats."

"What else can we do? We can't tell them somebody tried to poison their brother."

"Hardly. Did Dr. Werren say what it was?"

"He wasn't sure. Something that attacked the central nervous system. He thought it might have been metaldehyde poisoning."

"Metaldehyde? Isn't that what I use in the garden for slugs?"

"Could be." I shrugged. "Anyway, I asked him to hang onto the bag of tea until the police came for it."

"Have you rung them up yet?"

"No, and I wish we didn't have to, at least until morning. But everybody will be leaving for the holidays, so it can't wait. I suppose the police will have to talk to Haroun too. And that means they'll barge into Sadiq's place and disturb the girls."

"No, they won't," Kate said placidly. "It'll just be young Romang, and you needn't worry about him. He was a schoolmate of my two. Nice boy, and a good deal more competent than he looks. He won't cause any fuss."

Kate dropped back into second gear and turned up the Oberbort. "The children and their uncle went directly up from the vet's?"

"Yes, Sadiq said he'd get the girls into a hot bath. I thought it might help relax them. Though I doubt that anything will make them sleep."

"Oh, they'll sleep," Kate said. "After what they've been through today, they won't be able to help it."

Kate was right. She administered hot chocolate and quiet words of comfort, and soon Zora and Zafia were willing to be tucked in. Almost immediately they surrendered to total exhaustion. Kate tiptoed from their room and installed herself in an overstuffed chair to hold the fort with Haroun while Sadiq and I were gone.

Our round of explanation and interrogation took us from the police station to the school and back to Sadiq's chalet. The clock had already chimed one when the young policeman Romang finally finished with Haroun and left.

Kate padded in from the kitchen, a flannel robe wrapped around her comfortable figure. "Might I get you something?" she asked. "Coffee? Tea?"

"I think straight brandy will do us more good," Sadiq said. "Deirdre?"

I agreed, and so did Kate and Haroun. Sadiq raised an eyebrow at Haroun, but I saw that the snifter he poured for his young cousin was as generous as the rest.

"Well, did you find out anything?" Kate asked.

"Not really," Sadiq said dispiritedly. "Mrs. Payne was in the school office when the basket was delivered, but she was busy, so she didn't particularly notice the messenger. He was wearing some sort of uniform, she thought. And she just signed the invoice without really looking at it."

"Oh dear, that is a pity."

"The policeman didn't seem surprised. He said he'd order a check of the regular delivery services. But Dr. Payne was extremely annoyed with her. In fact," Sadiq said, his voice hardening, "Dr. Payne's whole attitude

*174*

was offensive. All he could think about was whether the story would get out and sully the impeccable reputation of his school."

"Oh, Sadiq, that's natural enough," I said mildly. "Though I can't imagine how he thinks it would get out. Dr. Werren won't say anything and, Lord knows, it's the last thing *we* want."

Sadiq looked at me with a small, quirky smile, and I realized I had unthinkingly ranged myself with the Qaimani family and not the school.

"Well," Kate said briskly, "if that basket had had its intended effect, it would be more than just a question of avoiding publicity."

"God, yes," Haroun groaned. "To think I actually offered those things to my sisters! I could have killed them. Thank heavens," he went on fervently, "Miss Sheridan wouldn't let them eat any."

Sadiq jerked his head toward me. "Then you did suspect—"

"No, at least not in any conscious way." I spread my hands helplessly. "Of course, I should have. But the basket looked so—innocent."

"Yes, somebody went to a lot of trouble to make it look that way," Sadiq said grimly. "The question is, who and how? Maybe the analysis will tell us something."

"Your young friend Romang," I explained to Kate, "is sending everything up to the police labs in Bern tomorrow for a good going-over. And of course they're going to try to trace the messenger. It's a shame the outside wrapping was already thrown away."

"It wouldn't have told them anything," Haroun said. "It was just plain brown paper with a typed card pinned to it. Very anonymous." He drew a shaky breath. "That's what bothers me most, the facelessness of all this. If somebody's going to try to kill you, he might at least have the grace to be around at the time."

Haroun drained his brandy snifter and held it out for a refill. Sadiq hesitated, then took it and moved wordlessly to the bar. Haroun was only seventeen, but he had just faced the fact that someone had been trying to murder him, and he was taking it better than most of his elders would have.

Sadiq handed the glass with its inch of amber liquid to Haroun. "When you finish that, we'd better think about getting to bed. We'll only have five hours of sleep in any case." He rubbed a hand over his eyes. "I wish I could let my copilot do some of the flying tomorrow."

"Copilot? Who, me?" Haroun said skeptically.

"God forbid!" Sadiq replied with a sardonic grin. "No, I've hired a copilot for the trip. At least, that's what the flight plan will say. Actually, the fellow has never flown anything bigger than single-engine models. But he has other accomplishments, particularly in the fields of security and small-arms handling. He comes highly recommended."

Haroun was silent for a while, then he nodded. "Yes, that was a good idea. Is he here now?"

"At the airfield. Sleeping in the plane."

"Good old Uncle Sadiq. You think of everything."

Sadiq finished his own brandy slowly, and set the glass on the bar.

"You can't ever think of everything," he said quietly. "That's one lesson tonight should have taught us. From now on, Haroun, you're going to have to look at every situation carefully and consider it twice. It'll take some of the fun out of life." Sadiq paused, letting the last word hang in the air. "But you'd better not ever forget it."

 *21*

I MANAGED to bear up for the next fifteen hours or so, but then the dam burst.

I was sitting in Kate's living room, staring into the fire, when suddenly the orange flames dissolved in a watery blur. I tried to fight the tears, but they would not stop. Finally I surrendered to them completely.

"Deirdre, dear, what is it?" Kate asked, her normally cheerful voice edged with solicitude.

"Nothing, Kate, except—just everything!" I blubbered. "The children looked so forlorn this morning when they left, and Sadiq was so drawn and strained and tired, and then at the school everybody laughing and looking forward to Christmas, and I had to pretend I was cheerful when I felt so miserable, and all those awful smiling things Dr. Payne said, and Cappy's dead and Milord maybe dying, and my ankle hurts, and—ohhh!"

I groped in my purse for a Kleenex and clamped it to my streaming eyes.

Kate moved to the fire, stirred it vigorously with the poker, and said sternly:

"Of course your ankle hurts. What do you expect, after traipsing about all last night without your crutches?" She sighed, and her voice softened slightly. "Here, have another cup of tea."

I snuffled and hiccupped and smiled crookedly in spite of myself. Kate was so unshakeably consistent! I wondered whether the crisis could ever arise for which she would not prescribe a good bracing British cup of tea.

I took the cup she handed to me. It was liberally laced with cream and sugar in the British manner, and Kate knew I did not like it that way. But I drank it obediently.

"Now," she said briskly, "what has Sidney Payne been saying to upset you?"

"Oh, Kate, he's such a *worm!* It was bad enough last night when he was fussing about the story getting out. But this morning he—well, you know how he harumphs and puts his fingers together and gets that owlish look on his face. This morning he said he was 'concerned that the Academy might not be the most secure environment for the children.' That's not what he's concerned about at all. He knows the children are happy at the school, and as safe as they'd be anywhere, short of being locked up. He's just worried that if anything 'unpleasant' happened, his precious school might get blamed. It's pure moral cowardice."

"Honestly," Kate snorted, "that man gives me the pip!"

"Kate, you don't think he'd actually tell them they can't come back?"

"I don't know, probably not. As you say, he's not a strong personality. If someone put up an argument—his wife, or the sheik, or your friend Yamali—he'd likely back down. But, Deirdre, that's not the whole question. Do you think the children really *are* safe enough at the school?"

I tossed my sodden wad of Kleenex into the fireplace and slumped back in my seat. "I don't know what's safe anymore, Kate. So much has happened, and there still isn't one piece of solid evidence. I hope Sadiq can find out something in Qaiman this week. Because it just can't go on this way, not knowing how or when the danger will come next. Oh, Kate, I've worried so much, and I'm so *tired!*"

"Yes, dear, of course you are," Kate said soothingly. "And I intend to see that you get a good rest. Jeanne and Théo and the baby won't be arriving until Wednesday, and Heaven knows whether Paul will be able to get up here even then. So you'll have three whole days to sleep until noon and potter about in the kitchen with me and perhaps take some short walks. Now why don't you just crawl into bed until dinnertime?"

The telephone rang shortly after seven. Kate answered it promptly and spoke in low tones, but despite her precautions, my nap was effectively interrupted. I decided to have a quick shower to wash away the last cobwebs of sleep.

By the time I was dressed, I was feeling fully awake and refreshed. Even my ankle was not as painful as it might have been, considering the punishment I had subjected it to last night. I replaced the elastic bandage, located my slippers, and made my way with the aid of a crutch into the living room.

Kate looked up from her newspaper and smiled. "Welcome back to the land of the living. Sherry?"

Without waiting for my answer, she went to the sideboard and returned with two glasses.

"Cheers," she said. "And we do have something to be cheerful about. Dr. Werren just rang up."

"Milord's—going to be all right?"

"Werren says he'll do. They've been giving him vitamin B-1 and such, and he's conscious now and getting stronger. We can bring him home in the morning."

"Oh, Kate, that's wonderful!" I said. "But are you sure you won't mind having another convalescent in the house?"

"Don't be silly, Deirdre. What earthly difference could one more cat make to this ménage? Now what about yourself? How are you feeling?"

"Better, thanks. You were right, I really needed some rest. It helps put things back into perspective." I twirled the stem of my glass and sipped thoughtfully. "You know, Kate, Sadiq said something interesting last night about the 'accidents'. He said that maybe the—whoever caused them—maybe he didn't care so much whether they were effective, so long as they threw Haroun and the rest of us into a panic. Maybe the purpose, or at least part of it, was to keep us off balance."

"That's possible," Kate said after a moment's consideration.

"In which case, it's important for everybody, particularly Haroun, to stay calm. And if Haroun can do it, so can I."

"Good! That's more like the old Deirdre." Kate finished her sherry and stood. "Now I'd best get that joint out of the oven. You Americans all like your meat raw."

It wasn't raw, but it was nicely rare, and dinner was accompanied by a stream of inconsequential chatter. Just being with Kate improved my spirits. Whether we discussed serious matters or trivia, Kate's matter-of-fact approach made the world seem an essentially rational and comfortable place.

After we cleared up the dinner dishes, I poured coffee while Kate burrowed in a storeroom and returned with several old shopping bags full of Christmas ornaments. "I'm so glad you agree," she said. "I just can't see waiting until Christmas Eve. I'd rather do it early and be able to look at it."

"Yes, we always had our tree trimmed a good week before—ohhh!" I bit my lip and put my hand to my throat. Suddenly, here in the warmth and love of Kate's home, the loss of Daddy and Conn was more immediately painful than it had been for many months. I struggled to hold back my tears. I did not want to break down in front of Kate a second time.

Kate looked up inquiringly.

"Coffee's still too hot," I stammered. "I burned my throat a bit."

"Oh dear, that can be so—*get out of there!*" Kate cried, lunging at a tabby cat that was industriously pulling tinsel garlands from a bag. The cat eluded her grasp and escaped to the back of the sofa, where it settled down and assumed a look of perfect innocence.

"I don't think you've met Delilah. She's a litter mate of Samson's, one of Libérale's progeny. The Bennetts had her, but they had to go back to England, and of course they couldn't take her, so—"

"—so Cousin Kate has just what she always needed, another cat. How many does that make?"

"Just seven," Kate said with a smile. "And they don't spend so very much time indoors. Deirdre, do you think you might manage to stand on a chair with that ankle? I'm a little too well padded for leaning over treetops."

I clambered onto a straight-backed chair with Kate's assistance, and under her direction placed the starburst

*181*

ornament on the top and began draping tinsel over the boughs. It was tricky work, as I did not trust my left leg to take much weight, and before long I was teetering precariously.

"Here, give me that," Kate laughed. "I can reach the rest from here. You look like a very unsteady stork."

I handed over the remaining loops of tinsel, then almost lost my balance completely as the telephone shrilled just behind me.

Kate reached around and answered it, listened briefly, then passed the receiver up to me. I heard the overseas operator give way to a crackling and finally, as I slid down onto the seat of the chair, the voice of Sadiq, distant but distinct.

"Yes," I said, "I can hear you perfectly. How was the flight?"

"Not bad. Grueling but uneventful. We only stopped twice, at Cilipi near Dubrovnik and again in Cyprus. We landed about an hour ago."

"And the children are—"

"With their father. He looks quite alert, considering that it's well past midnight here. But I expect he rested a good part of the day so as to be able to be up now. I really haven't had a chance to judge how well he is. The children wanted me to get straight through to you."

"Of course," I said.

Of course, I thought. The children. If it were left to Sadiq himself, he would not have bothered to telephone me at all. Well, he needn't have made the implication so explicit.

I shook my head and told myself to be fair. I was tired and overwrought, and Sadiq was even more so. There was no reason to read anything into his words.

"Tell Zafia I'll be picking up Milord and bringing him

here to Kate's in the morning," I said. "He's going to be just fine."

"I'll tell her. She'll be very happy to hear it." Sadiq did not sound happy. He just sounded exhausted. "Deirdre, would you do something for me? I meant to ask you last night, but with so much happening, it slipped my mind. I'd like a photograph of Hearn's man Abdullah. Do you think you can find an unobtrusive way to get one?"

I thought for a few seconds. "I can try. It may take a couple of days. Assuming I do get one, how should I send it to you?"

"Got a pencil?"

I pulled Kate's appointment book and a felt-tipped pen off the telephone table, said "Fire away," and took down the name and Geneva address that Sadiq dictated.

"Post it to him if you can't deliver it in person, and he'll see it gets forwarded by diplomatic pouch. Oh, and to be on the safe side, you might include an assortment of other photographs and some sort of innocent note."

"Right. I'll do my best."

"Good girl. I'll be in touch. So long."

I sat for a while with the dead receiver in my hand, then replaced it firmly on the cradle.

Good girl . . .

Good girl, indeed! It made me sound like some sort of faithful dog. Well, I would get the photograph as commanded. That was in a good cause. But I would not, for Sadiq Yamali or anyone, sit up and beg!

It felt almost sinfully late the next morning when I finally slid out from beneath the billowing feather-filled *duvet.* I pulled on my robe and slippers and wandered slowly through the silent chalet. In the kitchen Kate had left orange juice and coffee and sweet rolls, along with

*183*

a note. I polished off half a dozen rolls without a thought for the calories, then took a second cup of coffee with me to the telephone.

Abdullah answered: *"Quatre trente-et-un soixante-cinq."*

*"Mademoiselle Jenny, s'il vous plaît, de part de Mademoiselle Sheridan."*

*"Ne quittez pas."*

Jenny came on the line and said sleepily, "Miss Sheridan? What are you doing up at an ungodly hour like this?"

"Did I wake you? I'm sorry. But my cousin Kate's gone to Mass, so the hour isn't, strictly speaking, so ungodly."

"Yeah, I guess. I wasn't really asleep anyway. I promised myself I'd sleep till noon every day, but I must be out of practice."

"Me too," I laughed, "though I haven't given up hope of regaining the knack. Are you planning to spend the whole vacation here?"

"Uh-huh. You?"

"Same. I couldn't do much else anyway, until my ankle's better. But Kate's been nagging me to get out more," I improvised. "So I thought maybe I could talk you into inviting me to tea tomorrow or the next day."

"Hey, great! Why don't you come tomorrow, about four? I'll tell Abdullah to do something special. He can be a pain in the you-know, but he sure can cook."

"Right. And thanks, Jenny. I'll see you then."

I hung up, wishing I hadn't had to play on Jenny's trusting nature. But I hadn't been able to think of any other way of getting close to Abdullah.

Kate came in, stamping her feet and rubbing her hands together. She draped her ancient fur coat over a chair. "Lord, it's cold out there! Any coffee left?"

"Should be."

"I'll have a cup while you get dressed, and then we can collect Milord."

Kate got her coffee and followed me into the bedroom, perching on the edge of the bed while I rummaged for my warmest clothes.

"Kate," I said, tugging a turtleneck over my head, "what kind of camera do you use?"

"Mostly my old Retina Reflex."

"Mine's a 35-millimeter, too. But I don't think it'll work too well for what I have in mind." I outlined Sadiq's request and my plan to have tea with Jenny, and concluded:

"I'd better go down to Fäh's tomorrow and buy a Polaroid. Everybody likes to play with those."

"Yes, a Polaroid should look innocent enough. That sounds the best plan. I do have one other camera, though, which might be useful to you."

She went out and returned with a tiny Minox. "I use it when we're hiking or skiing, because it's so easy to tuck into a pocket. And it really gives surprisingly good results for its size. I once got some stunning shots in the Sistine Chapel, which of course is strictly forbidden, and I was practically under the guard's nose the whole time. So you might consider it."

I took the Minox from Kate and nestled it in my cupped hand. "It'd make a good back-up system, at least. It's certainly easy enough to hide."

"Look, I've got another packet or two of film somewhere. Why don't you shoot the rest of the roll that's in it, for practice? Then we can reload it, and if you want it, it'll be ready."

Adopting Kate's suggestion, I spent part of the afternoon practicing with the Minox. And the next morning, as soon as Fäh's was open, I bought a Polaroid and an

*185*

armload of film and set to work familiarizing myself with it.

Sadiq had said I should include some innocent-looking pictures. So I shot the Christmas tree, with the children's presents nestled underneath as promised. And I expended a dozen or more frames on Milord.

First I tied a red ribbon around his neck and photographed him sitting on a plump satin cushion. He made a docile subject; poor thing, he wasn't feeling very frisky. Then I moved him under the Christmas tree and flicked a low-hanging ornament. That caught his interest. For a couple of minutes he batted at the glass balls while I crouched nearby, busily snapping him. Then he abandoned the game and crept shakily to me, crying in soft meows.

I set the camera aside to lift him onto the sofa, wrapped my arms around him and nuzzled his fur, murmuring gently in babytalk. But he continued to whimper.

He could not know that Cappy was dead. But he knew that he felt weak and ill, and that he was in a strange place, and that he missed Cappy and his doting little Qaimani mistress. I told myself he would forget faster than a human would. And yet there was no doubt that Milord was now a very weary and dejected cat.

By the time I arrived at the Hearn chalet, the Minox in my purse and the Polaroid in a shopping bag together with a couple of gift-wrapped packages acquired on the way for camouflage, I felt reasonably adept with both cameras.

Jenny met me at the door, and Jeff behind her. I surrendered my coat and hat, but I kept the shopping bag as I followed Jenny into the living room.

"Off the crutches for good?" Jeff asked behind me.

"That's right," I said jauntily. "I got tired of the things, so this morning I chucked them in the corner and pronounced myself cured."

"Great. How soon are you going to be skiing with us again?"

"I think I'd better give it a few more—oh! Isn't that magnificent!"

The Christmas tree that stood in the corner of the Hearn living room was smaller than Kate's, but it was a work of art. Jenny had done it all in red and silver—silver swags, silver and red silk balls, and slender three-inch red candles in little silver holders clipped to the ends of the branches.

The tree delighted me, and for more than one reason. It gave me the immediate opening I needed.

"I've *got* to have a picture of that!" I exclaimed.

I set the shopping bag on a chair and tossed aside the packages on top until I could dig out the Polaroid. Ripping off the store wrappings, which I had painstakingly replaced only an hour before, I lifted the camera from its box and launched into my prepared speech:

"Jenny, look what I've just bought! I'm going to give it to Kate for Christmas. She's been so good to me, and it's her grandson's first Christmas, and I thought it would be nice if I could photograph the whole family for her, opening the presents. But first I have to learn how to use it. And I can't think of anything prettier to practice on than your tree. Would you mind standing over there beside it?"

As I had expected, Jenny needed no persuading. She moved over to the tree and posed with natural grace and only a touch of theatricality.

"Jeff, do you know how to work a Polaroid?" I said, trying to sound slightly female-helpless without overdo-

*187*

ing it. "The man in the store showed me how to load it, but I haven't had a chance to read all the instructions yet."

Jeff took the camera from me. "Nothing to it. You just line up the picture through here, and press here." I made a show of paying close attention while he snapped Jenny. He handed the camera back as the exposed frame emerged. "Now you try it."

"All right. You stand beside Jenny."

I shot a couple of pictures of Jeff and Jenny together and one of the tree alone. Then Jenny took the Polaroid to try it on Jeff and me. I summoned my most sparkling smile, and inwardly I wore a smile too, if a rather calculating one. I wanted this picture to turn out well. I had every intention of including it in the shipment of "innocent" photographs to Sadiq.

We gathered around the developing pictures, watching as the colors came alive. Then, to keep the camera center stage, I opened a window on the back yard of the chalet and did a landscape, the snow-laden spruces clustered in the deepening blue dusk.

So the camera was still in my hand when Abdullah brought in the tea tray.

"Doesn't that look delicious!" I exclaimed. "Abdullah's really outdone himself."

Hearing his name, Abdullah glanced up just as he set the tray on the cocktail table, and I caught him full face with the camera.

Still babbling ingenuously about how delicious everything looked, I begged Jenny to hold off pouring the tea while I finished the roll of film. The tea tray made a plausible still life, and it gave me a chance to convince Abdullah that my interest was in the burden and not in the bearer.

I laid the last two developing photographs on the arm

of my chair and packed the camera back into its box while Jenny played hostess, pouring out the three cups of tea, inquiring formally whether I preferred lemon, hovering over the platter of cakes and pastries as Jeff and I made our choices. By the time Jenny handed me my plate, the pictures were fully clear, and I swept them up casually and shuffled them into the pile that already occupied a corner of the low table.

For the next hour, I managed to listen and contribute to the conversation. I even succeeded in steering it to the theater and Jenny's manifest talents. I had promised Jenny that I would try to win her father over, and this was a perfect opportunity to do so. But my thoughts kept going back to the photographs resting beside my teacup.

The picture of Abdullah was a masterpiece of composition. The tray being lowered to the table, the face of the servant looming over it, were in perfect alignment and focus. There was only one problem.

Abdullah had chosen that moment to blink.

There was no question of using the Polaroid again; I had had only one chance, and the result was profoundly unsatisfactory. With his eyes almost closed, much of the essence of Abdullah was missing. Somehow the eyes, so important an expression of individuality in any face, seemed even more so in the case of an Arab. It was true of Haroun, and of Zora and Zafia. They all spoke volumes with their eyes. And Sadiq especially, with his dark and piercing—no, I had better not think about that now.

Well, I still had the Minox. Perhaps I might do better with that. I would have to try.

I excused myself and went down the corridor to the powder room, closed the door behind me, and ran water in appropriate ways for half a minute while I adjusted the Minox and turned the vanity mirror to the angle I wanted. Then I opened the door and turned back to the mirror as if in an afterthought for a final few strokes of my hairbrush. In my other hand I held the Minox cupped against my cheek.

When Abdullah stepped out of the pantry, my practice with the Minox paid dividends, and I caught him at about a quarter profile before he turned away with his tray to go to the living room. I had no idea whether photographing in a mirror would work. But this way I had had my back to Abdullah and he had suspected nothing.

The table was cleared when I rejoined Jeff and Jenny, and the hour had turned from teatime to cocktails, at least by Jeff's reckoning. I stayed until almost six-thirty, nursing a drink and asking questions about life on the Arabian peninsula. That seemed to flatter Jeff, as well as satisfying my own curiosity. Then, firmly refusing Jeff's offer to drive me home, I rose and began collecting my things.

When Jenny had gone for my coat and hat and Jeff to call a taxi, I wandered over to the Christmas tree and slipped among the gifts under it the little package I had brought for Jenny. I thought I was alone in the room, but when I turned I saw Abdullah, tray in hand, bending over the cocktail table.

My presence seemed to startle him too, for his elbow brushed the edge of the table and swept the stack of photographs to the floor. I hurried to help him retrieve them, but by the time I crossed the room he had most of them on his tray. I fished a stray one from under my chair, checked the surrounding floor, and took the others from Abdullah as Jeff returned to say the taxi was on its way.

When I got back to Kate's, she met me at the door with an expectant, "Well?"

"Just so-so," I said. Going straight through to the

190

living room without taking off my coat, I reached into my purse and spread the Polaroid photographs on the sofa.

Then I felt in the pocket of my purse and in the main compartment, fingered each of the photographs to be sure they had not stuck together, and turned back to the purse again. But I knew it was no use. I had already checked there thoroughly, just as I had checked the floor of the Hearn chalet.

The picture of Abdullah was gone.

 *22*

ON TUESDAY I went down to Geneva by the first train, but
it was already dark by the time I got back to Saanen late
that afternoon. It had taken a good deal of time and
persuasion to find a photography lab in Geneva that
would do a rush developing job on the Minox film at the
height of the Christmas season. And even then, after I
had examined the prints, it cost me a further delay and
an additional whopping tip to get the photograph of
Abdullah reprinted from the wrong side of the negative.
I had forgotten that the mirror would reverse everything
left to right.

   After a hasty stop at a stationer for a sturdy envelope
and a note pad, I dashed through the holiday crowds to
the Qaimani legation at the address Sadiq had given me,
only to be told by the receptionist that the man I wanted
to see had just left for lunch and would not be back until
two. I was left with time to kill, and the hope that my man

operated on Western, not Arab, punctuality.

At least, I decided, I could get the package ready. I found a cafeteria and installed myself at a small table with a tasteless sandwich in one hand and my pen in the other. I discarded several approaches, then wrote:

> Dear Sadiq,
> Would you be good enough to pass along the enclosed snapshots to Zora and Zafia? I thought they might enjoy seeing their Gstaad friends, feline and human, in their Christmas activities. I have a new camera, and I'm still appallingly clumsy with it, so I'm afraid the results aren't very professional—and to make matters worse I have somehow, frustratingly, managed to mislay the best of them. But I hope you'll all like them anyway.
> Yours,

I read over what I had written, hesitated, then signed it. If I were to follow Sadiq's directions and sound innocent, it was the best I could do. He would just have to read between the lines.

I culled a representative sample from the thirty-odd photographs, wrapped them together with the note in several blank sheets of paper, and sealed them in the envelope.

Leaving the cafeteria, I found myself outside a quietly elegant dress shop. I still had an hour on my hands and Sadiq on my mind, and the combination was fatal. At the end of the hour, I left the dress shop with a large box, trying not to think how much it had diminished my bank account.

When I got back to the Qaimani legation, the man Sadiq had directed me to see was still not there, but he was only twenty minutes late in returning. He heard my request without apparent surprise, addressed the envelope in flowing Arabic script, and assured me he would place it personally with the urgent despatches. So I made my train with a few minutes to spare.

It was not until the train pulled from the Geneva station that I realized how much tension my errand had made me feel. I drew a deep breath of relief, and immediately fell asleep.

Jeanne and her husband Théo and the baby arrived in Saanen early the next afternoon, and despite Kate's doubts Paul managed to get away from the hospital in Lausanne in time for Christmas Eve dinner.

My cousins were much as I remembered them from ten years before, Jeanne bright and vivacious, Paul tall and serious. They both seemed genuinely glad to have me with them for the holidays.

"Were you really on Broadway?" Jeanne wanted to know.

"Well, I wasn't exactly the star, and it was a short run, but yes."

"I want to hear all about it."

I started to tell her, flattered by her interest, but before I had gone very far she leaped up and cried, *"Non, chéri, ne touche pas!"* and hurried after her small son. When she had rescued him from his crawling explorations and diverted him with some favorite toys, the subject was somehow lost.

Paul too, when he arrived, was attentive at first.

"I hear you've been exercising the rescue patrol. Let me check that ankle for you."

"Oh, Paul, you've been seeing patients all day," I protested.

"No, let's have a look at it." He prodded the ankle with strong fingers, flexing and rotating the joint. "Good. You can ski whenever you like. Do you get much free time? I imagine they keep you pretty busy at the school."

We chatted for a few minutes, but then Paul's attention was claimed by his nephew crawling over his shoetops. The baby monopolized everyone until dinner was ready. By the time he was put to bed, I was content to see him go. Still, I had to laugh at myself. It was unbecoming to be even mildly jealous of a ten-month-old infant.

The meal Kate produced was mammoth. "This is superb, Mother de Villiers," Théo said.

"Always is," Paul agreed. "We've had roast beef and Yorkshire pudding on Christmas Eve ever since I can remember. Why is that, Mum?"

"To stretch your stomachs for tomorrow's goose. Here, have some more," Kate said complacently. "Do you remember the Christmas when Père Viret was with us and—"

Dinner progressed with a current of small talk. Every so often someone tried to include me in the conversation, but it invariably returned to gossip and reminiscences about people I did not know.

My interest revived when, over coffee, Kate asked Théo: "What's new in the foreign service?"

This was the signal for Théo to launch into a series of anecdotes about life in the diplomatic world. One stuffy ambassador in particular seemed to be a staple character in his stories, and though I missed half the references that were familiar to the others, I was fascinated. Théo was a good storyteller, and as he talked I could envision the diplomatic circles in which he moved. They were the circles Sadiq moved in, too. I smiled privately; no doubt that accounted for much of my interest. So I was disappointed when, after half an hour, Jeanne reminded Théo they would have to be up early in the morning with the baby.

We were all up early. After breakfast I got out the Polaroid and a stack of film and installed myself near the tree. "It's not a surprise," I told Kate, "so I didn't wrap it. But I meant it when I told Jenny I was giving it to you for Christmas. I thought you'd like to have the whole family photographed together for once by an outsider."

"Deirdre, you're not an outsider, you *are* family!"

"Absolutely," Paul said firmly, lowering himself to the floor beside the tree and crossing his legs yoga-fashion. "And I think you should have the honor of opening the first present. What about this one?"

"If you don't mind, I'd rather have that little one there. I promised Zora and Zafia I'd open it first thing."

As I peeled off the wrapping, I smiled at the girls' thoughtfulness in remembering me with a token gift on what was, after all, not a holiday in their religion. But when I raised the lid, I saw that the gift was more than a token. Nestled on a bed of cotton was an intricately worked pair of filigree earrings, two masterpieces in spun silver. I lifted them from the box, and the light seemed to be caught and held inside the cages of swirling cobwebby wire.

"I've never seen anything like them," Kate said. "They must come from Arabia."

"May I?" Jeanne asked. "Oh, feel how light they are! You could wear them for hours and never know you had them on." She held them up to her ears, and I gazed at them dreamily, planning how I would wear my hair to show them to best advantage on New Year's Eve.

Beside Jeanne, the baby hauled himself onto one knee and groped toward the glinting objects in his mother's hands. She gave them back to me hurriedly, reaching for a package to distract him. That reminded me of my self-appointed task, and I took up the camera.

As Paul distributed the gifts, the baby showed more interest in the wrappings than in the contents, and he had soon surrounded himself with a fine mess. He had some help, too. Most of Kate's menagerie were outside, but Cléopatre was in attendance by the tree, and so was Milord. I was glad to see that he was a bit more lively this morning. He hid himself under tents of wrapping paper, rolled himself in ribbon, and intruded his nose and paws into my efforts to undo presents.

My cousins had seen that I was not neglected. Jeanne and Théo had brought me a lovely shawl of Brussels lace. Paul, with a bachelor's lack of imagination, contributed a bottle of perfume. And Kate, by luck or last-minute design, gave me a pair of silver evening shoes that would be perfect with my new gown. But the most original gift came from Haroun.

The tubular package in gold foil proved to contain a flimsy twist of tissue paper inside a scroll. I unrolled the crackling parchment, my smile broadening as I scanned the lines of meticulously executed lettering. Then, at my cousins' urgings, I read aloud:

### THE ROYAL ARABIAN SOCIETY
### FOR THE DEFENSE
### OF MALE SUPREMACY

meeting in rump session
and with blithe disregard
for quorum requirements
does hereby
declare and decree

### DEIRDRE SHERIDAN

admitted to the
honorable estate of

### ARAB WOMANHOOD

with all the duties
and responsibilities
thereto appertaining.

Done this 25th day
of December

Haroun had signed it with a bold flourish and finished it with tails of ribbon embedded in sealing wax.

I handed the scroll to Kate and untwisted an end of the tissue paper. At first I thought it contained nothing, it was so light. But then a square of gauzy fabric slithered onto my lap. I held it up and saw that despite its gossamer lightness it was quite opaque. It was an old-fashioned Arab face veil.

"Of all the impudence!" I grinned. "I suppose he means women should be seen and not heard."

"If that much," Jeanne said. "It looks as though he thinks women shouldn't be seen, either."

"What a sly boots he is," Kate laughed. "I've got an idea he means more than that. He means our fair Deirdre's face is altogether too distracting to his Uncle Sadiq."

I lifted the veil under my eyes to cover the flush that was mounting my cheeks. It was unlikely that Kate's teasing suggestion was true. But it would be nice to think so.

When the others had gone off to Mass, I got the baby settled in his playpen with a few stuffed animals and picked up the litter of gift wrappings that surrounded the tree. After the festivities of the last twenty-four hours, the chalet seemed eerily quiet.

But the tranquility did not last long. When my cousins returned, they brought with them a couple of former schoolmates, and as the day wore into late afternoon, the stream of visitors continued and with it the babble of voices. Most of the conversation was in Schwyzerdutsch, which Paul and Jeanne spoke as well as French or English, but which was incomprehensible to me. The more people arrived, the more left out I felt.

I was about to go for a twilight walk when the cowbell that hung outside Kate's door clanged again, and I discovered with pleasure that this pair of callers was for me.

Jenny bounced into the room with her father in her wake and gushed, "Miss Sheridan, it's absolutely perfect! I just love it!" She turned to Kate. "Have you seen it, Madame de Villiers? Isn't it beautiful?"

She proudly exhibited the gift I had tucked under her tree. From its slender chain around her neck hung the twinned masks of Comedy and Tragedy, exquisitely wrought in enamel. While Jeff was occupied with introductions, she leaned over to me and whispered, "It was a brilliant idea. And he didn't suspect a thing."

Jeff's words, when he made his way across the room, were at odds with Jenny's, but his tone was bantering. "I think you two are conspiring to persuade me Jen is going to be the next Ingrid Bergman."

"Not really, it was just an impulse," I said with shaded truthfulness. "But when I saw it in the shop window, I couldn't resist it. It had 'Jenny' written all over it."

"As a matter of fact, so does this, literally," Jeff said, producing a prettily wrapped package from under his arm. "But we hope it will interest you. Merry Christmas."

I felt a sharp twinge of guilt as I took the package from Jeff. I had not meant my impulsive gift to Jenny to invite

*199*

reciprocation. But my misgivings ended when I un-wrapped it. While it was a handsome book, filled with pictures and text about Arabia, it was obviously well-thumbed.

"It's a wonderful book," Jenny sighed. "We got it before Dad took Mom and me out to Arabia for the first time. I think I was four. I learned to read on that book."

"You needed considerable help, as I remember," Jeff said indulgently. "I bet I can still recite whole chapters by heart."

I smiled. "And I bet I'll be able to before long. It looks fascinating."

While I riffled the pages, Kate produced fruit cake and tea, and Jenny shifted her attention to Jeanne's baby. As she sat on the floor entertaining him with a hand puppet, it struck me how close she was herself to the age of motherhood. Jeff was watching her too, and I thought he might be thinking the same thing.

"Jenny has a date Saturday night," he said presently, "so I'll be on my own. Can I talk you into having dinner with me?"

I agreed without hesitation. It would be nice for Kate to have her children to herself for one evening. And it would be nice for me to get out. Jeff was good company. Not exciting, perhaps, but comfortable in a familiar American way.

When he and Jenny had departed with the last of the afternoon visitors, I paced the chalet restlessly. Paul was telling Jeanne the news of some childhood friend, and Kate, in the kitchen again, said she didn't need any help. I picked up the book on Arabia, leafed through it, and sat down to read.

But I found it hard to concentrate. The book reminded me of Haroun and his small sisters, now with their father for what might very well be the last time. I knew the pain they would soon be feeling, for I was feeling the full force of it now.

Just a year ago I had been with Daddy and Conn, not knowing it would be our last Christmas ever. The memory of that happy time was more painful than I could bear.

Milord, sensing my misery, crept into my lap and began to lick my hand. But his instinctive sympathy only made me feel worse. Sitting here in Kate's chalet, I was surrounded by a warm and loving family. But I had never felt so desperately, wrenchingly alone.

 *23*

By SATURDAY I was more than ready for a gala evening out, and I was glad that Jeff had chosen the Palace Hotel.

Every table was occupied in the cocktail area adjoining the grill room, but we found a pair of stools at the bar. Jeff handed me up and gave the barman our order.

"I must thank you properly for the book," I said, "now that I've had a chance to read it."

"Did you find it interesting?" Jeff asked eagerly.

"Completely absorbing. I read it through in one sitting."

That was a polite exaggeration. But my thoughts were so much with the Qaimani children lately that the book on Arabia had managed to hold my wavering attention as no other subject could have. When I finished it, I had even felt motivated to dig out the book Sadiq had sent me and apply myself to the study of Arabic. It was good mental exercise. And I thought Zora and Zafia would be pleased if on their return I could ask them about their vacation in their own language. But my vocabulary was still severely limited.

When our drinks arrived, I picked up my glass and asked Jeff, "How do you say 'Cheers' in Arabic?"

"Mostly, you don't. Drinking isn't exactly encouraged in those parts."

"No, I guess not. The Koran is pretty explicit on that point."

"And in Arabia the Koran is literally the law. Not that there aren't ways around it. You can get just about anything for a price." Jeff grinned. "I once laid out a cool grand for a case of Johnnie Walker Red."

"Good Lord," I said. "At that price, I'd stick to beer."

"No, you wouldn't. Not at seven bucks a bottle. You'd do what we do." Jeff drained the rest of his Scotch and signaled to the barman. "That's one good thing about the oil business. It needs chemists, and chemists are very handy fellows to have around. We whip up a little home brew called *sidiki*. Kind of like Pernod, but with a lot more kick. Luckily, we haven't been caught so far."

"I imagine that could be fairly expensive," I said, trying to sound worldly.

"Expensive? They'd lock us up and throw away the key. You can get five years just for possession."

The prospect did not seem to affect Jeff's cheerfulness. He applied himself steadily to making up for the drought in Arabia, meanwhile regaling me with an American oilman's view of the quaint local customs. He had worked his way through several Scotches and several stories, and was winding up a hilarious account of how to ride a camel, when the head waiter announced that our table was ready.

We moved into the grill room. After we ordered, I remarked, "You must find even the Palace's menu a little tame after all that exotic Middle Eastern cooking."

"Who, me?" Jeff laughed. "I'm a Texas boy, remember? Nothing I like better than a good steak. Not that we can't eat as Western as we like in Arabia. You can find most things there nowadays. The Saudis are getting Westernized fast. You should see the amount of Coke they drink."

"Strange, isn't it? After everything America has accomplished, what do we give the world? Coca-Cola."

"Oh, we export a few other blessings to the Saudis, too. Big cars. Television programs."

"Don't tell me, let me guess. *Bonanza* and old John Wayne flicks."

"Yup. And *I Dream of Jeannie,* believe it or not."

"Oh no," I groaned.

Before long our food arrived, claiming our appreciative attention. Around us the tables were crowded with holiday-makers. Their polyglot chatter rose over the more muted sounds of the orchestra. It was only when I was almost through the main course that I noticed Jeff's change of mood. He hadn't spoken for a full five minutes.

I looked across at him from under lowered eyelids. He was staring down at the tablecloth, his brows knit in concentration, his blunt fingernail tracing lines in the crisp white linen. The tournedos in front of him was barely touched, but beside the table the waiter was already extracting the cork from a second bottle of wine. When the glass was filled, Jeff reached for it automatically.

I lifted my chin and put on a bright smile. "This is all just lovely, Jeff. I can't think of a more perfect place to spend Christmas than Gstaad."

Jeff came out of his reverie and made a visible effort to remember what I had just said. His answer was appropriate enough, but it seemed to be chosen at random.

"Yeah, I guess it's all right for families, but for a single person it can get pretty dull. What are there, four halfway decent nightclubs? This town doesn't even have a casino."

He turned to summon the waiter, and I contemplated his remark. It was not the first time I had noticed a certain restless streak in him. Of course, he had been a widower for some time now, and I doubted that the oil fields of Arabia offered much in the way of a steadying influence.

"If you want a casino," I said, "isn't there one just down in Montreux?"

Jeff's grin was lopsided. "Big deal. The Swiss have a maximum bet of five francs. What's the good of hitting a hot streak if you can't parlay your winnings? Thank God we're just around the corner from France. They take a more sporting view of it there."

France. In a few days I would be going over to France with Sadiq. I wondered whether he took a sporting view too. There were so many stories of oil-rich Arab play-boys dropping whole fortunes at the tables of Deauville or Las Vegas. Gambling fever seemed to be endemic to the Arabian peninsula, if Jeff was any indication.

Jeff ordered coffee and cognac. He had evidently forgotten about dessert. That did not particularly bother me—I would have declined it anyway—but Jeff had hardly eaten anything.

When he had signed the bill, we moved on down to the GreenGo, the nightclub of the Palace. Here Jeff apparently found the young and lively crowd more to his liking. We wedged ourselves around a tiny table and stayed there. The floor was too crowded to think about dancing. And the incessant blare of the discotheque music made conversation almost impossible.

I suspected that was what Jeff liked best about the place. He nodded his head and drummed his fingers in time to the music, but his thoughts were once again patently elsewhere. From time to time a frown creased his forehead. He was downing his drinks roughly three to my one.

He was still distracted as he drove me back to Saanen. Once he started to say something, then lapsed back into silence. At Kate's door he roused himself long enough to say:

"Remember you promised Jenny you'd ski with us tomorrow."

"Right. I'm looking forward to being back on skis," I said. I was less sure, now, that I was looking forward to so much time in Jeff's company, if his present morose mood continued.

"I'll pick you up at ten."

He slipped an arm around my shoulders and bent over me. I did not pull away, but the good-night kiss he gave me was distinctly half-hearted.

As I let myself into the chalet, I tried to puzzle out the change in him. The Jeff I had seen before was freewheeling and hearty. I had half expected him to make an aggressive pass, and I was cheerfully prepared for it. But tonight's Jeff was withdrawn and indifferent, his kiss perfunctory. It was mystifying and, I admitted to myself, not very flattering.

My vague annoyance deepened to disappointment when I reached my room. Kate had propped a note against my pillow:

> Your Mr. Yamali telephoned just after you left. He said thank you for the excellent snapshots, the children are fine, and he'll call for you at two on Wednesday.

When I was ready for bed, I reread the note before snapping off the light. Then I folded my arms behind my head and stared into the darkness.

Perhaps it was just Jeff's unaccountable mood that made me feel the evening was wasted. But I would gladly have traded those five hours at the glamorous Palace Hotel for five minutes on the telephone with "my" Mr. Yamali.

"I told Daddy it was only fair," Jenny said, shuffling forward in the Wasserngrat lift line swollen by holiday skiers. "After all, if he hadn't abandoned you on the afternoon of my birthday, you wouldn't have been out of commission for three weeks. We have to take better care of you."

"I've seen your father's skiing," I said, "and I would not say it was any guarantee of safety."

Jeff removed his sunglasses and scowled at me, then winced and replaced the glasses hurriedly.

"Aren't you feeling well this morning, Jeff?" I asked, my tone more wicked than sympathetic.

"It's nothing I don't deserve," he said sheepishly. He looked very boyish then. "Anyway, it's bad form to complain about a hangover."

"Never mind, Daddy, you'll feel better after a couple of fast runs," Jenny said with a practicality that spoke of some experience. She passed her skis to the lift attendant, who swung them into a pocket on the outside of the tiny waiting cable car. I handed over my own skis and followed her into the two-man bubble.

As the car glided onto the cable and up over the road, I saw Jeff and a Swiss boy of about twelve climb into the open chair that was next in line. I was glad that Jeff's limited chivalry had extended to sending Jenny and me up together. I would not have minded riding with a stranger. But I did not feel like being suspended in mid-air alone with Jeff this morning.

"Why don't you and Jenny go on up," I suggested when we had reassembled at the middle station, "and I'll join you later. I'd better stick to the bottom section until I see what sort of shape I'm in."

"Okay. If we don't see you before, we'll be on the terrace at noon." Jeff gave a sketchy wave and moved with Jenny toward the upper-stage lift line.

Outside, I put on my skis, then paused before shoving off. It was a perfect day, with crisp air and warm sun. Despite the crowds of holiday skiers, there were still places where the fresh snow that had fallen during the night lay untouched and inviting.

I began slowly, taking the first right turn with apprehension, but my ankle bore my full weight without protest. Even the torsion of the turn did not seem to bother it. I increased my speed and, filled with the exhilaration of being back on skis, cut over to the Bissen run. It was little more than a long training slope, and I could enjoy the feeling of letting myself go while I was still warming up.

I soon regretted my decision. On the expert trails, the skiers flashed by with regularity, picking their lines of descent swiftly and surely. But here, where the slope was gentle, the struggling beginners stood all over the *piste,* moving haltingly if at all. Dotted among them were the blue jackets with the red arm stripes that identified the instructors of the Swiss Ski School.

I managed to thread my way through the hesitant groups that cluttered the *piste* until I was almost at the bottom. Then, just as I had worked up some speed, a girl shot into my path, sitting helplessly on the tails of her skis. I had the choice of running her over or falling deliberately. I accomplished the latter with only inches to spare.

Regaining my feet, I slapped ineffectually at my clothes. I had snow up my cuffs, snow down my neck, snow caking the hair under my hat.

Just below me I heard a burst of laughter. The unfortunate girl's instructor had helped her up, and now he was voicing his amusement at my predicament. A tart remark rose to my lips. Then I saw that the face above the blue instructor's jacket belonged to Ruedy Messerli.

"Miss van Allyn, Miss Sheridan," he said with a nod of introduction. "I recommend in future, Miss van Allyn, that you stay clear of this young lady. She specializes in collisions." Ruedy was still holding the girl's arm, and his tone was both jocose and familiar.

I gave Ruedy what was intended to be a baleful look. Really, it wasn't *my* fault the wretched girl couldn't stay on her feet! Ruedy needn't try to make his client feel better at my expense. Of course, the customer was always right, but—

I took a closer look at the girl, remembering Ruedy's dreams of developing his hill and his casual remark about marrying an American heiress. Standing, the girl no longer looked so ungainly. And judging from her clothes and ski equipment, she was hardly poor.

I raised a sardonic eyebrow at Ruedy, and he shrugged deprecatingly.

It was only after I had shoved off again that it occurred to me to worry about the effects of my fall and to rejoice that my ankle was still intact.

After lunch Jenny claimed she was too full to ski again right away, but she still had enough energy to entice Jeff and me off the restaurant terrace and into a snowball fight.

Lunch had been a merry affair, with Jenny bubbling as usual and Jeff largely recovered from his hangover. Now as we stood outside in the warm sun, Jenny pointed downhill at the tiny figures of skiers crawling toward the village far below. Jeff and I turned to follow her pointing finger, and she caught me squarely in the back with a snowball, crowing in triumph. I charged her, scooping up a double handful of snow on the way, but she dodged me and ducked behind Jeff for protection. Within five minutes we were all gasping for breath.

When Jenny pointed again, neither Jeff nor I dared to take our eyes off her. But this time, she insisted, she was serious. "Look, just over there. At the Eagle Club. I think it's a wedding."

As we looked at the impressive gray stone clubhouse just across from us, members of the party poured outside and clustered around the door. Half a dozen girls emerged in a group, dressed in identical striking pink jumpsuits, followed by an equal number of young men in black ski clothing. Each of them carried a pair of ski poles. They moved a bit beyond the other guests, formed two even ranks, and turned expectantly back to face the door.

"There's the bride!" Jenny breathed.

The bride stood framed in the doorway. Every detail of her costume was white—white ski boots, white fur-trimmed suit, white mittens. From her white fur head-band fluttered tier on tier of veil, barely long enough to brush her shoulders. Beside her the groom, like his ushers, was all in black except for a spray of lily-of-the-valley pinned to his jacket. He bent to speak to her, and with an answering smile she lofted her bridal bouquet over the guests to the outstretched arms of her bridesmaids.

Then the groom seized her hand and they ran uphill in a shower of snowballs.

They stepped into the skis that had been laid out for them—hers white, his black—exchanged a kiss for the benefit of their guests, and shoved off in unison. As they approached the double file of their attendants, the ski poles swung smoothly up to form an arch over their heads. To the accompaniment of cheers, they slid beneath the arch and downhill out of sight.

"Wasn't that fabulous?" Jenny said rapturously. "Just like a military wedding, with crossed swords when they come out of the chapel and everything. I hope, when I get married, it'll be as beautiful as that." She sighed. "Gosh, I love weddings!"

Jeff had been standing close beside me as we watched, but at Jenny's words he unconsciously moved a step away. I glanced up and saw that he wore a look of intense unhappiness. Was it, I wondered, because Jenny had reminded him how soon she would be grown up and married? Or was he perhaps thinking of another wedding, years ago, and of his dead wife?

He stood staring into the distance for so long that at last I reached across and touched his arm gently. He transferred his gaze to me, his face as unhappy as before. For a moment I thought he was on the verge of speaking. I looked back at him steadily, waiting to receive his confidence.

Then he shook his head slowly, took a deep breath, and said:

"Come on, let's ski."

## 24

"WHERE are we going?" I asked.

Sadiq finished locking the doors of the Citroën, parked now in the lee of a small airport shed. He squinted speculatively for a moment at the gathering clouds overhead, then picked up my suitcase and started across the Saanen airstrip, gesturing with his free hand at the gleaming blue and white twin-engined plane that sat fifty yards from us.

"Yes, but—where are we going, Sadiq?" I repeated, hurrying to keep up with him.

"I thought I told you. To France. I hope you brought your passport."

"Yes, but—in that?"

"Of course, 'in that'. Why? Don't you trust my flying?"

"Yes, but—" I stopped, hearing how foolish I sounded. It seemed the only words I could utter were "yes, but."

I had assumed, when Sadiq said we were going to France, that we would be driving around Lake Geneva to Evian, or perhaps up into the mountains of High Savoy, to Chamonix or Megève. It had not occurred to me that we might be going further, let alone faster and higher.

Sadiq stopped in front of the port wing and opened a hatch in the nose. He swung my suitcase up to stow it in the neatly carpeted luggage compartment beside his own handsome leather bag. Then he ushered me around the wing to the door in the side of the fuselage, and up the single step.

"Mind your head," he warned.

In the cabin, it felt strange not to be able to stand upright. At my height, I had never had to worry about low doorways and the like. But the cabin was barely over four feet high. I sank into the nearest seat.

What the cabin lacked in headroom it more than made up in luxury. The four seats that faced each other in pairs were deep and comfortable. The padded leather overhead and the curtains at the wide windows were a restful bone color, and the fitted carpets a rich solid blue. But the tapestry that covered the seats and the side panels, its blue picking up the color of the carpet, was quietly opulent and clearly Oriental. Sadiq must have supplied the fabric for custom upholstering.

I had barely begun to examine the fittings and accessories when Sadiq, forward in the cockpit, called: "Sorry I can't give you a tour now, but we'll be taking off in a couple of minutes. I want to get in while it's still light."

I moved between the forward seats and stuck my head into the cockpit to reply, but my words were drowned by the igniting engines. Sadiq revved them in turn, then absorbed himself in a check of gauges and controls.

Glancing at my watch, I saw that it was past two-thirty. Sadiq had been a little late calling for me at Kate's, which probably accounted for his desire to lose no time now. We would have a scant two hours of daylight after we were airborne. I wondered how far that would take us. Paris? The Riviera?

"Deirdre!" Sadiq bellowed.

"Yes, Sadiq?" I answered quietly.

He looked up. "Oh, sorry, I didn't know you were right here. Sit down and strap yourself in. We're going up."

I slipped into the copilot's seat as Sadiq eased the airplane forward and taxied to the end of the runway. He wheeled and began the takeoff immediately. It was only seconds before the uneven bumping of the wheels on the runway was replaced by the smoothness of flight and we were skimming over the snow-laden roofs, climbing steadily and banking to the south. Then we bored into a dense white fog. When we emerged the clouds were below us, and in the spaces between them the chalets in the valley showed as tiny dots. Around us was the limit-less expanse of the clear, bright sky, punctuated by the highest peaks. We were alone in the magical world of the mountaintops.

"You can unbuckle now. I'll show you our route." Sadiq reached for a chart beside his seat, then dropped it again. "No, you'll be able to see better on a regular map. There's a book of them in the pocket of the right rear seat. Would you get it?"

I ducked into the cabin and brought back the book of maps. Sadiq propped it against his control wheel, flip-ping through it with his free hand. Then he laid it, open to a map of southeastern France, on my knee.

"We're here now, and Aline's villa—that's our hostess —is on Cap Ferrat, here. So we'll be landing in Nice. You can see our course is just about dead south. We'll be flying over Italy most of the time."

A moment of misgiving assailed me when I heard our

destination. Cap Ferrat's reputation as a Mediterranean playground for the wealthy was as exalted as—as Gstaad's was in the mountains. Well, I reminded myself, I had been living in Gstaad for four months now, with no great sense of awe.

"That's the Grand St. Bernard pass just ahead," Sadiq said, pointing through the windshield. "Have you been over it before?"

"Only by car. And I thought *that* was breathtaking."

"We should be up to altitude by the time we cross it."

A look at the altimeter on my side of the instrument panel told me we were already above sixteen thousand feet and still climbing. "I'm surprised I don't feel it in my ears yet," I said.

"We're pressurized automatically to about five thousand. You wouldn't notice anything unless I took it right up to twenty-five or thirty. We won't be going that high today."

I nodded, examining the other instruments in front of me—compass, air speed, rate of climb—then rested my fingertips on the copilot's control wheel, lightly tracing the letters BEECH and the Maltese cross in its shield. "Is this a Beechcraft Baron?" I asked.

"Beechcraft Duke B-60."

"Oh," I said in a small voice. I might have known, if there was a higher-ranking model, Sadiq would have it.

He smoothed his mustache, hiding a smile. He must have known what I was thinking.

"It's not so extravagant, really," he said. "These things have a solid resale value. And I managed to talk the Qaimani government into picking up the operating costs. At that, they're saving money."

I supposed that was true enough. Sadiq's travels were apparently on the scale of the fabled Henry Kissinger's.

"Will you be going back to the Gulf to pick up the children?" I asked.

"No, there's no sense in my making a special trip. Their father will send them up in his own plane." Sadiq grinned broadly. "His idea of a private plane makes mine look like a windup toy. He's got a 727."

I laughed along with Sadiq, and then I stopped laughing abruptly. The Sheik of Qaiman might possess oil money by the billions of barrels and the heady power of an absolute monarch, but they were worthless to him. In the prime of life, he would soon die, and he knew that neither wealth nor rank could do anything to prevent it.

"How does he seem to you?" I asked.

Sadiq too was sober now. "Quite strong, these past ten days. But I don't think anyone can predict how long the remission will last. Haroun is with him constantly, of course. There's so much Haroun still has to learn, and Sheik Sultan is doing his best to prepare him. But he's not really his old self except when the girls are with him. Then he's truly courageous, laughing and playing with them. I don't think Zora and Zafia can have any idea how much is weighing on his mind."

"Does he know all about the—incidents involving Haroun?"

Sadiq waved his hand in an expressive gesture that betrayed his French blood. "Just the bare facts. I haven't troubled him with my speculations. And that's still all they are, though they're getting more clearly formulated. Thanks for the photograph, by the way. I gathered from your note that you had a little trouble getting it?"

"A little." I told Sadiq how I had visited the Hearns and taken the two pictures of Abdullah, and how he had managed to make off with the one he knew about. "So I'm afraid he suspected what I was doing," I concluded.

Sadiq thought for a while. "Not necessarily. Arabs

don't like to be photographed. Supposedly it's because of the Koran's prohibition of graven images, but knowing the Arab mind, I think it's more apt to be pure superstition. Our friend Abdullah may just have an aversion to having his picture taken. That's his real name, incidentally."

"You found out who he is?"

"Yes. He's Qaimani, all right. And he's got a police record that goes back a long way. Petty crime, mostly. Strangely enough, it stops a couple of years ago. He's been picked up several times since then, but never convicted."

"Friends in high places?"

"So it would seem. And I'd give a thousand to one it's the sheik's brother Ahmed. But I haven't been able to uncover a direct link. I haven't found out how Abdullah came to be working for Hearn, either. But I did learn something about the third side of that triangle."

"A connection between Ahmed and Jeff Hearn, you mean?"

"It looks that way. You see, I started to think it was altogether too handy a coincidence that Abdullah worked for somebody who just happened to have a child at the same school as Haroun and his sisters. It had to have been contrived."

"Something like that occurred to me too," I said. "But it can't be. This is Jenny's fourth year at the school."

"Sure, but look at it from the other end."

"The other end?"

"Haroun and the girls. They're the ones who are new at the Academy of the Oberland. After all, there are quite a few top schools in Switzerland. I wondered how the sheik had hit on this particular one. So I asked him, casually."

"And what did he say?"

217

"He thought someone had suggested it to him—his brother, maybe. He had an idea Ahmed had a friend, an American oilman, who had a daughter there."

"Jeff and Jenny," I said slowly. I thought about that. "Then it would be at Ahmed's suggestion, too, that Jeff hired Abdullah?"

"It makes sense, doesn't it?"

"Yes. But it doesn't tell us what Jeff's role is. We don't know whether he took on Abdullah just to oblige a friend, or whether he's in this up to his neck."

"No," Sadiq agreed. "And I'm tired of thinking about it." He busied himself adjusting the controls, then put the plane on automatic pilot and shifted to face me. He lounged comfortably in his seat, one arm draped over the headrest. His smile was easy as he said: "Today I'm on holiday. So let's both relax and enjoy ourselves."

Sadiq threaded the rented car through the last of Nice's crowded streets and onto the Lower Corniche, adjusting his speed to the flow of late-afternoon traffic that wound its way eastward along the Mediterranean coast.

"Do you want to tell me now what it was all about?" he asked, not unkindly.

"Of course, Sadiq. Really, I wasn't nervous about the landing. I do trust your flying. I meant it when I said I wasn't frightened."

"Well, *something* upset you. When I looked at your hand, the knuckles were white. You were gripping that armrest for dear life."

It hadn't been fear for myself that I felt, or even shock. I had known that the sea was there. Indeed, at our altitude, we had been able to see the Mediterranean for much of the flight. I had kept a firm grip on my nerves, forcing myself to sit calmly, admiring the magnificent scenery that unrolled below us, fetching coffee willingly from the drink dispenser, and in general acting resolutely normal. But that was only until we began our landing pattern.

Then the sea rose to meet us with sickening speed, and I could no longer stave off the irrational terror and loathing I felt. Before long Sadiq noticed it too. But I could not tell him then. He was too busy radioing to the control tower and taking the airplane down.

So I told him now.

He listened quietly while I talked of the accident that had claimed the lives of Daddy and Conn, talked of it fully for the first time. His manner was sympathetic and encouraging, but he did not say anything during my recital, or for a full minute afterwards. Then he said:

"It's ironic. When I asked you to come with me, I thought a trip to the Riviera was something you'd particularly enjoy. It seems I couldn't have been more cruelly off the mark."

"No, Sadiq, it's all right. I have to face it. And talking about it helped, helped a lot. I'm grateful."

Sadiq moved his hand deprecatingly.

"Besides, it didn't happen here, and that helps too. The Mediterranean was always a favorite of Daddy's, and of all of us. I just have to concentrate on remembering the happy times we spent here."

Sadiq agreed that was wise, but he did not allow me to put my resolve into practice then. He filled the next few minutes with a series of comments on the lovely seaside towns through which we passed, anecdotes about the people who lived in them, and observations on human nature. At first his efforts to divert me sounded a trifle forced, but before long his stories caught my interest. We had swooped down onto Villefranche and through Beaulieu toward Èze before I realized that we had passed the turn for Cap Ferrat. Once again it seemed our travel plans were more complex than Sadiq had bothered to mention.

I turned in my seat and looked back at Cap Ferrat, the loaf-shaped bulge of the peninsula looming over the charming little harbor of St.-Jean. "Where is Aline's villa?" I asked.

Sadiq glanced over his shoulder. "Right up there on the crest. The view from her upper terrace is magnificent. It's too bad you won't be able to see it by daylight. But of course Aline was full up by the time I told her you were coming. The Réserve was booked solid too. So we'll be staying at the Hôtel de Paris in Monte Carlo."

I nodded, suppressing a smile. It was typical that Sadiq, on finding the Réserve in Beaulieu was full, would opt to drive the extra ten miles into the Principality of Monaco rather than stay in a less luxurious hotel. On this glittering coast, every inch of which catered to the affluent tourist, he found only a handful of establishments worth considering. I wondered briefly whether my presence had influenced his choice. No, I thought, he was probably guided solely by habit.

I wondered too whether it was habit for Sadiq to take girls to hotels in strange cities overnight. Kate had joked only this morning about my Arab playboy transporting me across international borders for immoral purposes. But we had both assumed I would be staying in the home of the hostess. Somehow the possibility of this unchaperoned commercial arrangement had not suggested itself to us, and it made me a little uneasy now.

Well, I decided, times had changed. I was years past the age of consent and presumably able to take care of myself. If I had known, I would not have raised any prudish objections.

Still, I wished Sadiq had thought to mention it.

# 25

SHIELDING my eyes and taking a deep breath, I loosed a cloud of aerosol spray at my head. The mist on the back of my hand felt cold and sticky. It was months since I had used hair lacquer—since my short run on Broadway—but from what Sadiq said, Aline's party would last well into the wee hours, and I did not want my hair to collapse before I did.

I unpinned the towel around my shoulders, put on the silver filigree earrings, and surveyed the result.

The Deirdre who looked back at me from the mirror above the Louis XV dressing table was immeasurably more sophisticated than the tousled creature who had arisen from her nap an hour ago. Now my hair was swept back over the tips of my ears and up into a swirling crown. I remembered Sadiq, the first evening we had dinner together, saying he preferred my hair long and loose. But there was no doubt the present arrangement set off the earrings effectively.

A glance at my travel alarm told me Sadiq would be here shortly. Checking the contents of my evening bag, I went out into the sitting room, closing the door firmly behind me.

When I had found, on our arrival at the hotel, that Sadiq had taken not a room but a suite for me, I had been slightly abashed. But I could see a great advantage now. I would not have to receive him in my bedroom.

Standing before a full-length mirror, I examined myself critically. The short cape that was draped over a brocade chair was, it was true, only fake fur. But that was all right. Nowadays movie queens and crowned heads were refusing to wear real fur on principle. My other accessories, from the spun silver earrings Zora and Zafia had given me, to the silver shoes, were fine. And the dress was perfection itself.

In cut and fabric it could not have been more classic, a simple, long white silk sheath, sleeveless, with a modified mandarin collar. Delicately graduated bands of silver embroidery at the hem were echoed at the waist and collar, relieving, and yet somehow reinforcing, the gown's elegant austerity.

I stepped back and twirled experimentally in a series of short steps. Kate must have chosen the confections of interlaced silver straps on my feet as soon as she had seen the dress, for they harmonized admirably. But there was nothing to give support to a weak ankle. I would have to be careful not to dance too long.

A tap at the door brought me up short. I glanced once more at the mirror and smoothed my skirt automatically. "Come in!" I called.

Sadiq entered, tossed his coat over a chair, and looked across at me, smiling wordlessly.

I had not seen him before in dinner clothing, and the

effect was striking. With his dark coloring, trim mustache, and even white teeth, it seemed to be made for him. And he wore it with the ease of long practice. I realized with a start that, for Sadiq, black tie was not the exception in evening attire but the rule. Unless the rule was white tie with orders.

If I had been staring, so had he. Finally he moved forward, reached one hand toward my ear and said simply, approvingly, "Yes."

That brought me a glimmer of understanding. "I think I have to thank you again," I said. "You chose these earrings, didn't you?"

"The girls did ask my advice," he admitted. He withdrew his hand and turned to examine the bowl of roses on the low table beside him.

Trying to match his casualness, I said, "But of course you had nothing to do with Haroun's gift."

He looked up with a quirking eyebrow. "That was Haroun's own idea," he said. "I prefer my women emancipated."

There did not seem to be any answer to that. I picked up my long white gloves and drew them on, wondering uncomfortably how numerous "his women" were, and how emancipated. The thought occupied me while Sadiq, attentive but silent, slipped my cape onto my shoulders and escorted me to the elevator and across the crowded lobby.

People were entering the Hôtel de Paris in a steady stream, and just across the way at the imposing baroque palace that was the Casino, the scene was intensified. Limousines and taxis disgorged little knots of elegantly dressed revellers arriving for the New Year's gala. The traffic around the Casino square was becoming more snarled by the minute.

Sadiq's rented car stood waiting in front of the hotel,

*223*

and before we reached it, the venerable doorman materialized beside us. He held my door, then sprang around to the other side to open Sadiq's with a speed that belied his years.

"Thank you, Alex," Sadiq said. "A Happy New Year to you."

"Thank you, Your Excellency." Alex stepped in front of the car and, with a few waves and blasts of his whistle, accomplished the seemingly impossible, clearing a space for our departure.

Sadiq nosed the car through the Monte Carlo traffic, down into la Condamine and up the rue Grimaldi toward Monaco proper. As we passed under the brow of the palace gardens, I remarked how much I liked the Grimaldi palace. "It manages to be impressive and rather graceful and still unpretentious."

"Like the people who live there," Sadiq agreed. "I'm sorry I won't be able to present you to them. Aline will have her share of glittering people at her party, but Rainier and Grace won't be among them."

I thought that it was Sadiq who was now a bit pretentious, so I said artlessly:

"Oh, I doubt that they'd remember me, anyway."

"You know them?" Sadiq almost concealed his surprise.

"Not very well. Of course, Prince Rainier has always been immensely interested in the Oceanographic Museum here, so he and Daddy got to know each other over the years. But I was only sixteen the last time we were here."

After a moment Sadiq said, "I suspect that even at sixteen you were fairly memorable."

I let the compliment pass, knowing what he was really thinking. And it was what I intended him to think. I knew there was a good chance I would feel ill at ease tonight among so many jet-setting strangers. But not for worlds would I have Sadiq consider me out of my depth.

I smiled, remembering the letter I had received from Maggie yesterday. She commiserated with me, left behind to rusticate in Saanen while she had flown off to her fiancé in the States. Well, my flight had been shorter than hers but vastly more glamorous. And now I was driving along the Riviera to an exclusive party, talking casually with my escort about a reigning prince who was our mutual acquaintance.

If Maggie could see me now, I thought, she would retract her sympathy.

My mood of confidence carried me through our arrival at the villa on Cap Ferrat and the initial wave of introductions.

Our hostess was a tall and flamboyant redhead with an expansive personality to match. She welcomed me warmly, then turned to Sadiq with a probing look.

"You've been holding out on me, you wretch."

"Down, Aline," Sadiq laughed, propelling me past her and into the next room.

Aline, he explained, had acquired her string of residences and race horses by being widowed in a timely fashion. Now she showed no interest in remarrying, but expended her considerable energy on partygiving and matchmaking.

She obviously had a talent for the former. Her guest list included painters and performing artists, captains of industry and prominent sportsmen, with just enough genuine titles and old money thrown in for leavening. Everyone mixed well, and Sadiq seemed to know them all.

I was surprised to hear several of them call him "Your Excellency." I had thought that the doorman Alex at the hotel had merely been flattering him, but now I remembered that he held ambassadorial rank. A few others used the title "Your Highness," about which I was less sure. Most of them simply called him Sadiq. One overweight and undercorseted Englishwoman hailed him as "Dickie," but at that, I noted with amusement, he could not suppress a wince.

There was even someone I knew at the party, a honey blonde named Roxanne who had been a year ahead of me at Wellesley. We had not been particular friends; in fact, our chief point of contact had come when she had stolen from me the affections of a rather sweet but not too intelligent Dartmouth fullback. But now she fell on me with coos of delight. I had a keen idea why.

A glance at Sadiq reassured me. He was smiling as easily as ever, but I recognized amused tolerance in his eyes. He listened for a while to Roxanne's gushing, "Who would ever have believed?" and, "You must tell me all about it," and then he said firmly:

"You girls have all evening to talk. But Miss Sheridan promised me this dance."

He guided me into the other half of the vast double drawing room, now cleared of furniture, toward the orchestra at the far end. "Would you like to dance?" he asked. "We don't have to. I just wasn't quite sure you wanted to talk to her."

"You mean you were quite sure I didn't," I laughed. "Thanks for the rescue. And I'd love to dance, if the orchestra would only play something resembling music."

Sadiq looked at me quizzically. Around us the final bars of the latest Wings number pounded in inexorable crescendo.

"I know, I'm a disgrace to my generation," I admitted.

"But I never could appreciate hard rock. I had a conservative upbringing."

"So did I. I can't see the point in dancing if you don't have a girl in your arms." He listened as the last thundering notes died away and the orchestra swung into the next set. "Did your conservative upbringing happen to cover the *paso doble?*"

"It did. Daddy was an acknowledged expert." I smiled, thinking of my father teaching me to dance. The memory was tender but for the first time not overwhelmingly painful.

"Then I'm on my mettle."

Sadiq whirled me onto the dance floor and into the intricate steps of the *paso doble.* He led with sureness, moderating the size of his steps to accommodate the restricting narrowness of my skirt, but sacrificing none of the stamping staccato rhythm and shifting of hips that made the dance as dramatic as a tango. As he spun me into a tight circle and then back to arm's length, I gave a low laugh of pure delight.

"Well, how do I compare?" he asked.

"Different, but very nice."

He smiled in gratification, and I smiled back. But I had not meant his dance steps, which were familiar enough. I had meant the firm pressure of his arm across my back, and the gentle support of his hand holding mine. These sensations were different in a subtle way from any I had known, and very nice indeed.

The orchestra slid into the next number, a slower one. Sadiq drew me closer until I was encircled in his arms, my forehead brushing his cheek. We did not talk anymore, but drifted in unison to the dreamlike strains of the music. When it ended and we left the floor, my hand still rested lightly in his.

227

We danced together only once in the hour that followed. But as we moved from group to group, sometimes joining in the conversation, sometimes dancing with other partners, I felt in quiet harmony with Sadiq. From across the floor his eyes would meet mine for an instant, so that I seemed never to be apart from him.

It was almost midnight when he claimed me as his partner again and we had barely begun to dance when the orchestra, in the middle of a bouncy bossa nova, stopped abruptly. The lights went out for a few seconds, and when they came back on, the familiar notes of *Auld Lang Syne* rose, almost drowned by the raucous sounds of party noisemakers and the wild cries of "Happy New Year!" All around us people were kissing each other and tossing streamers and blowing horns.

Sadiq grinned and bent his head as though to kiss me. Then he straightened suddenly and, his arm still around my waist, steered me through the crowd and out of the drawing room. In the deserted hall, he drew me into a shallow alcove and, away from the other guests, he bent over me again.

His arms closed around me, and I leaned gratefully on their support, for my legs were suddenly reluctant to hold me. I could not breathe. I could not hear the din of blaring horns and festive shouts, but only a distant roar. I could see nothing but Sadiq's dark expressive eyes approaching mine. I could feel nothing but the touch of his lips, gentle at first and then insistent.

After a minute that stretched endlessly, he eased us apart, his arms still supporting me, and said:

"Happy New Year, Deirdre."

As I raised my lips to meet his again, I could not imagine how any moment of the long year ahead could be happier than this one.

\* \* \*

The remains of the lavish buffet were almost cleared away. In front of the bandstand servants were fitting additional sections of portable stage, preparing for the entertainment Aline had planned. Beside us a hovering waiter offered champagne.

Sadiq finished the glass he held and set it on the tray, declining a fresh one with a wave of his hand. "Would you excuse me for a few minutes?" he asked me.

I watched him start across the room, then turned back to the waiter with a shake of my head. I did not want any more champagne. The little I had drunk, I knew, was not the cause of my lightheaded euphoria. I tried to listen with interest to the bright chatter of the people beside me, but my private thoughts enveloped me like a sound-proof cloud.

When Sadiq had been gone for five minutes, I began to feel in turn restless and, as I identified my mood, amused with myself. Foolish Deirdre! I thought. In the four months I had known Sadiq, I had seen him perhaps ten times. And now I was regretting a separation of a few short minutes. At least, I decided, I could take advantage of his absence to repair my appearance.

Outside in the hall, I paused uncertainly. There was a powder room, I thought, next to the room that held our wraps. It was on the right, not far down one of these corridors. But Aline's villa was a sprawling twenty- or thirty-room affair, and three corridors led from the hall on the side opposite the drawing room. In the bustle of arriving guests, I had not paid attention to the layout. And the decor was no help. All the walls were the same cool Mediterranean white, all the floors the same terra cotta tiles.

There was no servant in sight to give directions, so I moved hopefully into the middle corridor. I wished that Aline had marked the appropriate doors with little wrought-iron señoritas and caballeros, but unluckily for my present purposes, she had better taste than that. All the doors looked alike, and most of them were closed.

But one stood ajar. It seemed about the right place, so I pushed it gently wider.

It was clearly not the room I sought. The wall that revealed itself was lined floor to ceiling with books, and as I checked my hand from opening the door further, I saw in the corner of the room a heavy mahogany desk and on it a telephone, the receiver off the hook. At the limit of my vision was the black-clad shoulder of a man.

I pulled the door quietly toward me again, but as I turned to leave I heard a voice, urgent and angry and unmistakably Sadiq's.

"That's not possible!" he said.

His voice, so different from the warm and gentle tones he had used minutes ago with me, froze me where I stood. I heard him repeat his words in French, and I realized he had spoken the first time in Arabic. A brief silence followed. Then Sadiq said:

"Just take care of your own end, and keep your eyes open. I'll be responsible for the rest."

There was another silence, longer this time, before Sadiq said with weary finality:

"I don't expect any more false alarms. This time he *is* going to die."

I stood immobile for another moment. Then I caught up my skirt and ran.

As I flew down the corridor toward the main hall, Sadiq's words pursued me, French and Arabic, grim and determined. He must not know that I had been listening. And he would not, for I ran so fast that my heels never touched the hard tile floor. At the end of the corridor, I almost careened full tilt into a tray-bearing waiter.

The waiter recovered from his surprise with professional smoothness, and assumed a mask of imperturbability. He heard my stammered request and gave me directions.

Inside the powder room, I sank onto a bench before the vanity bar and cradled my head on my arms. I could not move. Sadiq's words echoed about me, draining my strength, beating me into a sick helplessness. "This time he *is* going to die," they chanted. "This time he *is* going to die."

No! I screamed inside my head. That can't be what he meant. He must have meant something else, someone else. The sheik. Of course, he meant the sheik. The sheik was going to die. He didn't mean—no, I would not even think it. It was too horrible. How could I, however briefly, have thought such a thing?

But his voice had been so unnatural, so grim and harsh, when he was talking to—whom? All I knew about the person on the other end of the line was that he spoke French. And perhaps Arabic, though not necessarily; Sadiq had repeated those words. He might have been talking to someone here in France, or Switzerland. Someone in Gstaad. But that would mean—no, it was impossible! Perhaps it had been someone in Qaiman. But it was the middle of the night in Qaiman, a secretive time for a phone call.

Of course, I told myself, that was the point. Sadiq had to be extremely careful. There was nothing in his words that did not have a perfectly innocent explanation. I had only to ask him—but I could not ask him about it. He must not know that I had been eavesdropping. And most of all, he must not know that I had let myself be swept by such wild and horrible suspicions.

I raised my head and looked at my reflection a foot away. Even in the soft pink lighting of the powder room, my face wore a ghostly pallor.

It must be fatigue, I thought, or the champagne, which had made me so irrational. I had overheard a few ambiguous sentences and erected a baseless tower of hideous conjecture.

Sadiq loved Haroun and the girls, I had seen that often and clearly enough. He was not posing. He was not playing a part with Haroun, with Zora and Zafia. With me.

I would trust Sadiq, I resolved. He had done everything to earn my trust. And if he did not trust me in return, it would only be what I deserved.

 *26*

"I'M BEGINNING to think there are too many people here. What do you say? Shall we go somewhere else, just the two of us?"

I smiled up at Sadiq and nodded.

"Good. Let's fine Aline and make our escape."

As I followed Sadiq, working our way through the crowded room, thanking our hostess, finding our wraps, I was relieved. The last hour had not been a total success.

The show had already begun when I got back from the powder room. Sadiq was waiting for me, and he maneuvered a space where I could see the stage. While we watched the trio of flamenco dancers, he stood relaxed beside me, an arm draped over my shoulder. And when the show was over, we danced again. But some of the sparkle was gone from the evening.

It was my fault, I knew. My mood was still unsettled, and I thought that it had somehow communicated itself to Sadiq. Even if it had not, if his slight preoccupation was the aftermath of the telephone call, I should have been able to charm it away and bring back the magic spell of midnight. But the nagging awareness of my lapse of faith dragged at my spirits. The conversation that floated around us on a wave of champagne suddenly sounded too brittle, and the orchestra too brassy.

Outside the villa, Sadiq took my elbow and said, "Let me show you Aline's garden before we leave."

The irregular flagged area to which he led me was surrounded by a rocky plantation of cactus, a dozen or more varieties. Strategically placed spotlights illuminated the spiky plants from below, accentuating their exotic shapes. Above them rose the trees, umbrella pines, fan-like palms, and feathery mimosa. A half-risen moon filtered through the branches, giving a striking contrast with the grotesque forms below.

Sadiq, behind me, rested his hands lightly on my shoulders. "I'm sorry to drag you away from the party so early. But I'm afraid I'd had enough of crowds."

"It's all right, Sadiq. I felt the same way."

He pulled me gently back against him, brushing the side of my neck with his lips. I shivered at their touch, as my self-reproach deepened. Sadiq was crediting me, I knew, with more intuition than I possessed. It was I who should be apologizing to him.

Feeling my shiver, he wrapped my cape around me more closely. Then he led me to a stone bench, seating himself at an angle to face me, and reached into his pocket deliberately.

"There's something I'd like you to have. It's late for Christmas, but I wanted to give it to you myself. Close your eyes?"

I obeyed, feeling Sadiq's fingers moving at my wrist. Then I opened my eyes and looked down at what he had placed there. My other hand moved slowly to my throat. I was speechless, not with delight but with dismay.

The bracelet that was clasped over the white satin of my glove was clearly the work of the same master craftsman who had made the earrings Zora and Zafia had given me. But the earrings were only of silver filigree. This was something more. Nestled among the spun threads of shining metal that encircled my wrist, tiny points of fire winked in the moonlight, ten, twenty of them. They were small, but they were unmistakably diamonds.

I caught my lower lip between my teeth. Accepting a pair of fur boots from Sadiq had been questionable. But about this there could be no question at all.

Finally I raised my eyes to meet his. "Sadiq, I can't accept this."

His eyebrows came together, and the shadow of a palm frond dipped across his face, accentuating his look of disappointment. "Don't you like it?"

"You know I do. It's beautiful."

"Then it's yours."

I shook my head slowly. "No, it wouldn't be right. If a girl accepts this kind of gift from a man, it means she's—" I stopped, not knowing what to say.

His fiancée? His mistress? It could mean either of those things, and neither was a word I could bring myself to speak.

Sadiq lifted the arm that wore the bracelet and kissed my fingertips and the palm of my hand through the glove. Then he leaned forward and kissed my trembling lips. He said softly, "I'd like to think you will be."

I continued to sit unmoving, unsure what he meant, unsure how to answer.

After a moment, Sadiq smiled philosophically, stood, and reached out to help me up. He said:

"Wear it at least for tonight, then? Maybe, if I'm lucky,

you'll get used to the idea."

I could not think of any way to refuse without being ungracious. So I smiled back and nodded.

I still did not know what the "idea" was. But I suspected it would be all too easy to get used to.

Sadiq did not drive recklessly, but he drove fast, and we were back in Monte Carlo within half an hour, pulling up before the hotel.

I had expected to go straight inside. But when Sadiq had handed over the car keys, he lounged at the curb, his hands in his pockets, his head tilted speculatively.

"Where to, now?" he said. "Régine's opened up a new place across the way. I expect we could get in."

He said it negligently, and I reflected that he was used to having doors opened to him without a reservation.

"A nightclub? If it's anything like her places in Paris, it'll be noisier and more crowded than the party we just left. I thought that was what you wanted to get away from."

Sadiq looked at me in mock reproof. "Well, we can't just go to bed. It's barely three o'clock. What about the Casino? Have you ever—no, of course not, you were only sixteen. Come on, I'll show you the tents of wickedness."

Allowing myself to be persuaded, I accompanied him across the street and up the broad stairs. I waited in the lobby while he went to the admission desk.

The tents of wickedness, he had said. That reminded me of Arabia, and of how I had speculated about Arabs and gambling the night I had dined with Jeff Hearn. Now I would see how those speculations applied to Sadiq.

At the admission desk I heard him patiently spelling his name in French. That answered part of my question right away, I thought. If Sadiq was not known at the Casino in Monte Carlo, he hardly ranked among the world-class gamblers.

He joined me, and as we entered a vast room, its gaming tables dwarfed by glittering chandeliers, huge mirrors, and frescoed ceiling, I reminded myself to give him a bright smile. He was at such pains to entertain me, to make up to me for blighting our festive mood. And the fault, if he had only known, was easily half mine. The least I could do was show him that I was enjoying myself.

The room into which we passed next was more crowded, but the murmur of voices was lower and more serious. In this private room, the stakes were higher. Sadiq paused at the door, surveying the scene, then steered me to a roulette table near the center.

He passed some large French banknotes to a croupier at the end of the table, who stuffed them into a slot and shoved back to Sadiq the counters he had requested.

"Here, have some toy money to play with," Sadiq said, nudging most of the chips along the table to rest in front of me.

I was about to protest, when I saw that the round red chips stacked before me were of a much smaller denomination than the few that Sadiq retained. Those were in fact not chips at all. They were solid rectangular plaques, as substantial as the sums they represented. Compared with them, my gay little red chips were indeed toy money. Sadiq had exercised a nice, tactful piece of judgment.

"Thanks," I said. "Prepare to watch a truly expert loser."

I had never gambled, but I had seen plenty of films with casino sequences, and I thought I could handle the part. It would be fun to play the role of a pampered darling of the sporting set. I dropped my evening bag and cape carelessly on a chair behind me, twitched off my gloves, and tossed them after with a controlled flourish.

Then I leaned over the table.

"*Messieurs, 'dames, faites vos jeux,*" intoned the croupier.

Pretending to consider my bets, I studied the table and watched the other players, trying to remember what I knew of the game. Tentatively I placed a chip on black, and another on high. Then, more daring, I put a pair on the third column. Anxiously I watched as the wheel spun and slowed.

For a moment it seemed that the little ivory ball would stop on double zero and all bets would lose. But then it dropped into the next slot, twenty-seven. My even-money bets had split, but the big one had come in. I had four more chips than I had started with.

I clapped my hands and glanced up at Sadiq with an impish grin. He was regarding me indulgently, the way I had often seen him look at Zora and Zafia, the way Jeff looked at Jenny. I moderated my grin and tried to assume a more mature expression.

On the next round I put two on the third column again, two on black and, in a burst of recklessness, two on the thirteen-to-eighteen block. All my bets converged on number fifteen. That had a good feel to it. As an afterthought I placed two chips on odd.

The croupier again set the wheel in motion. Just as he said, "*Rien ne va plus,*" Sadiq reached out beside me and casually dropped one of his plaques on number eight.

I had thought I was playing recklessly, but a single number was a thirty-eight-to-one shot, and the bet was not a small one. I looked at him in astonishment as a buzz ran around the table and the little ball clicked and fell silent.

When I looked back at the table, the losing bets were being raked away. Of mine, only the black had won. Then I finally saw what was causing the stir. On the wheel, the smooth white ball nestled in the number eight slot.

"Sadiq!" I gasped.

He motioned to the croupier to cash in our chips, then moved away from the table, away from the center of attention. I followed, matching his nonchalance with effort. I knew his bet had been a cavalier gesture and had won by the merest luck, but I was impressed in spite of myself.

"Sadiq," I whispered, "do you do this kind of thing often?"

"It all evens out in the long run." He smiled at me crookedly. "At least I've won back the cost of the bracelet you just tossed away."

I looked down at my bare wrist in horror. Then I looked at the chair where my gloves lay haphazardly on my cape. I must have sprung the clasp when I jerked the gloves off, completely forgetting the bracelet fastened on top.

"Oh no!" I moaned. "Sadiq, I—I—"

My eyes swept the floor around the chair frantically. I was about to drop to my knees and search the area when Sadiq touched my arm, bringing me back to face him reluctantly.

He continued to smile crookedly as he reached into his pocket, slowly withdrew the bracelet, and dangled it in front of me. I gazed at it in speechless fascination, as if it were a snake.

His voice was wry as he said, "Is it the gift you're so indifferent to, or the giver?"

I shook my head weakly, my mouth opening and closing without a sound. I was struck dumb with relief, and shame.

Sadiq reached toward my wrist to refasten the brace-

*239*

let, but I lifted a hand and forestalled him. When I could speak, I said shakily:

"No, Sadiq. I don't believe in omens, but—I think it would be better if you kept it."

His expression did not change as he stood with the bracelet dangling from his fingers. Finally he slipped it back into his pocket and said in a conversational tone:

"It's rather stuffy in here. Shall we get some air?"

"I'm afraid I'm not cut out to be a gambler."

My voice still did not sound quite natural to me, but Sadiq pretended not to notice as he took my arm and we descended the steps of the Casino.

"Neither am I," he said. "I've never understood its appeal. In almost every aspect of life, what you do can have a real, positive effect. It's senseless to waste time on something that's pure chance."

He guided me out of the path of a taxi and across the square.

"Are you tired?" he asked. "Or do you feel like walking for a while?"

"No, I'm not tired. But let's walk in that direction," I said, gesturing uphill. "I like to have gravity on my side on the way back."

We mounted the steep streets toward Beausoleil, turning at random along broad avenues and into darkened side streets. Occasionally a burst of merriment filtered down to us from an upper story, or a car full of revellers sped by. But we had the sidewalks to ourselves.

As we walked, climbing into Beausoleil until we were well over the French border, and then turning back toward the bright lights of Monte Carlo, we talked. Or, rather, Sadiq talked. I contented myself with interposing encouraging remarks and questions. And I found myself enjoying this part of the long evening that was stretching into morning more than I had the party on Cap Ferrat or the opulent casino.

Sadiq talked of Qaiman, of his hopes and aspirations and disappointments, of the progress that had been made and of the staggering task of education and development that remained. As I listened, I realized that I was learning a great deal, not only about Qaiman but about Sadiq Yamali. This was a contemplative side, profoundly analytic and broadly philosophical, which I had only glimpsed before. Sadiq was someone who saw clearly, and who cared deeply about what he saw.

"But too often," he was saying, "what we're trying to accomplish, for simple justice, runs straight across the grain of the Arab character. Take something as basic as the emancipation of women. We've made some strides, but if you saw what remains to be done, you'd throw up your hands in despair."

"Oh, I doubt it," I said lightly. "I'd be more apt to roll up my sleeves in determination."

Sadiq laughed. "I apologize. Of course you would. And I'll bet you'd make a scrappy fighter. That's something I'd very much like to see."

I basked in his approval, feeling the warm pressure of his hand on mine, as we strolled back along the Casino square. Once again we passed the entrance of the hotel, heading toward the overlook beside the Casino. Beyond the balustrade lay the harbor. The sinking moon spread a shimmering silver path across the water.

"It can be discouraging," Sadiq was saying now, "to see the public health problems we still have to conquer, and the substandard housing. But Qaiman can be very beautiful, too. Sometimes in the clear air of the desert night I stand on the roof of my house and look out across the Gulf, with the moon shining on the water the way it is now, and—"

*241*

At that moment I checked my strolling steps involuntarily. On the side of the Casino was a showcase window containing a jeweler's display, a few pieces of understated elegance in precious metals and stones. They reminded me of the bracelet in Sadiq's pocket, and my mood of contented well-being evaporated in a wave of regret. I was sure now that Sadiq had intended nothing improper. But I had had to reject the gift, and with it I had seemed to reject Sadiq as well. I could not expect him to renew the implicit offer.

Feeling my steps halt, he too came to a stop. He looked at me questioningly, and then his face creased in pain. He pulled me abruptly into his arms, cradling my head against his shoulder, kissing my hair, whispering urgently:

"Deirdre, I'm so terribly sorry. I simply didn't think. Oh Lord, of all the awful things to say—"

At first I did not understand what he was talking about, and then I did, and everything was suddenly soaringly right again.

I leaned back in the circle of his arms and smiled up at him. "It's all right, Sadiq. Truly," I said. "Come, I'll show you."

I slipped away from him and walked steadily to the balustrade of the overlook. As he came up behind me, I said:

"I'm not afraid of the sea anymore. The loss of Daddy and Conn still hurts, of course. It always will. But I can be rational about it now."

Sadiq lifted my hand from the balustrade and squeezed it encouragingly. As we stood hand in hand looking out over the moon-streaked Mediterranean, I thought that he could not possibly know how much I owed my new-found peace of mind to him.

When my father and brother had died, I had lost the

two men in the world whom I loved. And with them I had lost a part of my reason. But now in the space of a few short hours, the wound had closed and the healthy healing begun. It could not be a coincidence. For in those few hours I had made a discovery.

There was after all another man in the world I loved.

# 27

In my sitting room, Sadiq slipped the cape from my shoulders and draped it over a chair.

I wondered nervously what I should do next. The traditional thing would be to invite him in for a drink. But I had nothing to drink here. And besides, he was already in.

Sadiq solved the problem by saying, "It occurs to me we haven't had much to eat tonight. Are you hungry?"

"I'm starving," I admitted.

"Let's see what room service can do."

He crossed to a door in the side wall, unlocked it, and turned. "I'll be a few minutes. Why don't you get into something more comfortable?"

As he went through the door and closed it behind him, I caught a glimpse of a sitting room the twin of mine. Apparently Sadiq's suite and this one were communicating. I might have known.

Suddenly I was more amused than apprehensive. Even Sadiq's parting words, though he had uttered them unconsciously, had been predicable. They were a stock line in every risqué comedy.

Well, I decided, I could do one of two things. I could run screaming down the corridor. Or I could get into something more comfortable.

As I hung up my gown, I considered the few other items hanging in the closet. I could hardly put on a skirt and sweater for an intimate supper in the wee hours. I would look like a schoolgirl. Finally I pulled out the caftan I had brought to use as a dressing gown and wriggled into it headfirst. After all, it was every bit as modest as the dress I had just taken off. More, for it had sleeves. I stuck my feet into soft Moroccan leather slippers and sat down at the dressing table.

My face still looked fairly fresh, but the hairdo was getting a bit tired. I started to push it back into place. Then I changed my mind, ripped out the hairpins, and picked up my brush. Sadiq preferred my hair unbound, so I would wear it that way. I did not think he considered me a loose woman, and loose hair would not alter his opinion.

I was back in the sitting room in a comfortable chair when Sadiq reappeared. He still wore the black trousers with their satin stripes at the seams, but he had changed into a soft shirt and what I thought was called a smoking jacket. He was followed by a waiter, more formally clad even at this hour, wheeling a large cart.

The waiter departed, and Sadiq turned his attention to an ice bucket of impressive dimensions. In it reposed four tulip glasses, stems up, and an equal number of foil-wrapped bottle tops. Sadiq twirled one of the bottles in the ice, withdrew it, wrapped it in a napkin and worked off the cork with a satisfying pop.

*245*

"I ordered the champagne in splits," he said, "so it won't have a chance to get flat. And if there's any left, we can have it for breakfast."

"Breakfast?" I echoed. "I thought this was breakfast."

"My dear young lady," Sadiq said with elaborate patience, "this could not possibly be breakfast. Champagne, yes. Caviar, yes. But one never, never begins the day with cold lobster and mayonnaise. Cheers!"

I took the glass he handed me, touched it against his, and drank. The bubbles made my nose wrinkle, but the wine was light and crisp as only the best champagne can be. Sadiq handed me a wedge of toast liberally spread with caviar and prepared one for himself. Then, his mouth full, he motioned me to go ahead and help myself.

Before long the glasses were empty. Sadiq plunged them back into the ice, extracted the other pair, and filled them. By this time, we were eating the plump grains of pearly gray Molossol caviar with spoons. It was, I decided sagely, the only way.

Sadiq opened another split of champagne and we attacked the lobsters, rapidly reducing them to an untidy heap of shell. The bubbles of the champagne no longer bothered my nose. They seemed to rise straight up through my head and burst softly at the top. I took another sip and giggled.

"This all feels deliciously wicked," I said.

Sadiq nodded. "Like a private dining room at Maxim's at the turn of the century."

"It reminds me of a limerick. Daddy collected limericks," I confided, "and this was one of his favorites. I think it went:

> There was a young lady from Kent
> Who said that she knew what it meant
>     When men asked her to dine

And plied her with wine—
She knew what it meant, but she went."

Oh dear, I thought too late, I wonder what Sadiq will make of that. I hadn't meant it the way it sounded. At least I hoped I hadn't.

Sadiq laughed obediently, but he sounded half serious when he said, "But you're not from Kent."

"No," I agreed soberly. "I'm from New England. Home of the Puritans, you know."

"Just my luck," he said, peering into his glass sadly. "Oh well, it's nothing new. Things are even more strait-laced in Qaiman. I'm used to pretending that my intentions are honorable."

He looked up and smiled almost shyly. After a puzzled moment I realized that, for all his sophistication, he felt as awkward as I did.

Finally he stood and pulled me to my feet. Holding both my hands, he leaned forward and kissed me gently on the forehead.

"It's been a long evening. I think we could both use some sleep."

"So then what happened?" Maggie wanted to know.

"Then we went to bed."

Maggie raised her eyebrows.

"He went to his bed. And I went to mine," I said firmly. "And the next afternoon he flew me back here."

"Deirdre," Maggie said patiently, "I have the feeling you are leaving out considerable chunks of the story."

It was true. My recital to Maggie had not contained any actual falsehoods, or even any intentional misdirection, but in the telling I had left great gaps.

Maggie had been pestering me ever since she had seen Sadiq's latest floral offering, a compact bunch of sweet-

247

heart roses surrounded by baby's breath, on the corner of my desk. She saw it as a step forward. I knew it to be a considerable, and delicately considerate, step back, but I did not enlighten her.

The first night after her return from Cleveland I had turned aside her questions with a question of my own about Fred, which had its intended effect. The next two days I had pleaded the press of renewed work. But now, in the slack time before dinner on Wednesday, she had cornered me.

I felt rather guilty, after four months of exchanging girl-gossip, depriving Maggie of her fun. But my memories of the trip with Sadiq were something I wanted to treasure, to hug to myself. I had sidestepped Kate's restrained inquiries on my return, and now I was evading Maggie's more determined interrogation.

My protestations of candor sounded unconvincing, and I was relieved when a tap came on the door. Zora's neat, dark head peeped through.

"Come and see, Miss Sheridan! Oh, hello, Miss Cline. You come too."

Across the hall, we followed Zora and Zafia to their window. For the hundredth time, I noted the wrought-iron grille, and for the hundredth time forced myself to show no awareness of it.

"You see, Miss Sheridan? They've come right to the edge of the school grounds. I've never seen one come so close to people."

Thirty yards away in the lingering dusk, a pair of deer browsed quietly by the protected base of a tree. Two lines of delicate tracks showed where they had walked unimpeded over the snow-drifted hedges.

"We had a lot of snow while you were away," I said. "The deer can't find enough food higher up, so they've had to be brave and come down to the valley."

As we watched, the deer suddenly lifted their heads and froze. Then they wheeled in unison and bolted with great bounding strides into the deepening shadows.

Zafia turned from the window and went back to her bed, where Milord lay curled in a relaxed doze. But Zora continued to stare out into the darkness. She looked, I thought, like a deer herself—soft-eyed, timid, and exquisitely graceful. And she looked very sad.

She was missing Cappy, I knew, and she was almost alone in doing so. The rest of the school community, on hearing that one of the cats had gotten into something poisonous and died, had expressed distress and promptly forgotten about it. They had a whole vacation to discuss.

There was another absence, too, which was of no interest to the school community, but it was of great interest to me. I had learned of it the morning school recommenced, when Jenny hailed me on the way to the first class.

"How are things at Chalet Hearn?" I asked.

"I've been managing all right, but now that school's started again, I don't know what Daddy's going to do."

"What?" I said blankly.

"Oh, I forgot. You didn't know, did you? Abdullah's gone."

"Gone? Where? When?" My surprise had reduced me to monosyllables.

"About three days ago. I don't know where. He just disappeared. Back to Arabia, I guess. Daddy's absolutely furious."

We had parted then to go to our respective classes, so I could not question Jenny further. I doubted, anyway, that she knew more. But there was clearly more to be known. If Abdullah was really gone, what did it mean? Had he become discouraged, or perhaps frightened?

249

Had he, or whoever was working with him, decided that the risk was too great? In any case, I must tell Sadiq immediately.

But no, I reminded myself, even this would not give me an excuse to telephone Sadiq. There were well-established channels now for me to go through.

For the absconding of Abdullah had not diminished the population of Gstaad. There was an addition, too, in the comforting presence of Haroun's de facto bodyguard and chief of security, Bernard Favre.

This Bernard Favre now seemed to be permanently in Sadiq's pay, or the sheik's. Since Sadiq had first hired him as "copilot" for the flight to Qaiman, he had remained with the children, accompanying them on the return flight to Cointrin and convoying them to Gstaad. Now he was ensconced at the school.

I did not know what Sadiq had said to Sidney Payne to induce him to accept Bernard. But it had been effective. Dr. Payne had passed off the addition of Bernard to the school staff with the greatest air of plausibility. And it was quite true that Ruedy was now busy enough with the racing team and his other ski classes to need help with his more routine duties. But it was also true that Bernard, although he occasionally drove a school bus or performed some physical labor, was usually to be seen wherever Haroun was. He had even been given a room by the foot of the stairs in Haroun's dormitory.

I was thinking of the two of them, and now I saw them as I came into the office to drop off some papers before dinner. Haroun was just picking up a heavy manila envelope.

"More homework," he said, waving the envelope at me cheerfully. "As if you slavedrivers didn't pile enough on, my father has to make things worse."

"Is this a new development?"

"No, it's been going on all year. He sends up a packet once a week with the minutes of the cabinet meeting and the economic reports and all that stuff. God, you should have seen it at annual budget time!"

"I can imagine. That envelope you have there looks pretty staggering."

"Oh, I'm getting better at it, learning how to skim for the important parts. This lot's fairly standard. Usually I just glance through them when they come in, then I sit down and go through them on Friday nights."

"Not this week, though, I hope," I said. "That's when the ski party is."

Haroun nodded. "I'll have to find some other time. I could do with a couple of forty-hour days." He turned to Bernard and nudged him, switching to French. "What do you say, Favre? I'll read the reports, and you write the essay for Miss Sheridan on 'Social Conscience in the Works of Hemingway and Steinbeck'."

Bernard grinned. "Not a chance. I'll do your physics homework, if you like. But literature is something I can't handle."

As the two of them walked away, I reflected that literature was probably one of the few things Bernard could not handle. Compact and muscular, he gave an impression of physical and mental competence. Certainly Haroun not only liked but trusted him.

With Bernard here, I thought, we would all be more confident and safer.

As it turned out, I was only half wrong.

# 28

I WAS getting uncomfortably full, but at the larger table the students were still attacking the row of fondue crocks with adolescent gusto. Sixteen long forks speared chunks of crusty French bread, plunged them into the bubbling cheese mixture, and waved them to cool before popping them into sixteen eager mouths. At the restaurant on top of the Eggli, the Senior Class Fondue and Ski Party was in full swing.

Jenny Hearn worked her fork into a cube of bread, dipped into the pot and pulled out the fork, empty, with a convincing little cry of dismay. Beside her, Peter Duncan claimed his forfeit of a kiss. Jenny acceded with pretty grace. That girl, I thought, is not only a born actress but an instinctive flirt.

I laid down my fork and pushed my plate slightly away. Across from me, Ruedy leaned back and lit a cigarette.

No one at our table, the "adult" table, had any more interest in eating.

There were six of us. Ruedy, of course, and his two ski instructor colleagues who had been engaged for the evening. And Bernard and Sadiq and me. Bernard was there in his ostensible position as Ruedy's assistant. I was there as senior class advisor, a largely ceremonial post, since Adam Ngomutu as class president needed less than no advising. And Sadiq was there for reasons of his own. I did not know how he had sold his presence to Dr. Payne —probably as smoothly as he had accomplished the hiring of Bernard—but I knew what his reasons were. He was determined that Haroun would not move an inch without the surveillance of Bernard or himself, and preferably both.

He had paid only a minimum of attention to me tonight, but I thought I understood that, too. His pressing business was with Bernard. So I did my best to entertain Ruedy and his two fellows, keeping up a cloud of chatter under which Sadiq and Bernard could talk unheard.

After the fondue was cleared away, the students persuaded the proprietor to turn on some music. They shoved back the tables, kicked off their ski boots, and danced in their stocking feet. I took a few snapshots of them with Kate's Minox. Then I sat back to watch, marveling that they could dance now, on full stomachs and in full ski gear. Just watching them made me tired. Somewhere between their age and my present exalted twenty-three, I had lost that limitless supply of youthful energy.

Finally we were ready for the high point of the evening, the descent on skis by torchlight.

"Okay, does everybody know his position?" Ruedy asked. "Now remember, just take it slow and steady. Watch the line of the person ahead of you, and don't let gaps open. If you have trouble, call ahead and we'll stop. Everything's going to look different than it does in daylight."

We assembled at the departure point, with the torchbearers occupying every third place in line. There were eight altogether, the five men and a trio of boys chosen by Ruedy as steady enough. Haroun had wanted to be among them, but Sadiq had vetoed that. Haroun and I would follow him, with Bernard bringing up the rear.

The leading instructor shoved off, followed by a student and another and then the next torchbearer. As they began to snake down the mountainside, I wondered whether I could catch the play of light on the snow with the Minox. I would just have time for a quick shot or two.

I reached behind me and exclaimed in annoyance.

"Darn it, I've left my waist pack in the restaurant," I told Sadiq. "I'll only be a minute. Don't wait for me. Stay with Haroun. I'll catch up."

I slid out of line, kicked off my skis and dashed back to the restaurant.

The pouch was not where I had been sitting, and I hunted fruitlessly for a few seconds. I had almost decided to give up when I spotted it on a serving table. I snatched it up, belting it around me as I ran outside.

It had taken longer than I estimated. The last torchbearer, Bernard, was already far below, halfway to the great bend in the trail that would take him out of sight.

I jammed my boots into my skis and grabbed my poles, not bothering with the loops. Glancing at the moon, I plunged downhill.

This part would be all right. The floodlights of the cablecar station cast light as far as the bend. But after that I would have to have Bernard well in sight, for I would be dependent on his torch. I could not rely on the moon. It was strong enough, only a few days past the full, but it was now intermittently obscured by patchy clouds. If I fell behind, I might be hours picking my way down the mountain. If I did not freeze to death first.

I was skiing now as fast as I had ever skied by daylight, and by the time I reached the bend, I thought I had made up a good deal of distance on Bernard. I took the turn high and tight, to give myself the widest field of vision, and skidded to a stop in the lee of the trees. I needed to get my bearings, and my breath.

There, I saw with relief, was Bernard's torch, advancing at a sedate pace not more than a hundred yards ahead. I wormed my hands through the loops of my poles and went forward again, not so fast now, but still gaining steadily. I would overtake Bernard in a minute or two.

I kept to a high line, working just at the edge of the shadows of the trees, guarding against a sudden, unremembered turn. The gap closed to seventy yards, then fifty. Beyond Bernard I could now see other skiers and two more torches. Adam, that would be, and Sadiq.

As I drew closer, I could go a little faster, for the light was better. But I still had to pay close attention to the terrain. The moon and the distant torchlight cast weird shadows. There remained some distance to cover, under unfamiliar conditions, and on my own.

And then suddenly I was not alone. Below me a figure detached itself from the shadows and slid toward Bernard, silhouetted in the halo of his torch.

At first I was surprised, and then increasingly uneasy. For I knew that figure. Even from the back and in this uncertain light, there could be no mistaking his style of skiing.

I slowed instinctively and drew back into the shadows. I knew that no one was expected to be here, to witness what happened next.

It happened with chilling rapidity. The figure swooped down beside Bernard and delivered a vicious backhand blow to the head. Bernard fell heavily on his side, skidding into an inert tangle of limbs wrapped around a hummock even before his torch, looping through the silent black air, buried itself with a hiss in the snow.

Then the figure, with one brief backward glance, dove on down the hill. Haroun was caught turning, warned perhaps by the sudden change of light, but the blow, though off center, was effective. Haroun dropped as silently as Bernard had.

A second figure emerged from the trees and dragged Haroun into the shadows while the first followed with his skis. The two of them struggled to load him onto a low, bulky object. I knew what it was, for I had ridden on one only a month ago. But then it had been in the hands of the rescue patrol.

I watched motionless as Haroun was strapped onto the luge and pushed through a gap in the trees. I had to do something, I told myself frantically. But what? I could not go after them alone. That would just mean two victims. And I could not go back. The slope I had descended in scant minutes would take ten, twenty times as long to climb.

There was only one way I could go. Down, to Sadiq.

The cold night air knifed at my lungs as I fought for speed. Sadiq was now as far ahead as Bernard had been, and every second was crucial, increasing the lead of Haroun's abductors, increasing the danger that the faint moon would cease giving me its light altogether.

I abandoned every thought of prudence and took the straightest line possible, driving over obstacles and irregularities on sheer instinct. My mind was far ahead, and my legs would have to carry me there by themselves.

Already my knees were throbbing from the repeated shocks.

When I thought I was close enough, I forced my flayed lungs to take in more air and screamed, "Sadiq!"

If he had not heard me, I do not think I could have screamed again. But he stopped, and turned with a welcoming smile. Then, as he looked above me and saw the dark, empty mountainside, his expression sharpened in alarm.

I slid to a stop beside him, trembling and fighting for breath. Somehow I managed to speak.

"They've got Haroun," I gasped. "They came up behind Bernard and knocked him out. He's lying up there. Then they hit Haroun and put him on a luge and dragged him off through the trees. Jeff and—I think Abdullah." I choked and gulped air. "They don't know I saw them."

Sadiq mastered his shock rapidly. He asked a couple of short, sharp questions, then his face set. "All right," he said, reaching the same conclusion I had, "the quickest way up is down. Come on."

I struggled to keep pace with him as he overtook one skier after another, passing the undulating line as if it were standing still. As he approached the third torch, he called "Messerli!" and checked his speed to match Ruedy's.

"Haroun and Bernard are in trouble," he said, low and urgent. "I want you to take us down this hill as fast as you know how."

Ruedy did not ask any questions. He just nodded with stolid Swiss imperturbability. Then he shot forward, leaving us in his wake.

At the head of the line, Ruedy held up his hand to stop the leader. His voice was steady and emotionless as he told the instructor:

257

"Bernard and Haroun need help. We're going ahead. You'll have to reorder the line. When you get them down, take them back to the school. Here are the keys to the bus."

Then he turned to us and said: "Let's go."

Of that headlong descent I do not have a complete memory, only a confused set of impressions—

Pain, lancing through my left ankle, throbbing in my knees, tearing at my lungs.

Speed, far greater than anything I would ever have attempted in daylight.

And, strangely enough, security. Ruedy was ahead of me and Sadiq behind, their torches bright and reassuring. Now there was someone else to do the planning and acting. It almost felt as if someone else were skiing for me.

Ruedy was an expert's expert. He led us with a sureness that allowed us to match his pace, telegraphing his moves and choosing his line far in advance. Almost before we had begun, it seemed, we were sliding into the runoff and across the bridge.

We kicked off our skis and chunked them into the snowbank as Sadiq told Ruedy what had happened. He continued:

"I'll call from the Arc-en-Ciel and get the police moving. Then you—here, Deirdre, get my car and bring it around to the door of the hotel." He held out a bunch of keys and turned back to Ruedy. "Then you arrange help for Bernard, and try to get a flare planted where it happened. That'll give us a bearing when we. . . ."

As I ran to the parking lot, Sadiq and Ruedy moved toward the hotel, and I caught only snatches of their conversation.

". . . roadblocks on all three . . ."

". . . Bern for reinforcements by helicopter . . ."

". . . too long. We'll have to start the . . . set up a communications center and keep lines open to . . . radio frequency with . . ."

The door of the hotel banged behind them as I found the car and slid inside. I left the door ajar for light, flipping through the keys to find the one for the ignition. Then I surveyed the dashboard. Yes, here were the head-lights, high beam, low. The handbrake was beside me. The seat adjustment must be—no, Sadiq would want it where he had left it. I edged forward in the seat and reached for the pedals. Accelerator, brake, clutch. They were uncomfortably close together. Even the advanced Citroën CX-2200 had not been designed for driving in ski boots.

I slipped the key into the ignition, started the motor, and experienced a moment of total panic as the car heaved under me. I had broken it!

No, it was all right. It was only the hydropneumatic suspension system pumping itself up.

Get a grip on yourself, Deirdre! I told myself. If you can't even start a car without going to pieces, what earthly good will you be to Sadiq? He needs every clear head and steady hand he can find. God knows what can be done, but hysteria won't help.

I eased the stick shift into gear and brought the car out of the parking lot. In front of the hotel I double-parked, leaving the motor running and the driver's door open, and slid over the console into the passenger seat.

In less than a minute Sadiq slammed himself into the car, jerked it into gear, and sped off. I did not ask any questions. I could not have heard the answers.

Finally I shouted, "Where?"

"Airport," he said.

We screamed into another tight turn. Sadiq was driv-

259

ing with total disregard for traffic regulations and common sense. On the straight stretch between Gstaad and Saanen I simply held on and prayed. And then we were through the village and slewing into the entrance to the airfield.

By the time I had climbed aboard the plane, both engines were coughing into life. Sadiq revved them, then dropped back to idle and, waving to me to stay there, ducked out and ran back toward the airport office.

Another car was just pulling in, and soon the office lights blazed on. Sadiq was inside for perhaps a minute. When he emerged, he held something in his hand. Running toward the plane, he looked up at the windsock and shook his head.

I could see what was bothering him. The wind was strong now and gusty, and it was blowing straight across the runway. It would not be an easy takeoff.

Sadiq came headfirst into the cockpit and dumped his burden in my lap. As he belted himself in, flicked on lights, and began checking gauges, he said:

"Aerial flares. They only had three, but it's better than nothing. When it's time to drop one, hand it—there's a map light under your control wheel, here—hand it to me with this end forward, and I'll drop it through the bad-weather window. Okay?"

I nodded, looking past Sadiq to the little round porthole in the left-hand window of the cockpit.

Then we were surging forward and taxiing to the end of the runway. As we turned and began the takeoff, Sadiq spoke. I had to strain to hear him above the engines.

"Of course the wind would have to be dead foul. No help at all either way. We might as well take off to the west, so by the time we bank and get back to the Eggli, we'll be at altitude. Damn it, it wouldn't have hurt them to add a few feet to this thing!"

*260*

We lifted, the landing-gear lights raking the end of the runway, then the roofs of chalets, and the tops of trees. Sadiq had been talking, I realized, for sheer relief of tension. This was a lot of airplane, and it was not a lot of runway. We had barely cleared the end.

We continued to climb over the highway to the westward for half a minute. Then Sadiq banked sharply and we passed over Saanen, rising along the flanks of the Eggli.

"I've left the landing gear down," he said. "It reduces the stall speed anyway. So we'll be able to use the landing lights to track them once we pick up the trail. Can you tell where they went into the woods?"

"It should be off the starboard wing in about—five seconds. Yes! There's the flare!"

God bless Ruedy, I thought fervently. He could not have wasted a second getting back up the mountain and down to where Bernard lay. The sputtering red light of an automobile emergency flare was planted right in the middle of the *piste.*

Sadiq peeled off to the left. "I'll circle around Kalberhöni and come back over the station. Get ready to pass me one of those things and tell me when."

I released my safety belt and, balancing against the tight turn, worked myself up and back until I was standing almost upright in the narrow aisle, my arms braced against the backs of the two seats, my head brushing the ceiling of the cockpit.

"What are you doing? Sit down!"

"No. I can see better from here. Steer ten degrees to the right. Here's the flare. Bank left. Now!"

Sadiq turned as tightly as possible, but it was still agonizing seconds until we had come around and brought the area back in view. A circle hundreds of yards wide was bathed in a ghostly glow. This flare was not like

261

Ruedy's little red marker. It was a great, bright, hanging ball of light.

I strained to see in the direction Jeff and Abdullah had dragged the luge. They had to have gone to the right of the *piste*, and they had to have gone roughly downhill. But here the trees were thick, and I could pick out nothing on the first pass. By the time we came around again, the light of the flare was fading.

Just as we passed out of the lighted area, I thought I saw a slash across the snow in the space between two stands of trees. I could not be sure, but it might be the track of the luge. It would be a couple of feet wide, easily visible from our altitude.

"See something?"

"I think so. Can you drop another flare—" I squinted over Sadiq's shoulder at the compass "—about three hundred yards east-southeast of the first one?"

Sadiq put the plane into another turn, dropped the flare where I indicated, and circled to come back over the area. He was using an airplane at perhaps a hundred miles an hour to execute maneuvers that called for a helicopter, and he was doing it with grim efficiency and precision.

As we approached the ball of light, I craned to see the patches of white between the trees rushing far beneath us. Sadiq had all he could do to keep us aloft and on course. I would have to pick up the track myself. But I had only seconds to do so with every pass.

"There! Fifteen degrees to the left. And beyond too, I think."

"Okay. I'll bring us around lower this time. The nose wheel light is steerable. Maybe it'll help. You direct me."

This time I was able to pick up a bit more of the trail, and form a clearer idea of the direction Jeff and Abdullah were taking.

As Sadiq circled again, gaining altitude, he reached for the radio and gave our bearing.

"Do you think the police can intercept them from below?" I asked anxiously.

"No," Sadiq said. His voice was heavy. "There are only a handful in the area. They'll have trouble setting up proper roadblocks, let alone surrounding a mountain. We have to find Haroun before—" He shoved his cuff back and looked at his watch. "We may be too late already. Even with the weight of the luge, they could be down by now."

"We still have a flare," I said. "If we hang it in the direction they were taking, but a lot further down, maybe—"

"Maybe," Sadiq said.

It was pure guesswork, but we both tried to sound confident as we came around and chose the spot to drop the last flare. If we lost the trail now, Jeff and Abdullah would have Haroun off the mountain and away long before the authorities could move.

And they would be desperate. The flares would have told them they were already hunted. Desperate kidnappers usually killed their victims.

Sadiq was silent now, but I could see the tension in his hands on the control wheel. My own hands were numb from fright, and from cold. I had removed my gloves to handle the flares. Despite the heater, the draft from the open bad-weather window made the cockpit icy.

This time Sadiq skirted the area illuminated by the flare, banking slightly to give me the maximum field of vision. It would take luck to pick up the trail now. The open spaces between the trees had become fewer and smaller.

Then I cried out in relief and triumph. "There!"

Sadiq had chosen his course faultlessly. The swath of

the luge lay revealed below, just off the starboard wing. It cut into a stand of trees, out again and into another. Beyond the lower trees, almost at the valley floor, was a broad white expanse of snow. But I could see no track across it.

"Can you come around the same way?" I said. "I think they're still in the trees."

Sadiq pulled up and into another dizzying turn. "Could you tell where they were heading?"

"I'm not sure. It looked like there was something at the edge of the light from the flare, a bit below the trees. Maybe a barn. If we can get the lights on it—" Again I picked up the trail disappearing into the trees. "Turn a little more to the right. Yes, there's the barn, see? And there's something below it. A car. Jeff's car!"

This time Sadiq did not pull up into a turn immediately. He shot on over the river and the highway, banking and climbing over the flanks of the Wispile. Then he said, "Hang on!" and stood the plane almost on its wingtip.

"They're not going to get to that car," he said grimly. "Because we're going to get to it first."

# 29

SADIQ leveled the plane parallel to the river and cut back on the throttle.

"Sit down," he said. "I'm going to belly her in. It'll be rough."

I edged into my seat, watching in fascinated horror as the snow tilted closer. In the lights of the landing gear I could see, not far ahead, the barn and the car. And just emerging from the trees above, two figures and a heavy sledge.

Sadiq had left the landing gear down until the last possible moment. But then it retracted, and with it the lights, and suddenly we were dropping into pitch blackness.

I had not had time to fasten my seatbelt, and I gripped the edges of the seat, bracing for the impact. But it was lighter than I expected. We settled onto the cushion of snow, slowing and sinking like a water-skier releasing the towrope.

Then something caught under the plane and whipped us counterclockwise, skidding us to a jolting stop, starboard wing foremost. I crashed heavily forward, my right shoulder hitting the circuit breakers, the right side of my face slamming against the panel eyebrow. The control wheel caught me in the chest and forced the breath from me.

Sadiq had snapped off the panel lights and left the cockpit before I could regain my seat. He was back in seconds.

"Here," he said, dropping something heavy into my lap. "There's an empty chamber under the hammer. You have to pull the trigger twice. Don't be afraid to use it."

Then he was in the cabin again, struggling with the door. He put his shoulder against it and heaved to push aside the piled-up snow. It gave six inches, a foot, and he was gone.

Turning back to the windshield, I watched him struggle through the unbroken snow toward the barn and the car below. In his hand he held an object that reminded me of its twin in my lap.

I lifted it and examined it in the light that came from the wingtip. It looked strangely unreal, like a child's toy from a game of cowboys and Indians.

Everything seemed unreal. I must still be dizzy from the blow on the head when we landed, I thought. My mind was filled with a jumble of half-remembered impressions. Hollywood Arabs riding across the desert brandishing rifles. King Hussein of Jordan, photographed unawares on a visit to a Western capital, with a handgun tucked into his waistband. Sadiq, at dinner in Weissenbach that long-ago, happier night, saying, "I don't particularly like guns."

But this gun was real, and so was the one Sadiq carried.

I looked up and saw that he had gained the shelter of the car, crouching behind it and peering uphill. I turned, but the plane had slewed too far on landing, and I could see nothing in the direction of the trees.

Perhaps from the cabin, I thought. But even through the parted curtains of the cabin windows, the angle was wrong. And I had to see, I had to know.

I slid through the open door and into the snow, wallowing through the track Sadiq had made, around the half-buried wing and up to the nose. I wormed forward, keeping the gun clear of the snow, almost surprised that it was still in my hand.

Now I could see. But it took me a while to register what I saw.

The light was unearthly. The moon was now veiled by cloud, and the only illumination was the mingled green and red glow from the strobe lights on the wingtips and tail. The wind-whipped snow rose and hung like colored confetti.

Descending from the stand of trees were three figures. Haroun, now released from the luge, floundered in the deep snow. The two others flanked him closely. Jeff was still on skis. He must have come down the mountain that way, steering the luge. Abdullah appeared to be wearing snowshoes.

They were halfway to the barn now, within hailing range. Their voices carried clearly downwind to me.

"Get away from the car, Yamali," Jeff shouted.

"You'll never make it out of the valley," Sadiq called back. "There are roadblocks on all three highways."

"I'll take my chances. Get away from that car, or you won't ever see the boy alive again."

"Listen to me, Hearn!" Sadiq's voice was strong and

urgent. "Make it easy on yourself. Let Haroun go. You can't escape."

"Who's going to stop me? You?"

"You're surrounded. Let him go."

"You're bluffing. You're alone, and I know it. Now come out from behind that car with your hands up, and stand clear. I'll count to ten. One!"

As Jeff counted, I tried feverishly to think. Sadiq was bluffing, and Jeff knew it. But he was wrong when he said Sadiq was alone. If I made enough noise here at the plane, maybe—

"Three!"

Jeff had to be convinced he was surrounded. Then he would let Haroun go.

"Four!"

I could let him know there were two of us. Now if only he thought the barn was covered—

I looked at the gun in my hand. No, I had better hang onto that. I shifted it to my other hand and wrenched at the pack belted around my waist. With numb fingers I dragged the zipper open.

"Seven!"

My hand closed around the Minox as I levered myself up. The camera was small but solid. If I threw it as hard as I could, it might work.

Nobody was looking in my direction. I drew back my arm and aimed at the barn. Pain tore through my shoulder, and I realized in an instant of surprise that it had been hurting for some time. Then I forgot it and heaved, just as Jeff shouted:

"Nine!"

The crack of the Minox against the side of the barn was not as loud as I had hoped, but it was loud enough. Jeff and Abdullah whirled to face it, crouching.

Seeing his chance, Haroun broke for the protection of

268

the plane. But Jeff, on skis, was quicker. Within a few yards, he brought Haroun down with a lunging sideways tackle. He kicked off his skis and, still holding Haroun, struggled to his feet.

Abdullah called to him sharply in Arabic.

"No," Jeff said, and more Arabic I couldn't understand.

Then Abdullah really screamed at him, an outpouring of venomous invective. He sounded crazed.

Jeff released Haroun and started back toward Abdullah, trying to argue with him. But Abdullah's voice rode over Jeff's as he raised his hand and fired.

Jeff fell, tried to rise, then dropped back onto the snow.

Haroun was closer to the plane now, but there was no one between him and Abdullah, and the hand was rising again, extending and taking steady aim.

I did not stop to think. I just swung the gun in Abdullah's direction and pulled the trigger, once, twice.

I had not expected to hit him. I only wanted to distract his attention from Haroun. And I accomplished that, almost too well. A bullet whined past my ear and another struck the nose of the plane before I could duck behind it.

But those were not the only bullets fired. From below I heard two sharp cracks, then another, followed by a short, rising scream.

Ten seconds passed with no more shots. I raised my head cautiously and looked out over the nose. Sadiq had reached Abdullah. He rolled him over, nodded in grim satisfaction, and started toward Haroun.

I came around the nose of the plane and waited while they approached me. My right shoulder was hurting more now, and the arm hung straight down, still holding the gun. Sadiq reached out to take it from me, but it

*269*

slipped from my numb fingers and dropped to the snow.

"Are they—"

"Abdullah's dead," Sadiq said wearily. "I don't know about Hearn."

I nodded dully and began to trudge through the snow to where Jeff lay. All of me felt as numb as my frozen hands. Poor Jenny! I thought. She loved her father so fiercely. It was bad enough to lose an adored father, I knew. But to lose him this way. . . .

The wind was full in my face, but my cheeks were hot with tears as I knelt beside Jeff and touched his forehead. It was cold, as cold as my hand. But then his eyes flickered open.

Behind me I heard Sadiq say, "Haroun, get back to the plane and radio for an ambulance."

Jeff was speaking now too. I had to lean close to hear his words above the shriek of the wind. There was blood at the corners of his mouth.

"I swear I didn't . . . I thought they only wanted me to . . . and then I'd be free of them . . . but then . . . everything all wrong . . . so sorry . . . tell Jenny . . ."

He coughed weakly, spitting more blood.

"I'll tell Jenny," I said gently, trying to keep my voice from breaking. "I'll tell her how much you love her, and how brave you were. I'll tell her how you saved Haroun's life."

Jeff blinked, and tried to smile. Then his eyes closed again, finally, and his head rolled sideways on the cushion of blood-streaked snow.

I rose unsteadily, swaying in the buffeting of the wind. Sadiq's arm came around my waist.

"He knew," Sadiq said heavily. "He must have known. He wasn't that stupid."

"Oh, darling, does it matter now? He's dead."

*270*

"I suppose not." He turned me slowly but firmly away from Jeff. "Now I'm taking you back to the plane. You look like you're about to—"

And that was the last I remember.

 *30*

WHEN I woke up, the first thing I noticed was the smell.
It was a strange mixture. Antiseptic? Yes, and something
sweeter too. Roses.

I opened my eyes a slit, and then closed them quickly.
The light was too bright. I would have to work up to it
gradually.

I lay still, trying to get my bearings. Even my body
seemed foreign territory, to be explored.

I began with my feet, wiggling them under the bedclothes. They seemed all right, though the left ankle hurt
a bit. So did the knees. I continued the inventory upward.
As far as the waist, everything was relatively normal. But
then the trouble began.

Above the waist, every inch of me seemed to be
swathed or wrapped or bandaged or taped. My chest was
tightly bound, and the upper part of my right arm with
it. My head too was bound. Though my eyes and nose

and mouth were uncovered, I felt like an Egyptian mummy. And my left arm was strapped flat and immobile.

I opened my eyes again, carefully. It was not as bright as I had thought at first. Actually, the blinds were almost shut. And the walls were a dull pastel, of the sort hospital designers consider restful, and which I have always considered depressing.

So I was in a hospital. Under the circumstances, it seemed like a good idea.

Beside me I heard a voice. It sounded faint, but when I turned my eyes to follow it, Kate's face was only a foot from mine.

"Don't try to talk," she said. "You're not supposed to talk. Just lie back and rest. I'll bring my chair over."

She moved away, and I closed my eyes again. Then I opened them to continue my exploration. This bed, for instance. It was propped up at a slight angle. And the arm, the left arm that was so firmly anchored. That was laid out across a table beside the bed, with tubes taped into the crook of the elbow. My eyes followed the tubes upward to the bottles ranged one beside another, inverted and impersonal. Plasma, I supposed, and glucose and whatever they gave people who had whatever I had.

Kate pulled a chair beside the bed and sat down. "Now I expect you want to know what's wrong with you?"

I nodded. The slight movement made me dizzy.

"I must say, Deirdre, I'm impressed by your thoroughness. Here it is only three weeks since you got off those crutches, and already you've added pages to your medical history." Kate gave an exaggerated sigh. "First, there was the frostbite. But that wasn't serious, and it's cleared up now. The concussion—'cerebral commotion', they called it—was a bit more severe. You also managed to acquire three cracked ribs, a dislocated shoulder, and several loose teeth. And a broken cheekbone."

She held up her hand quickly. "Now, don't worry about that! Everything's all back in place. Paul came up from Lausanne and did it himself. You'll be just as pretty as ever. You just won't be able to talk for a while."

I nodded again, more carefully this time.

Kate smiled sympathetically. "I know, it's a dreadful thing for a woman to be told she can't talk. But I've worked out something so you won't be completely helpless." She cranked the bed to a slightly higher angle, then brought an object and settled it on the bed across my hips. "A reading stand, and a pad and pencil. So at least you can write."

I moved my right hand tentatively. The upper part of the arm was strapped to my chest, but below the elbow it was free. I picked up the pencil and scrawled, *What day is . . .*

Then my eyes saw what was on my wrist and the pencil slipped from my fingers.

Kate turned to see what I had written. "It's Sunday," she said. "Four o'clock on Sunday afternoon."

She looked back at my face and finally saw where my eyes were staring. Her smile was broader now.

"Oh yes," she said. "Your Mr. Yamali was most particular about that. He said you should be wearing it when you woke up. He said you'd know what it meant."

I stared for a moment longer at the bracelet, turning my wrist so that the muted light was reflected by the spun silver and tiny diamonds. Then I closed my eyes.

I wanted to be alone with my thoughts. I would let Kate think I was asleep.

And before long I was.


The next day they began letting me have other visitors, for short periods. My room took on the look of a hor-

274

ticultural exhibit. Everyone knew that candy and fruit would do me no good, so they all brought flowers.

Except Maggie. She brought me a book, bless her. And she brought an even more welcome surprise.

"I talked my way around the regulations," she told me. "They're not supposed to let children in, but these two wouldn't believe you were all right until they saw for themselves."

Zora and Zafia tiptoed to the end of the bed and peered at me doubtfully. I took my pencil and wrote:

*Hello, darlings. I'm all right, really. I feel a lot better than I look. I just can't talk for a while. But I can listen. So tell me everything you've been doing.*

Maggie lifted them onto the end of the bed and they perched there gingerly. They told me how lonely they were at the school. Everyone missed me. And Haroun and Sadiq had gone off to Qaiman. Even Jenny was gone. Her grandparents had flown in from Texas, and they had all gone back there together for the funeral.

That surprised me for a moment. I had thought of Jenny as being alone in the world. But then I realized her grandparents would only now be nearing retirement age. I had become so accustomed lately to people losing their parents unnaturally young—Jenny, these little Qaimani girls, myself—that I had almost forgotten what a normal life span was.

The girls chatted for a few minutes more, and then Maggie lifted them off the bed and shooed them out. She pulled up a chair beside me.

"Don't worry about your classes," she said. "Just concentrate on getting well. I called an old schoolmate of mine in Germany—her husband's in the army there— and she agreed to come down and fill in until you're better. She's even moved into your room. I hope you don't mind?"

275

I shook my head.

"Actually, it's kind of nice to see her again. But I'd rather have you there." Maggie grinned mischievously. "I was looking forward to planning our weddings together."

I lowered my eyes.

Maggie laughed merrily. "Oh, Deirdre, don't look so innocent! Of course he's going to marry you. He'd better, after all you've done for him. You practically broke your neck saving him and that cocky young nephew of his."

I sighed, and wrote, *Cut it out, Maggie.*

She got up and dropped a kiss on my forehead. "Okay, clam. I'm going. But remember, I expect to be a bridesmaid, if I have to go all the way to Qaiman to do it." She tilted her head reflectively. "I doubt that I'll be matron of honor. Unless I miss my guess, you'll beat me to the altar—or whatever it is they have."

Ruedy came in the evening, looking freshly scrubbed and uncomfortable. Kate took the flowers he brought and found another vase for them while I scribbled, *They're lovely. Thank you, Ruedy. Thank you for everything.*

He did not have much to say, being Ruedy, and I could not talk at all, so the burden fell on Kate. After a few minutes he waved awkwardly and left.

Dear, dependable Ruedy, I thought. As soon as I was able, I would have to have a talk with him.

I remembered him telling me of his dream of developing his mountain, and joking that he would marry me for my money. In fact, he did not know that I had that much money. And I did not plan to give it to him as a dowry.

But I thought that it might be rather fun to invest in a mountain.

\* \* \*

276

By the next morning I was looking a little less pitiable. The intravenous apparatus had been dismantled, and I was now taking liquids through a glass straw.

Kate had brought one of my own nightgowns, and she had brought me a frilly nylon cap, the kind that is worn over hair curlers. She pulled it over my bandaged head and handed me a mirror.

I studied my reflection critically, then dropped the mirror and picked up my pencil. *I look,* I wrote, *like the wolf playing Little Red Riding Hood's grandmother. But it's an improvement. I used to look like I'd just undergone a lobotomy.*

Kate roared with laughter. "Deirdre, I do believe you are showing signs of recovery."

She moved about the room, rearranging flowers, adjusting the blinds, straightening my bedclothes.

I reached for the pencil again. *What is all this about? Are we expecting a Royal Presence?*

She smiled. "Close. And I think he's here now."

She went out, and when the door opened again it was not Kate but Sadiq.

He took the hand I held out to him in both of his and stood for a while looking at me wordlessly.

Then he raised one eyebrow in the quirky way that was so familiar, and said wryly, "At the risk of insulting you, my dear, I've seen you looking better. I'm afraid the airplane will be mended long before you are."

I took up the pencil and wrote, *Kate wouldn't like to hear that. She tried so hard to pretty me up.*

"Has she been taking good care of you? I told her I wouldn't leave unless she promised to stay with you every minute."

I nodded. Then I wrote the question that had been gnawing at me ever since I awakened two days ago. *What was Jenny told?*

"Why, exactly what you said to tell her."

I frowned in perplexity.

"Don't you remember? You were in pretty bad shape when we got you here to the hospital. But you wanted to see Jenny, to tell her yourself. You kept saying, 'I promised Jeff.' Of course, it was out of the question. But before you let them put you under anaesthetic, you made me repeat the story Jenny was to be told.

"And it was quite a story. The gist of it was: Jeff was helping Ahmed because he owed him money—you said not to mention gambling, to call it 'a debt of honor'—but he thought it only involved kidnapping, for some kind of political stunt. He didn't find out until the very end that Abdullah meant to kill Haroun. He tried to stop him, and when he couldn't, he threw himself in the path of the bullet to save Haroun's life.

"There was a lot more, but those are the bare bones. I don't know where you got the details. I suppose you made them up as you went along.

"Actually, it was true about the gambling debts. There was probably more to it, too—the offer of a lot of money. And just possibly it appealed to the daredevil streak in Hearn. At least until he found out the object was murder.

"He must have suspected it for quite a while. He might not have known about the poison, but he'd have known about the 'accidents'. Maybe that frightened him, or maybe he just wouldn't let himself believe it.

"Because when he and Abdullah were yelling back and forth in Arabic at the end—you couldn't understand that, could you?"

I shook my head.

"Well, Abdullah told him to kill Haroun, and Jeff said no, now that the kidnapping had gone wrong, Haroun was still their passport out of there. Abdullah called Jeff a fool. He said he could handle me, he said Ahmed had never needed Haroun alive, and now that they were

278

down off the mountain, he didn't need Jeff. And then he shot him.

"So maybe you were right. Maybe, in the end, Jeff couldn't bring himself to kill anyone. Maybe the story you made up for Jenny was true in a sense.

"Anyway, it worked just the way you wanted it to. Jenny firmly believes her father died a hero."

I took a deep breath and squeezed Sadiq's hand. *Thank you,* I wrote. Then I added, *Where is Haroun now?*

"Oh, he's still in Qaiman. As soon as we got you taken care of, and checked on Bernard—who, incidentally, escaped with a knot on his head, which is less than he deserved—Haroun telephoned his father. He told him to clap Uncle Ahmed in irons and send up his plane to meet us in Athens. We were in Qaiman by noon on Saturday.

"The sheik was all for standing Ahmed up against a wall and shooting him. But Haroun was more humane, or legalistic, or something. He pointed out that with the star witnesses dead, we didn't have any case. And it would be bad for the national image.

"Ahmed's defense was a bit inconsistent. He swore he had nothing to do with it, and he'd never do it again. Well, that last part is true enough. He's under close house arrest, and the Interior Minister and the commander of the army have been fully informed. Ahmed will never leave the second floor of his house, let alone Qaiman."

I wrote, *Then if Ahmed is discredited, who will . . .*

Sadiq nodded before I had finished the question. He paced around the end of the bed.

"The sheik has named me guardian of Zora and Zafia," he began hesitantly.

I raised my hand in a gesture of approval.

"Of course I'll need your help with that."

I nodded, wishing I could breathe more freely.

*279*

"And he's announced plans for the succession. I think he knows it won't be long now. He's named a council of regency for Haroun. I'm to head it." He looked at me steadily. "You realize, this will make a big difference to us. I'll have to spend far more time in Qaiman for the next three or four years. Will you mind terribly?"

I spread my hands noncommittally. Did he mean, would I mind being separated a great deal? Or would I mind living in Qaiman?

He came to the side of the bed and lifted my hand, toying with the bracelet on my wrist. He smiled crookedly. "In Arabia," he said, "it's customary not to consider a refusal as sincere unless it's made at least three times. You've only refused this bracelet twice. Do you accept it now?"

I looked up from the bracelet to Sadiq's eyes, then dipped my head in assent.

Suddenly he grinned. "You know, my darling, when I consider the trouble I've had, forcing a flimsy silver bracelet on you, I shudder to think what it will take to talk you into a solid gold wedding band."

When he had left, Kate came back into the room. "Everything all right?" she asked.

I nodded.

Yes, everything was all right. I would have many days to think about it, many days before I could talk again. But when I could, I knew that Sadiq would not have to ask three times for my answer.